RESILIENT SURRENDER

A Deaf-Experience Suspense Novel

Praise for RESILIENT SURRENDER

Peter Quint has written more than a novel. He has created a mirror for the Deaf community and a powerful invitation for others to understand it. *Resilient Surrender* confronts trauma, identity, and resilience with honesty and depth. This story does not just speak for Deaf experiences, it honors them.

–Amanda Brewer,
ASL Instructor at Illinois State University

Resilient Surrender moved me deeply. As a Deaf reader, I was drawn into a world shaped by silence but rich with meaning. The story gave voice to a child's struggle for identity, belonging, and autonomy in ways that felt both intimate and universal.

What makes this novel unique isn't just its suspense or setting but its Deaf-centered lens. The use of sign language as storytelling, the emotional truth of being named—and renamed—by others, and the longing to reconnect with one's origins all resonated in powerful, lasting ways.

This book is a gift. It challenges assumptions, invites empathy, and amplifies a perspective we don't see often enough in fiction. Readers of all backgrounds will walk away changed.

–Emily Rakassi, reader and advocate for inclusive stories

In *Resilient Surrender: A Deaf-Experience Suspense Novel*, Peter M Quint enables the reader to experience not only what it is like to be Deaf, communicate in American Sign Language, and have to rely on others to interpret with others with the hearing world, but also what it is like for American Deaf individuals to suddenly find themselves having to communicate in another country's sign language, which in this case becomes necessary for Amy's and Julius's survival.

Quint wonderfully explores the issues of oppression, abandonment, and forgiveness. His descriptions of Mumbai will draw you in, make you feel as if you yourself have flown to India and suffered the humidity, noise and traffic, but will also leave you with the sensation you have enjoyed the wonderful aromas and tastes of Mumbai cuisine and the warm hospitality of its people.

–Linda Drattell, award-winning author and poet of
Remember this Day and *The Lighter Side of Horse Manure*;
and the children's book, *Who Wants to Be Friends with a Dragon?*

Peter Quint's writing is strongly evocative, yet compelling and easy to read. It will transport you from Spokane, Washington, USA, and then to the slums of India, in this exploration of language deprivation, finding oneself via developing a Deaf identity, friendship and exploring one's roots.

He delves deeply into language-based conflicts and the struggle of a fiercely intelligent young Deaf woman for independence. It is the exact same struggle I saw in some of my students, whose parents underestimated both their ability to thrive independently and the strength and power of their newfound community to help them navigate the world. A beautiful book that will expand your understanding of all the topics, richly, and underlying all of them, the experience of being Deaf, in any part of the world.

–Rachel Zemach, author of *The Butterfly Cage*

Readers are able to journey through the character's lives in imaginative ways and identify with many of the actions and choices they make within this story. Obviously, this book is one of a kind and must-read for anyone who wants their loved ones to understand themselves.

–Dr. Lewis S. Lummer,
Deaf Education Supervisor at Baylor University

Resilient Surrender is a powerful and emotional journey that gripped me from beginning to end. As a reader, I was deeply moved by [Amy's] determination to uncover her true identity and find her birth mother in India, despite the pain and chaos surrounding her. Watching her navigate life as a deaf woman—through loss, betrayal, and hope—felt incredibly real and personal.

Peter M. Quint masterfully brings deaf characters to life in a way that feels authentic and respectful. As someone who understands sign language, I appreciated the representation and the nuance in their communication. The bond between [Amy] and Julius, and the way faith and love guided their path, touched me in unexpected ways.

This book isn't just a thriller—it's a story of survival, identity, and the human spirit. I wholeheartedly recommend it."

–Catherine Worrall, Deaf runner with a bachelor's
in cybersecurity information systems

Peter M. Quint's *Resilient Surrender: A Deaf Experience Suspense Novel* offers a layered and culturally rich narrative that explores the journey of a Deaf Indian girl adopted by a white American woman. Far from a nurturing presence, the adoptive mother distances herself from the Deaf Community and imposes an isolating upbringing devoid of cultural or linguistic affirmation in the home. Against this backdrop, the protagonist holds on to vivid memories of her birth mother and her early life in poverty-stricken India. These core memories serve as emotional anchors, compelling her eventual return to India in search of identity, closure, and reconnection.

The novel deftly integrates themes of Deafhood, ethnic identity, audism, and the complex dimensions of love and independence. Quint does not shy away from the often-silenced experiences of intersectional Deaf individuals—those whose identities stretch across multiple marginalized communities. The protagonist's identity is not solely Deaf; she is also Indian, a woman of color, and an international adoptee. This intersectionality enriches the narrative and reflects the broader spectrum of the Deaf Community, including subsets such as Black Deaf, Jewish Deaf, and others. The tensions between self-definition and imposed identity, especially under the gaze of an audist, hearing-centered society, are explored with both tenderness and grit.

Quint's storytelling is as suspenseful as it is culturally illuminating. His portrayal of the protagonist's search for her birth mother is not just a geographical journey but a symbolic reclaiming of self. Through her navigation of love, betrayal, and community, the novel becomes a compelling meditation on what it means to belong *Resilient Surrender* offers valuable insight into Deaf experience and identity formation, making it a significant contribution to Deaf literature and an essential text for scholars interested in Disability Studies, intersectionality, and cultural Deaf narratives.

–Dr. Lisalee D. Egbert,
Professor and Coordinator: ASL & Deaf Studies,
University of Texas–Arlington

From the very first page, I was completely drawn in. Peter Quint, who is Deaf himself, offers a powerful and authentic perspective, writing from the lens of Deaf-experience in a way that hearing readers may never have considered. His attention to detail—how Deaf individuals see and move through the world—is both eye-opening and beautifully written. Each character's journey is rich with struggle, growth and success. I couldn't put it down—this is a binge-worthy read for both Deaf and hearing audiences alike.

-Karlie Waldrip, author of the
Deaf-initely Can children's book series

PETER M. QUINT

RESILIENT SURRENDER

A Deaf-Experience Suspense Novel

Quintessential Deaf Press

This story is dedicated to all who search for Truth.

This is my commandment: Love each other in
the same way I have loved you. There is no
greater love than to lay down one's life for one's friends.

(John 15: 12-13)

Please scan this QR code for an author introduction and explanation which includes Deaf character dialogue representation, the use of bolded words and QR codes to demonstrate character's signing and a way to obtain the companion course/workbook for this novel.

Please visit the Author's Note at the back of the book to see an expanded explanation plus examples of the various ways dialogue and communication is presented in English text to represent the main Deaf character's understanding and experience.

PROLOGUE

June. Mumbai, India.

During the dark night the rain fell in large, heavy drops. The bright lights of a train station shimmered behind a sheet of water cascading from the overhead metal roof. Trudging across the adjacent street in ankle-deep, muddy water, a thin woman adjusted the sack hanging from her shoulder and pulled her little five-year-old daughter with a firm grasp on the wrist.

As they neared the elevated platform of the train station, behind the sheet of water, the girl saw the shimmering outlines of many people milling about while waiting for the next train. She did not know why she and her mother struggled to cross the flooded street. If her mother explained the reason, she could not hear it. Hot anger welled inside the little girl's chest. Even in her limited understanding of the world, she knew it wasn't right to be jerked across a flooded street against her will.

"S____a!" she saw on her mother's lips. It was the first time she had seen that word. She did not know what she was called because words never registered on her ears.

Past the street curb, the mother pulled her daughter throughthe waterfall from the roof and grabbed her around the waist. With surprising strength in spite of her thin frame, the mother hoisted the girl up and deposited both the wet sack and her sopping daughter upon the cement platform.

Slowly, the mother raised herself up and sat next to the girl. Her shoulders rose and fell as she panted heavily while looking back the way they had come.

With quick intakes of breath, the girl tried wiping the mud off her legs and only managed to smear it on her tiny hands. She looked at her mother who slowly shook her head. The furrowed brows of rage and confusion were what the girl saw on her face. She had seen this expression before when the other people on the street stole their things while she and her mother were away begging. But this time it was different. There was an agony etched on her mother's face which matched the dark fury of the storm.

This was very near the street entrance of the train station where they usually did their begging when the weather wasn't like this evening. The tracks were on the other side of the platform.

The girl noticed a crowd of people milling about, waiting for the next train. A small, glass-enclosed office stood in the middle of the area where people stood in line to exchange rupee notes and pieces of paper with a man in the office.

Off in a far, darkened corner of the platform near the exit stairs was a small group of the other beggar children older than herself. None had a mother or father with them. She didn't like them. They were always trying to steal the few rupees she and her mother had managed to get from the rich folk. All of them were barefoot and wore the same thin, dirty kameez as herself.

As the other children slept, bunched together for warmth, one older girl sat up, her intense, severe eyes focused on a small bracelet she was making. As she strung a pink bead on a leather strap, this girl paused and looked up, locking eyes with the wet little girl next to her mother at the edge of the platform. Fear tightening her chest, the little girl crouched next to her mother. She wanted to melt into the hard, gray platform to escape from these intense eyes.

The mother stirred and grabbed her daughter's arm. The girl looked up and saw her mother's downcast eyes and the straight mouth above a set jaw. Again, there was that expression that meant trouble was brewing. Slowly, the mother stood and picked up the bag with her other hand. They walked to the brightly lit area behind the office near the wall, opposite from where the people exchanged rupees and paper with the man. Reaching into the bag, the mother pulled out a dirty-brown blanket, dripping from the rain water. She slapped it onto the ground and spread out its edges. The girl felt the cold wetness of the water seep through her clothes as her mother placed her on the blanket and sat next to her with her back against the office wall.

Nothing changed in train station. People continued to mill about or line up for pieces of paper. Across the platform, the older girl's eyes returned to the bracelet she was making. The little girl felt her mother's hand guide her head to her lap. The overhead tube lights illuminated the woman's face. The deep brown eyes, which had previously shifted in fear, now registered something the little girl had seen a few fleeting times before; the furrowed brow and gaze of concern illuminating a discord of emotions deep within. The mother's hand patted a rhythm. One, two, three, four…pause…one, two, three, four…pause. Then nothing. The blackness of sleep.

• • • • •

She opened her eyes and blinked. The bright lights at the roof blurred her vision as she sat up and stretched. Her hand fell onto a lump and she looked down, recognizing it as the sack her mother had carried. She could feel the items inside, some hard, some soft. Looking up she frowned. Something was wrong. Suddenly her heart pounded crazily in her chest and she froze. Her mother was nowhere to be seen!

She was completely alone!

On the wet blanket there was no place to go, so she did the only thing she knew, which was to close her eyes, open her mouth and wail. The vibrations registering in her throat and chest provided a modicum of comfort that she was doing something about her predicament.

Suddenly there was a jab at her leg and she opened her eyes. Standing above her was the older girl with the intense eyes, her foot poised to strike again should the wailing continue. Instinctively, the little girl shrunk back and grabbed the sack with the bundle inside. She noticed the other girl was quite tall and assumed she was there to steal her sack. The older girl put her foot down and stood, observing while holding the now completed bracelet. It seemed she was thinking about what to do. She looked around the station then back at the cowering little girl and made a "come-here" motion. Her mouth moved.

No response came from the little girl who frowned and glared at this impostor who meant no good. The older girl sighed and shook her head. She leaned forward and said something, opening her mouth wider.

"Nuhhh!" the little girl yelled back.

Surprised, the older girl stepped back with a puzzled expression. After a while, she looked around the station and then back at the little girl in front of her. The older girl nodded and appeared to decide something. Stepping forward, she held out the bracelet, softened her eyes and nodded with a "take it" expression.

The little girl frowned. This was not expected. Things were always taken from her, never given. With a quick motion, she grabbed the bracelet and examined it. It had pretty, multicolored beads and the smooth texture brought some comfort to her fingers. She looked up to meet the eyes of the older girl.

They nodded in mutual understanding.

PART I

Taken Away

Chapter 1

Hear-Nothing

The next morning dawned hot. Between the high-rise buildings above the endless expanse of blue tarp that covered the slums below, the sun had not yet tickled the standing waters covering the street below. Even then, the wafts of heat began rising like thousands of invisible little furnaces evaporating from the water.

At this early hour, in the midst of the ankle-high water, the city was alive with people going about their daily business, sloshing across the streets, getting wet from the spray from the wheels of the multicolored buses, trucks and automobiles hurrying past. Rickety wooden and metal carts pulled by black, sad looking buffalo proceeded past, their spoked wheels lapping like the water wheels which turned to generate electricity in the villages out in the country.

During this early morning, a row of four-wheeled flat carts was already attended and lined up along one side of the street a few blocks down from the train station. Two carts held the boiling pots, bottles, and containers used for the preparation of pani-puri. One supported the little oven and fresh cut cornhusks made ready for the roasted corn-on-a-stick snacks popular among the passing people who could afford them. On another cart, protected by an overhead tarp supported by a roughly welded rebar scaffold, a rather large pot of boiling chai perched precariously on a small burner as the chai walla poured the brown liquid in long thin streams from a large ladle into small metal cups.

Down the street, the little girl with her newly acquired bracelet watched as the older girl with the intense eyes instructed her small army of street kids. This girl grabbed a boy and a girl by their dirty kameez and shoved them, pointing in the direction of the pani-puri cart. They walked to the line of customers and began the poking, prodding and extended their cupped hands in the begging movements they were taught to perform. Several other children were gathered by the older girl and prodded in the direction of the roasted corn cart.

"Come-here." The little girl with the bracelet recognized the downward motion from the hand of the older girl. The other hand grabbed the arm of a boy about the same age as the little girl. His thick black hair stood up straight resembling little spikes on top of his head. The older girl knelt down and moved her mouth with instructions and looked at the little girl.

The little girl's eyes widened and she took a step back, shaking her head in confusion.

Spiky Hair's eyes became hard and his lips curled as his mouth moved. He stepped forward and shoved the little girl to the ground.

The older girl stood and slapped Spiky Hair across the face. His head jerked sideways, leading his body into a twisting turn as he crumpled to the dirty sidewalk.

The older girl stood over him and yelled. Her foot was poised to kick as a finger pointed to the little girl who observed from her seated position. The older girl's finger pointed to the chai cart down the road. Spiky Hair gathered himself up, wiping tears from his eyes and shooting a glare at the little girl as he approached the chai cart line to beg.

The older girl stepped toward the little girl and squatted. In the midst of the chaotic street scene, the two of them observed each other.

Very slowly, almost imperceptibly, the older girl nodded and raised her eyebrows in realization. She placed an open palm on her own chest.

"Bisha," she said and added a few other words the little girl did not recognize. "Tum?"

The little girl's eyebrows lowered. She recognized the question as referring to herself. With a little index finger, she pointed to herself and slowly shook her head. She knew that people were supposed to be called something, but in the mumbo jumbo of moving mouths, she never recognized what she, herself should be called.

Bisha looked down the street to check on her little army of beggars.

Then she turned to the little girl and pointed to her ear, shaking her head with a questioning expression. In this clarity of communication, the little girl relaxed. No one, including her mother, had ever slowed down and done this with her. Like a bee to a flower, this connection drew her in. She pointed to her own ear and shook her head. Bisha's hard face relaxed and she smiled slightly in recognition. With a nod of affirmation, she pointed to herself.

"Bisha," she said then pointed at the little girl. "Tum." She pointed to one of her own ears then closed her hand, shaking it while extending the thumb. "Bahara," Bisha pronounced the word slowly.

The little girl pointed at her own ear and nodded, copying the same sign. From her mother's begging on the streets, she recognized the shaking hand sign as meaning "nothing." That meant she was to be  called "**Hear-Nothing**."

Bisha stood and placed her hands under Hear-Nothing's armpits, raising her to a standing position. The older girl pointed to the bracelet and placed an open palm on the chest of the little girl.

"Hear-Nothing," Bisha signed. "Tum," she said with her voice and beckoned for her to follow toward the chai cart.

Hear-Nothing walked next to Bisha and smiled. For the first time in her very young life, she felt the warmth of verification—the affirmation that she was important and cherished enough to be given a special item and called something in a way that she recognized. She looked up at this older girl with the hard face who apparently was to be called Bisha. There was a connection with this new stranger which she had never felt before with others. She felt the smooth beads of the bracelet as they joined Spiky Hair next to the line leading to the chai cart.

Bisha surveyed the scene and nodded. Hear-Nothing saw the other children complying with Bisha's instructions at the corn roasting and pani-puri carts. They approached the short lines of adults, jabbing at their hips and holding out their hands in a begging stance.

As it was still early in the morning, this particular cart in front of her had a much longer line of adults waiting for their beginning-of-the-day dose of warm chai. Most were of the working class who plied their trade along the shops and small businesses of this particular street. Their clean shalwar-kameez and sandals a step above the bare feet and dirty rags that covered the children. A few adults wore the pressed shirts and pants complete with polished leather shoes that identified them as office workers from the high-rise buildings towering above the chaos of the street below.

A brown-uniformed police officer emerged from an alley and casually swung his black club as he sauntered up to the chai cart.

Bisha made a gesture to the other children and grabbed Hear-Nothing by the wrist, pulling her into the crowd of people mingling and traversing along the sidewalk.

With rehearsed actions, all the children casually disappeared into this street-side crowd. As they hid, all of their little eyes remained on the policeman as he rudely cut into the front of the line and demanded his customary morning chai. The chai walla complied, and the cop drained the little cup, casually surveying the scene and then moved on his way.

Like little flecks of dirt emerging from a pile of sifted rice, the children emerged from the crowd and re-assumed their places by the lines.

Bisha and Spiky Hair pick pocketed the office workers near the chai cart and jabbed at their hips while Hear-Nothing stood apart and fiddled with the bracelet on her wrist. The adults glanced sideways dismissively and turned to their cell phone screens as they waited for the chai.

Getting no response from his target, Spiky Hair frowned and looked at Hear-Nothing. She saw the same glare in his eyes from the night before. Hear-nothing took a few steps and shrank a step closer to Bisha who was busy jabbing at the hip of her next target.

Also getting no response, Bisha paused and looked at Hear-Nothing. The little girl recognized the contemplative look from the night before when Bisha was trying to figure out how to communicate. Again, there was that slow, almost imperceptible nod of an idea. Bisha squatted on her haunches to be at the little girl's level. She pointed to her own ear.

"Hear-nothing," she signed and held out her hands in the begging stance while her hard face assumed the most pitiful expression possible.

"Huh?" Hear-Nothing screwed her face into confusion.

Bisha tilted her head and pointed at Hear-Nothing. "Go-ahead, Hear-Nothing," she signed, and once again assumed the pitiful beggar stance, then pointed at one of the finely dressed office workers who stood in line.

Hear-Nothing looked at the man who took a step closer in the line while staring into his phone. Her eyes narrowed in recognition that she was asked to do the same with this man. She glanced at Spiky Hair whose eyes were narrowed, challenging her to perform the task. She jerked her head quickly away to face the challenge ahead.

As Bisha and Spiky Hair stood to watch, Hear-Nothing took a deep breath and stepped up to the man, jabbing him in the hip.

Being one of the adults not yet harassed by the children, this man glanced down at the source of the jab. The little girl's dark brown eyes widened and her mouth pouted into the most pitiful expression she could muster.

"Hear-nothing," she signed and held out a hand, palm up in his direction.

Strong hands grabbed her shoulders and pulled her away from the line.

Hear-Nothing looked up. Bisha was staring across the street, a look of panic on her face.

The same cop pointed his club at her while his mouth said something to his partner, who stood next to him, ready to pounce.

Spiky Hair bolted, darting behind a crowd of adults.

Bisha swooped up Hear-Nothing by the hips and ran in the opposite direction toward the entrance to a nearby bazaar.

Carried along in Bisha's arms, Hear-Nothing looked back and saw the cop with the club step toward the curb while his partner dashed across the street to chase the other children. The club holder paused and looked down at the flooded street. Hear-Nothing and Bisha escaped toward the bazaar.

They rounded a corner of a shop at the entrance to the bazaar. Bisha's head hit something hanging overhead. Hear-Nothing felt a sharp pain at her temple as something on a chain hit her head and wrapped around her neck. She grabbed it and glanced down. It was a small pendant of the man hanging on a cross. The bottom cross piece ended in a sharp point.

The girls crashed into a cart. Plastic idols of the elephant-god scattered into the alley. As Bisha paused to sidestep the idols, Hear-Nothing looked back and saw the cop pursuing them from across the muddy street. Small tsunamis emanated from his black boots. They were swallowed into the labyrinth of the slum. Like a mouse pursued by a cat, Bisha darted around many obstacles in the alley.

A woman balancing groceries on her head was nearly upended.

A fruit walla stopped his cart suddenly. Piled-high mangoes scattered onto the street. Like a sure-footed cat, the cop sidestepped the mangoes.

Riding on Bisha's hip, Hear-Nothing saw him move his mouth in a curse as he sprinted forward. They approached a cross street—

Whomp!

Hear-Nothing's shoulders crashed into some metal bars. She and Bisha tumbled to the ground and separated.

Hear-Nothing looked up to see a green and yellow rickshaw. The driver leaned out with an angry face and gestured with outstretched hand and arm. She had seen people do this at crowded traffic intersections.

Bisha stood and crouched in a defensive position.

The cop stopped at the opposite side of the clearing created by their chaos. He extended his baton toward Bisha and they glared at each other.

Hear-Nothing noticed a sudden, strange pause come over this little section of the alley. Like a swarm of bees in a collective pause prior to attacking a threat, the chaos of the alley stilled as people casually stopped to observe this sudden drama between the policeman and children.

Bisha's eyes darted quickly to the side. An escape. She looked down at the little girl.

Hear-Nothing saw a fleeting expression on Bisha's face. The older girl's shoulders sagged in a sigh. With a shake of the head, she blinked and darted to the side, away from the policeman to disappear, becoming one with the crowd.

Once again, suddenly alone, Hear-Nothing crawled back a few feet. She gathered herself into a protective ball near the rear wheel of the rickshaw and glared up at the cop.

He glanced in the direction Bisha had escaped.

The rickshaw moved. Surprised, Hear-Nothing scrambled out of the way.

The rough hands of the cop grabbed her arm.

Her hand tightened around the necklace pendant. She buried the point in the officer's leg.

Chapter 2

AMY

A tall, stern, pale-skinned woman in a white dress firmly pulled Hear-Nothing into a tube.

Hear-Nothing jerked her hand back, fed up with constantly being pushed, prodded, and jerked around.

She remembered waking up in a strange place after being whacked in the head by the club of the brown-uniformed man after she stabbed him in the leg with her necklace.

She also remembered the past couple of months at the large building where she stayed. There, other white-attired adults yelled, pushed, prodded, and backhanded herself and the other children.

After a series of short visits during the past couple of weeks, suddenly this strange woman with a stern-looking white face arrived earlier this day to shove Hear-Nothing's few belongings into a small white suitcase then whisk her away in a car.

Now it was dark outside. The narrow windows that lined the cream- colored walls of the tube in which she and the woman followed a line of people proceeding slowly toward a large hole up ahead.

Hear-Nothing's fingers were beginning to go numb from the vise-like grip of this tall, thin woman. Hear-Nothing twisted her wrist to try escaping from the grip, but it only caused the woman's hand to tighten more. In her other hand, the woman held the small white suitcase.

Arriving at the hole, Hear-Nothing saw a thick, curved door

propped open above a strange, squished rubber threshold over which she was guided to step. A soft hand touched her back. She looked up to see the pleasant white face of a woman. This face was nicely framed by perfectly manicured hair topped by a small hat of a pleasant red hue. This same color adorned her dress and matching shoes. She smelled nice.

Prompted gently from behind and jerked forward from the hand in front, Hear-Nothing advanced down the aisle between rows of high-backed seats and people jostling to deposit bags and small suitcases in open bins above. The pleasant smell of the woman behind was mixed with the sour stench of sweat from the armpit of a man reaching up to close an overhead bin.

Now the tall woman deposited the white suitcase into an overhead bin. Three empty high-backed seats faced forward. At the wall near the farthest seat was a small, thick-glassed oval window. The woman's mouth opened.

Hear-Nothing saw a long finger point her toward the far seat. She complied and sat, her feet extending not far from the edge of the seat. The woman sat stiffly. Hear-Nothing noticed how the woman's knees stuck out about the same height as the seat.

The nice-smelling woman held out two small blankets and pillows.

The tall woman grabbed these items and placed them on her own lap. She leaned sideways and fastened the seat strap around Hear-Nothing's waist.

Hear-Nothing shifted closer to the wall. The feel of the woman's hands on her legs gave her a chill. One pillow and blanket was given to her while the others remained on the woman's lap.

Hear-Nothing observed the bustle as people settled into their seats. A little blue-eyed girl with yellow hair and her family occupied the seats directly across the aisle. A large, dark-skinned man with a protruding belly squelched into the aisle seat next to them. An elbow jabbed the tall woman, and she shifted like a plank as the man struggled to extend the strap around his belly.

Both the woman and man looked up and watched the pleasant-smelling woman pointing and moving her arms in strange motions. She held a tube to the ceiling under one bin and placed an attached mask over her mouth.

With a dismissive expression toward this display, the tall woman shook her head and turned. She pointed to herself, moved her mouth, and formed a fist, twisting it twice upward at the side of her mouth.

"Huh?" Hear-Nothing scowled with puzzlement.

"Sybil," the woman formed on her mouth and repeated the hand motion as before.

She pointed at Hear-Nothing. "Amy." Her mouth moved and the hand changed to a fist with thumb extended, touching twice on the cheek.

Hear-Nothing screwed her face into a frown. She recognized that this was regarding what the woman wanted her to be called. It didn't help that the intense blue eyes of the girl across the aisle were watching in calm, contented observation. Hear-Nothing felt like the little mouse trapped in the coils of a snake as she and other kids once watched its life being slowly squeezed out.

The woman waved her hand in front of Hear-Nothing's face and pointed at her.

"Amy." The mouth moved, then the long fingers wrapped around her little hand. Her little fingers were manipulated into the same thumb-extended handshape that the woman recently formed. Then the hand was forced up to her cheek, touched twice, and released.

"**Amy,**" the woman said again, nodding for her to copy.

The girl looked at her hand and frowned. Slowly, she moved this hand to her cheek and touched it twice. The woman bounced in her

seat and smiled gleefully, clapping with small, tight motions. It reminded the Hear-Nothing of a little toy monkey's toothy grin as it banged its cymbals in a scary movie she and the children at the orphanage had recently watched. Her eyebrows lowered as her frown

The woman paused, as if searching for something. She looked across the aisle, then excitedly pointed to the little blue-eyed girl who continued to watch them. The woman's finger pointed back and forth between the other girl and her mother sitting next to her. Then the finger pointed to herself and the hand changed to an open shape with thumb extended, touching the chin.

This was the first time Hear-Nothing had seen the concept 'mother' expressed. But between the contentment of Blue Eyes, who settled comfortably next to her mother and her own position near this rigid thing, the application of 'motherhood' was like a nail driven into her heart.

Slowly, adamantly, she shook her head. She closed her fist, striking it twice at the side of her mouth. "Sybil," she pronounced and flashed her eyes at the woman whose face was now frozen in surprise.

"Mother," the woman signed. She nodded her head in a command.

"No!" Hear-Nothing's eyes widened and her fist adamantly touched twice at the side of her mouth. "Sybil!"

"Amy!" the woman signed and spoke. "I..am…mother!"

Hear-Nothing twisted in her seat and grabbed the pillow and blanket from the lap of this offending woman. Hear-Nothing placed these items on the armrest between them. She took her own pillow and blanket and stacked them on top of the others.

Now there was a wall between them. Neither the blue eyes of the girl across the aisle nor the cold, gray eyes of the woman next to her could pierce this private little space she had created for herself.

Sitting still, she pointed to herself and shook her head. Then she pointed to her ear and twisted a closed fist with thumb extended.

"I Hear-Nothing." She concluded with an emphatic nod.

An unknown force pushed her body into the seat-back. Surprised, she hoisted herself up and looked out the little window. There, past a metal extension which she recognized as helping this machine fly, she saw the ground below move rapidly past. The buildings from which they just came filed quickly behind. A sudden ceasing of vibration and upward tilting brought the scene beyond into the window's view.

She saw the high-rise buildings over the blue-tarped river which covered the roofs of what she knew as home. There were the multicolored buses, green and yellow three-wheelers, and white cars twisting, turning, and maneuvering in a vain attempt to pass each other.

Secluded from the prying eyes of the others beyond her self-constructed wall, with one hand, she grabbed her necklace pendant, feeling the pointed tip of the post on which the little man hung. She thought about burying this into the woman's leg, just like she did with the policeman. She shook her head and let go of the necklace.

She stroked the smooth beads of her bracelet on her wrist. This bracelet reminded her of Bisha.

Outside the window she caught the last glimpse of the multitude of people milling about and hurrying along the streets. She wondered if Bisha was among them, commanding her small army of little beggars. Mostly she wondered if her own mother was down there sitting on the

streets in hopes of charity from the more fortunate passerby.

She missed her mother.

As the flying machine rose and left her home behind, an image of her mother enveloped her mind like the clouds into which the machine flew. It was the concern in her mother's eyes that moment which seemed so long ago at the train station as she fell asleep before this time of blackness and chaos. Was it a look of love? Would she ever find this comfort and belonging beyond the dark clouds in the places toward which she hurtled?

PART II

A Prison of Control

Chapter 3

JULIUS

January. Seventeen years later.

Julius McLellan leaned forward, poised on the inside lane of the running track at Spokane Community College that was being used by the distance runners of the Gonzaga University track team. Snow piled on the infield from the clearing of the first three lanes he and his teammates had shoveled the previous half hour.

Looking sideways as the coach perched on top a pile of snow just inside the track at the starting line, Julius's focus was not on the moving mouth but focused on the motion of the coach's hand which held a stopwatch. The hand jerked up as the thumb hit the button, and Julius was off running around the curve, leading a tightly bunched group of other male runners followed by an equally tight-bunched group of females.

It was a preseason track workout called at the last minute by their coach. "Meet at 10:00 a.m. Need to do mile repeat workout" was all the coach's text disclosed early that morning on Julius's cell phone. It now lay face-up on top of his athletic bag next to the starting line. This practice being arranged at the last minute, Julius had hesitated to attend. He knew the coach would not think to arrange an interpreter. Nevertheless, he needed to get in a hard workout and decided he would rather do it with others than by himself.

The task was easy enough for him; run the first mile in four minutes and thirty seconds, take a one-minute rest, and then run the next one five seconds faster, and so-on for four miles.

Julius led the men through the first mile and stopped just past the line where the coach stood, yelling out the splits.

As the women filed in and joined the guys to chat a bit before the next segment, Julius walked over and grabbed the coach's wrist. Four minutes and twenty-nine seconds is what he saw on the stopwatch. The coach said something, but Julius ignored him and returned to the group.

The runners all wore tights and layers to protect from the cold. Several wore caps which covered their ears. Unlike Julius, in spite of this covering, they could hear each other just fine. One rather attractive female runner slapped the arm of the guy next to her, her shoulders shaking in laughter. Apparently, this guy had teased her, and all except Julius laughed at what was being said.

Julius moved closer to try and lipread, but the background glare of the sun made it impossible to see the mouth of the guy who responded to the girl's slap. Plus, this guy's head swiveled away from Julius, cutting off his access.

Julius sighed. *All I want is to be included,* he thought as he moved to the line to wait for the next movement of the stopwatch. *Why can't these people value me? They know I am Deaf! At least they could slow down their speech and face me so that I can have access. But no, they don't care! They just want to meet their own needs.* He crouched forward to better propel himself forward and beat these rude people.

A flash of the cell phone screen alerted his eye and he straightened, stepping to the curb to grab it from the top of his bag. He pressed the green 'accept' button as the runners took off for the next mile section without him.

"Hi, Amy," he signed, smiling. He formed the 'A' name sign

on his cheek with one hand while holding the phone with his other.

Wide, brown eyes greeted him and a dark brown face nodded emphatically as a little gold nose ring glinted in the light on the screen. "**Julius**!" Amy formed the 'J' name sign on the forehead which she had  given him long ago when they were elementary school students.

Julius looked down the track at the departing runners and shook his head. He would rather talk to his friend who valued him much more than these dismissive teammates. His eyes turned back to the screen. "What's wrong?" he signed.

"Ugh! Look!"

Her phone screen turned to reveal the pale, thin face of a woman whose mouth formed into a straight line. The screen flashed back to Amy.

"Sybil's annoying me!" She twisted the 'sick-me' sign and practically punched the side of her mouth with the 'S' handshape name sign of the woman who had adopted her.

"Won't let me use the car! I gotta get to my tutoring job at SFCC. What!?" She turned her face. The phone suddenly jerked.

Julius saw flashes of Amy's small, brown hands as she argued with Sybil. He recognized a couple of swear sign handshapes and wondered if Sybil recognized them in Amy's rapid-fire signing style when she was angry. He knew Sybil would know her adopted daughter was talking about her job at Spokane Falls Community College.

The screen flashed back to Amy's face.

A hand tapped Julius's shoulder. "Hold on, Amy." Julius held his forefinger to the screen and looked behind him. The coach pointed at the runners approaching to complete their first lap and moved his mouth. His finger then pointed at the stopwatch with a questioning expression on his face.

Scowling, Julius picked up his athletic bag, moving it to the outside curb of the track as the runners passed. He would rather deal with his feisty friend's problems than face the jaded, oppressive attitudes of these people.

He looked back at the screen. "Why can't you use the car?"

"Says she needs it to go to work. Can drop me at SFCC in an hour. But I gotta be there in fifteen minutes."

"Can you take the bus?"

"Bus doesn't leave for thirty minutes. Plus, you know the b**ch won't let a poor little Deaf girl like me ride the bus alone because she thinks it's not safe!"

The screen jerked sideways. Julius saw the thin fingers of a white hand try to grab Amy's phone. He knew Sybil caught the swear sign. He also agreed with Amy's label of this woman but wished she would control her language so that Sybil would give her more of what she wanted. The screen turned back to Amy.

Julius could see trees behind her. He recognized these trees as lining her front yard.

"Can you come pick me up now and take me to work?" Amy stared at the phone with wide, dark eyes and **wiggled her finger in a question mark**.

"I can't..." Julius paused and looked at the clumps of runners making their way around the opposite side of the track and were on the last lap of the mile segment.

The coach had his back turned to him. It seemed he was calling out splits so the runners could hear him across the field. Clearly, it made no difference to this coach or the runners if Julius participated or not.

"Fine," he said to the screen. "I'll come pick you up. See you in ten minutes."

Amy smiled sweetly through the screen. Her dark eyes, framed by the darker hued skin under her eyebrows, drew him in and he returned the smile.

"Thanks! ILY!" she signed then blew him a kiss before hanging up.

Depositing his phone inside the bag, Julius shouldered it and looked at the group. They had finished the mile and resumed their banter while waiting for the next segment. No one thought to approach and attempt to communicate with him. He lowered his eyebrow and shook his head, reconsidering if he should join them just so he could get in his daily workout.

No, Amy needs me, he thought as he turned and left the track area, throwing a dismissive glance behind him. *Plus, she values my attention much more than these people do.*

He felt the snow crunching under his feet as he walked toward the old green Subaru his mother had given him as a high school graduation present the previous spring. Julius tossed his bag in the back then sat in the driver's seat.

The morning sun incubated the inside of the car and provided a bit of comfort as Julius looked out toward the scene on the track. He reflected on all the running he had done the previous two years, finishing among the money winners in the Bloomsday race, an accomplishment very few thought a person of his age at the time could attain. Following this performance, his dominance of the Washington State high school championship two-mile race was expected. The winning time he posted as being among best in the entire nation secured his status as one of the scholarship-earning athletes on the Gonzaga University track team.

He was proud of these accomplishments, yet the work and effort it would take for future glory all became meaningless in the realm of human relationships and interaction. Nobody really cared how fast he ran. He wondered if it was really worth the effort, especially among the ignorant people who continued their workout, oblivious to their dismissiveness of him.

He turned the ignition. *God, I hope I am doing the right thing*, Julius prayed as he exited the campus and left the runners behind.

Chapter 4

AMY

A broken snow shovel jutted at an angle halfway across he partially cleared walkway, with the severed handle laying nearby—Amy's latest response to Sybil's nagging.

Amy slouched at her small bedroom desk, chin on her hands. She stroked the multicolored bracelet on her wrist. Tiny cracks and worn patches on the original leather strap could be seen between the beads. Her fingers moved over the little knots she tied over the years as her wrist grew, and she needed to expand the strap. The bracelet reminded her of Bisha. In the faded memory of years past, Amy's only clear recollection was of Bisha's intense eyes.

Amy sighed and glanced back at the closed door to her bedroom. On the other side of that door lurked the woman who adopted her. The cold, gray eyes of this woman were always ready to notice any diversion Amy produced contrary to her approval.

Like the bracelet from Bisha, Amy wished her Indian birth mother had given her something. She couldn't remember her mother's eyes. All she recalled was a thin woman with a look of agonized concern on her face just before she made the choice to abandon her daughter.

Why did my mother make that choice? Amy asked herself. *What is it about me that a mother would want to throw me away?*

A car approached, diverting Amy's mind from her past. It was a green Subaru wagon which slowed to a stop at the curb. Out stepped Julius. He tossed his head and squinted in the bright morning sun.

Even at this distance across the yard, Amy could see his right eyebrow lower significantly more than the other. It reminded her of the name sign she had given him long ago when they were kindergarten students. That their friendship endured over the years was testament to their shared identity as Deaf friends—a bond that grew stronger the more they got to know each other. This bond was solidified during the time they spent the recent summer after high school graduation and made it clear to both the great attraction and affection they mutually shared.

Amy sat up and glanced at the round vanity mirror propped at her desk. She smoothed her long dark hair and stood.

Julius walked up the path, stepping to the side to avoid the broken shovel handle laying on the path. He slipped a bit on an uncleared, icy section, his leg jerking sideways. The jagged edges of the snow shovel handle pierced the calf of his black running tights.

Amy took a sharp intake of breath as she read a swear word on his lips. A hand went to her mouth, and her dark eyes widened as she observed him lean over to rub his leg. She exited her room in a hurried walk through the living room.

In the tight space between the TV and coffee table, Sybil was bent over, depositing items into a large shoulder bag. She blocked Amy's way to the door.

"Move!" Amy threw the sign in a command. Sybil straightened.

Amy sidled past, wishing the shovel handle had pierced this woman and not Julius.

"Are you okay?" Amy exclaimed as Julius stepped through the doorway. She kneeled and lifted the leg of his tights.

"I'm fine." He bent over and gently raised her by the shoulder. "It's nothing. Don't worry about me."

Amy let out a deep breath.

Sybil's cold, gray eyes observed their interaction.

It reminded Amy of the time she tried to sleep in the reclining patio chair on the back patio. The too-small blanket was only sufficient to warm her front while her back shivered in the chill of the night.

She glanced over her shoulder and saw that Sybil was still watching them.

Amy jerked a thumb toward Sybil. "She won't let me use the car-EVER!" Her body twisted with the **NEVER** sign. "I guess I gotta use your car from-now-on. That okay with you?" She leaned forward and poked him in the chest and continued without waiting for his response. "Plus, she insists the money I make at SFCC pay for rent at this dump. You, on the other hand, have your own savings account, and your scholarship at Gonzaga pays for everything else!"

Amy could feel Sybil's eyes burning into her. "Can I have some money so I can get lunch later?" she asked Julius.

"I don't have any cash, but we can use my debit card—"

"See!" Amy held the sign in Julius's direction and looked at Sybil. "At least HE has a debit card!"

Sybil stepped forward and held up a finger. "Wait…one…second," she signed in her Signing Exact English (SEE) style. "We..have…talked…about…this…before…Let's…talk…about …this …in…private."

"No!" Amy grabbed Julius's arm and hugged it close. "He is my best- friend and we will talk about it NOW!"

Sybil closed her eyes and continued. "When…you…prove…that …you…are…independent—"

Amy stepped toward Sybil and pushed her on the shoulder. "Hey! Open your eyes!"

Sybil opened her eyes. "Then…we…will—"

"**Independent**!" Amy held the 'I' handshape and glared. "I'm twenty-two years old now and deserve to have all these things and not be stuck in this sh*t hole!"

Sybil's shoulders raised and Amy knew it meant she caught her breath.

"Young…lady…watch…your..language!" Sybil stepped forward.

"Hold on!" Julius stepped between them, his hand on Amy's shoulder and his finger held up to Sybil. "The two-of-us will leave."

Sybil drew her mouth into a tight line. Her eyes narrowed, a warning to Julius for stepping across the line of control in her own home.

His right eyebrow lowered, and his stare hardened to match that of his friend's adoptive mother. For a short while, the three of them stood, the tension a thick curtain between them, which nothing could part. Amy grabbed Julius's arm and pulled him toward the door. "Yeah, let's leave this jail," she signed. "I'm late for my tutoring job at SFCC."

Sybil broke eye contact and looked out the window. She pointed to the broken shovel in the front yard. "Put...that..in…the…garbage …by…the…garage…before…you…leave."

"Fine!" Amy stalked into her room, grabbed her purse and backpack, then returned to the tiny living room.

Julius held open the front door, avoiding eye contact with Sybil. He and Amy left the house without a word.

Out in the front yard, Amy felt the snow crunch under her feet as they approached the different parts of the snow shovel. Julius retrieved the shovel head from the side of the yard nearest the garage and deposited it in the blue recycling bin. Amy picked up the shovel handle, twisted her body and, with the pent-up energy release of a discus thrower, heaved the stick which flew in an arch. It struck the side window of the garage, shattering it to pieces.

Julius watched the handle clatter to the ground. "Way to go!" he signed, chuckling and shaking his head as he walked to the car.

"Yes!" Amy pumped her fist and joined him in the passenger seat of his car.

"Feel better now?"

"A lot!" Taking a deep breath, Amy relaxed her shoulders, grateful for this short escape from the prison of Sybil's home. She buckled the seatbelt as the car pulled away from the curb.

Chapter 5

AMY

Later that evening, after a long afternoon of patiently navigating the halting communication with beginning American Sign Language (ASL) students at SFCC, Amy sat at the small vinyl-covered table in the corner that served as a dining area next to the small kitchen of Sybil's house.

The house had the stale smell of dust left to collect on items that had remained in place for years. A small clock ticked away the time above a shelf lined with porcelain dolls. On a faded picture hanging nearby, the painted, expressionless eyes of the dolls mirrored those of Sybil as a young girl holding one of these dolls while standing stiffly next to her equally rigid parents.

With the exception of sitting on the living room floor and eating at the low coffee table in front of the TV, this dining table stood as the only place to eat in the small house. Amy would much prefer to partake of her dinner at her desk in her room or with the welcome distraction of the TV, but Sybil made it clear that the food she cooked would not be delivered anywhere else but this table.

Sitting across the table from Sybil, Amy speared a fork into a pile of spaghetti, twisting it and then depositing it into her mouth. With what she hoped was a guttural, slurping sound, she sucked in the dangling noodles in the same way she recently saw on a YouTube video where a Komodo dragon devoured an octopus whose tentacles still writhed while the body was being chomped in the mouth.

Sybil sat stiffly, slicing her spaghetti into small, manageable bite-sized pieces.

Amy envisioned this woman becoming the octopus in the mouth of the dragon.

Sybil placed her utensils on each side of her plate, slowly chewed her food and swallowed. "You…have…spaghetti…on…the…side…of… your…mouth." She pointed to the side of her chin.

Amy shrugged. In spite of her thoughts, the pleasant taste of the spaghetti reminded her not to bite too hard on the hand that fed her.

"More cheese," Amy signed, looking at Sybil with expressionless eyes.

Ever since Amy could remember, this tolerance defined their interactions. Sure, she knew that Sybil provided a house and took care of her physical needs. She respected that. But such was their evolved, mutual tolerance driven by the rigid control of all that was Sybil, Amy was not about to grant more than a rudimentary acceptance of the caregiving. She nodded slightly and kept her eyes on the sprinkling snow of parmesan from the container.

The dinner passed in silence with Sybil's gray eyes observing her adopted daughter and Amy limiting her focus to the plate in front of her.

Amy chewed on a piece of buttered French bread and wondered if Julius or Denise had texted her about their customary Friday night pizza plans the next evening. She knew Julius had a late afternoon track practice so couldn't give her a ride. To break the silence and satisfy her mind by bringing her cell phone to the table was not worth the inevitable battle she knew would occur if she broke yet another of Sybil's mealtime rules.

The bread was swallowed and she made eye contact with Sybil. "So…You know tomorrow is my Friday night pizza with Denise and all. I need the car—"

Sybil broke eye contact to slice her spaghetti with a knife and fork.

Amy's eyes narrowed as she waited for the gray eyes to return.

"Can I use the car tomorrow?"

Sybil chewed, swallowed, and placed the utensils carefully on each side of the plate. "Is…Julius…not…available?"

"No." She didn't have the patience to watch Sybil finish her long, drawn-out Signing Exact English sentences. "You know he always has track practice late on Fridays."

"Let…me…think." Sybil paused to pick up a napkin, wipe her mouth, and carefully fold the napkin to place next to her fork. "I…need…to…check…and…make …sure…I… don't …need …the …car."

Amy pushed her chair back, stood, and picked up her plate. She looked at Sybil with a bored expression. "Can you check now?" she signed with one hand.

"First…you…need…to…do…the…dishes…while…I…check …my …work… schedule … for … tomorrow… My… calendar …is …in—"

"In your purse, in your room. I know." Amy put the plate back on the table. "You know, why don't you just give me that piece of sh*t car and go buy a new one like Julius's mom did?"

"I…am…not—" Sybil began her protest.

Amy held up a finger. "Listen! I think that would be a lot easier cause then we wouldn't always need to be fighting over YOUR car."

Sybil pushed her chair back and stood. Being almost a foot taller than Amy, she knew how to use her height to her advantage. "I…am…not…the…same…as…Julie…McLellan—"

Amy laughed. "That's the truth!" She shook her head with a smirk. "In…this…house… you…will…follow…my…rules… and… earn…the…privilege…of…getting…a…car."

The stares became hard as they stood facing each other. Amy

attempted to counteract the height difference with an even more intense glare. She hated it when Sybil brought up the earning of privileges; these same privileges which her friends' parents granted years ago. Amy curled her fingers around the plate in her hand. Sybil glanced down at the plate and, with some satisfaction, Amy recognized Sybil's fear that the plate would be thrown.

"Fine!" Amy jabbed her chest with the thumb of the sign. "You go check your schedule." She dismissed Sybil and walked to the sink to do the dishes.

As the dishwasher was nearly full and there were bowls and plates left over from breakfast and lunch, Amy turned on the sink faucet and rinsed a few dishes in the cool flow, waiting for the hot water to traverse through the pipes. She filled the remaining spaces in the dishwasher and shut it. She filled the pasta cooker with warm detergent lather and began scrubbing, placing each item in the drying rack adjacent to the sink.

As the sun set behind the roofs of the houses beyond the back alley, Amy immersed her hands in the warm, soapy water. It reminded her of the dilemma that clutched at her heart. Like the kinship she felt with her Deaf friends, her hands were comforted by the warm water, but the colder temperature of the house pricked her with the realization that her comrades were but a fleeting respite from the cold, harsh reality of this house she shared with Sybil.

As the sun's glow reduced to a sliver, she yearned to escape and run toward the light to once again bathe in the brilliant warmth of the sun. But no, like her current plight, she knew that would be an act of futility, and she was trapped in the cold reality of her existence which Sybil had constructed and controlled.

A bony hand grabbed a dish from the rack. Amy shuddered with a start.

"You…missed…a…spot…on…this…plate." Sybil placed the

dish in the sink.

Amy glared at the dish. The thought occurred to smash this dish on the floor, but she dismissed it. "Um…Tomorrow. The car?" she signed, her hands dripping soapy water on the floor.

Sybil looked at the floor then slowly brought her eyes back to Amy's face. "You…can…have…the…car…tomorrow." She pointed to the floor. "Now…wipe…that…up…and…finish…the… dishes." She turned to begin her nighttime routine of watching TV in the living room.

Amy returned to the dishes, completely ignoring the small puddles on the floor. After ten minutes, she pressed the button on the dishwasher, feeling its vibration then walked through the living room illuminated only by the flicking lights of the TV. She ignored Sybil's face, shrouded in the shadows as she sat in her recliner at the far corner of the room.

Entering her bedroom, Amy clicked the lock on the door and made a beeline for the cell phone on her desk.

"Got the car tomorrow!" she texted both Julius and Denise in a group chat.

She looked at the screen and waited for the dot icons indicating activity on the other end. None came. Just the static image of her own words staring back at her.

"Hey! Anybody home?" she texted again.

Amy stared at the screen, feeling the pangs of loneliness and clicked on the video icon for a live group chat. She could feel the phone vibrate as the call rang. Still no answer. She sighed and placed the phone face- up on the desk to let it ring. After a while a 'Caller not available' message flashed. She punched the button to hang up and tossed the phone into her purse.

Instinctively, Amy placed a hand on her wrist, feeling the smooth shiny beads of her bracelet. She thought back to that time when it was given to her and remembered feeling lonely on a cement platform. It was Bisha who cared enough to give her these beads and provide some warmth and protection from her cold, isolated reality.

Perhaps this same Bisha could provide some answers and an escape from her present circumstance. Certainly, this girl, who by now Amy knew to be a woman, might have an idea regarding the original name by which her mother called her. Bisha might even know some of the people from the beggar community to which Amy's mother belonged.

Amy shut her eyes as she turned the beads in the fingers of one hand. *What name did my mother call me before she abandoned me on that cold, dark night?* she wondered. With the other hand, she formed an 'A'  and, with a shudder, produced the **name sign** given to her by Sybil. *No,* she thought. *That's not my name.*

Slowly, she changed the handshape to an index finger pointing to her ear and then shook the thumb. *Hear-Nothing,* she recalled. *But that was not given to me by my mother.*

Amy sighed, glanced into her purse and saw that there was no reply to her text on the cell phone. On her desk was her school issued laptop computer. A large SFCC sticker on the back indicated the institution to which it belonged. She looked at this computer and considered attempting some homework.

Not in the mood, she thought and reached next to the laptop, opening up a clear-covered, shallow box with small receptacles inside. One long receptacle contained a pile of string. The other smaller squares held a variety of beads, each sorted according to shape, size, and color. She brought this box to her bed, opened it, and examined its contents under the single lamp on the nightstand next to her bed.

Picking up a leather string, Amy tied a knot at one end and picked up a blue bead, threading it onto the string. She grabbed another bead and proceeded to make a bracelet. The living room TV lights flickered between the threshold and bottom of her door. She kept these lights at the corner of her eye as she focused on the bracelet. Sure enough, about fifteen minutes later, the flickering lights were blocked by a shadow.

Amy paused to look warily at the threshold to wait for the vibrations of Sybil knocking at her door. None came, but the shadow remained. A ghostly reminder of Sybil's presence on the other side.

Amy picked up a bead and fumbled it onto her lap. Scowling, she steadied the bead between a thumb and forefinger and paused, watching the doorway.

A minute later, the shadow disappeared and the flickering lights stopped as Sybil turned off the TV before going to bed.

Letting her face relax, Amy slipped the last bead onto the string and tied together the ends of the string. The completed bracelet was placed into her purse.

She knew she must leave this house.

The thought of getting an apartment entered her mind.

At the pizza dinner tomorrow night, she would ask her friends to help her find one.

Mostly, Amy thought of India, the place of her birth. During the upcoming summer break after spring semester, perhaps she and Julius could take a trip to India and answer the questions that swirled in her mind.

She would escape from this place.

Chapter 6

JULIUS

The evening of the next day, just before dinner, Julius guided the car down the Rowan Avenue hill. The setting sun cast an orange glow reflecting off the snow in the front yard of a house he approached.

A woman with long braided, auburn-colored hair bent over a snow shovel picked up a scoop of snow on the pathway in front of the house, and heaved it to the side.

Forever working. That's Denise! he thought as he parked the car at the curb behind an old white sedan he knew to be Sybil's. As Denise's back was turned to him, Julius sat and observed for a minute.

Upon the porch in front of the house, the swinging couch, suspended by chains from the overhanging eave, and the two easy chairs next to it sat as a reminder of the many hours they spent during the summers in the Deaf-space of Denise's home, reminiscing, laughing, and helping each other understand the complexities of life.

The front door opened and out stepped Amy holding a mug containing a hot drink that steamed in the evening cold. She stopped and watched Julius as he exited the car.

"Shh!" he put a finger to his lips. Scooping up a snowball, Julius heaved it at Denise, and it smacked the back of her jacket, disintegrating to the ground.

The snow shovel clattered to the ground. "What!?" Denise signed as she looked quickly behind her. "Julius! You little jerk! I coulda had a heart attack!" She clutched at her chest in mock pain.

"Sorry!" Julius laughed and enclosed Denise in an embrace.

Something poked at his arm. Amy smiled up at him with a smirk and handed the mug to Denise. "This hot chocolate is for **Denise**," she emphasized the 'D' name sign twisting on the cheek. "I was planning on bringing you one but, no, because of what you just did, you gotta go get your own!"

Julius closed a fist on his chest in mock **anguish**. "Oh! That pains me!" He held up a hand and inclined his head low. "Fine. I will go get my own."

"That's okay." Denise patted Amy on the back. "I am pretty much done shoveling now. I forgive him, so now we can go inside and get him his hot chocolate."

Amy picked up the snow shovel and examined it. "This is all in one piece. If it snows again, looks like I'll need to borrow this."

"Huh? Why the need to borrow?" Denise screwed her face in puzzlement.

"Uh…" Julius grabbed the shovel from Amy and jabbed it into the pile of snow so that the handle stuck out. "Long story, but you know the plot." He rolled his eyes as he wiggled his tongue, emphasizing the PAST-INCLUDE-TO-NOW sign. "She just popped off and broke Sybil's snow shovel."

"**SYBIL**!" Amy rolled her eyes and hit her chin with the B**CH movement added to the name sign. "That woman makes my blood boil!"

"Oh my! Come-on!" Denise waved them toward her house. "Let's go in and get warm. You can tell me more."

They stepped between the solid oak columns of the front porch and entered the house. The gas flames flickered in the living room fireplace, and the heat wafted over them as they deposited their coats in the closet near the entry.

Denise placed her mug on the coffee table near the fireplace. "Go-ahead and sit while I get the hot chocolate for you both."

As Denise entered her kitchen to prepare their drinks, Julius and Amy sat on the loveseat near the fireplace.

She removed her small black purse from her shoulder and placed it on the floor. He slid his arm around her shoulder as they watched the yellow flickering flames above the blue gas of the fireplace. Her thick, slightly coarse dark hair tickled his chin as he leaned his cheek onto the top of her head.

He could feel her shoulders drop as she leaned into him and knew she was struggling to let go. He prayed, *Please, God, give her peace. Don't let Sybil affect her so much.* The restless flames in the fireplace reminded him of the chaos which encompassed his friend. *If only she could let go of it all,* he thought. *I, too, need the peace.*

They sat thus for a couple of minutes, just sitting and looking at the fire.

Denise entered the room. "Here ya go." She exaggerated the words on her lips as her hands were busy holding mugs. She placed them on the low coffee table in front of them and sat in an easy chair next to the fireplace. "So…What's up?"

Julius could feel Amy's shoulders rise.

"I HATE living in that house!" Amy used the double handed **PUKE** sign. "That woman is like a cop. I'm in prison! Rarely lets me use her car. I had to beg to use it today. Won't help me set up a bank account so I can control my own money. Won't even let me say a  word, NOTHING, about moving out and getting my own place. Why is she like that?"

Denise shrugged. "I have interacted with Sybil for a long time. Still can't figure her out."

"She is a **demon!**"

"Hold on a sec, Amy." Julius placed a hand on Amy's DEMON sign. "I agree with you, but…"

Amy frowned and twisted out of his arm, scooting a few inches away. "But what?"

"She can only have as much control over you as you let her." "As I let her? What do you mean? She is not even my mother! At least you have a mother who listens to you, takes care of you, and LOVES you."

"That's true—" Julius pointed a finger toward the window in the general direction of Sybil's house. "Why can't you just forgive and let-go of your anger?"

Amy shook her head adamantly. "No! I will not forgive Sybil. If I forgive her, she will see it as me telling her everything is okay. It would justify everything she has done to me." She leaned forward and slammed an open palm on the coffee table. The hot chocolate splashed, almost spilling out of the mugs. "No! I will fight her!"

Denise leaned forward and held up a hand. "Hold on a sec. Calm down please. Julius is right. I agree that Sybil is a bad influence on you, but you are much more in control than you think you are."

"But how?" Amy raised her hands in the air. "I don't know who is my real mother. I don't even know what is my real name. All that was snatched away from me on the streets of Mumbai, India, when I was a little girl. Then that witch had to come and"—she held her fingers in the 'quote' sign—"save me from it all."

Denise nodded. "True, but she did take care of you—"

"But," Amy interrupted, "why couldn't somebody like Julius's mother, or better yet, you, Denise, take care of me?" A tear welled and dropped from her right eye.

Julius's heart tightened in his chest. He hated it when Amy's emotions got so out of control. He scooted closer to her. "But I'm here." He pointed to Denise. "And so is she."

Amy wiped the tear from her face and sniffled. "**Cr*p!**" She 
jammed her thumb into her other hand and pointed to a box on the

coffee table. Now my nose is running. Denise, can you please hand me some tissues?"

Denise handed Amy the tissues then fiddled with the end of her braid and looked at it. They knew she was gathering her thoughts. She dropped the braid and looked up. "Right, we are all here for you and will always be. But I agree, it is time for you to move on from that house." She pointed to Julius. "Maybe tomorrow you can go with Amy and help her check out the Fort George Wright Apartments across from SFCC. I saw a sign advertising one bedroom units for a reasonable rent." She looked up at the clock on the wall and turned to Julius with a questioning expression. "I thought Jeremy and Maria were supposed to be here by now and bring pizza."

Julius shrugged. "I haven't got a text yet from my brother—"

The The door flew open and a blast of cold air hit them. Through the door jumped a young woman about the same age as Julius and Amy. The brown cords attached to her cochlear implant magnets swayed with her perfectly styled hair.

"Speaking of the devil." Julius laughed and rolled his eyes.

Chapter 7

JULIUS

"Hi, Maria," Denise greeted. "Where's Jeremy?"

Maria jerked a thumb at the door. "He's coming with pizza."

Jeremy walked in, his hands occupied by two boxes of pizza. He nodded at Julius and placed the pizza on the coffee table. His long, dark hair fell onto his face and he brushed it aside.

Julius saw that his older brother wore the green coat from his military days. That remained the only reminder of his brother's former life which now seemed so long ago.

"What did you get?" Julius pointed at the boxes.

"Uh…how do you say it?" Jeremy paused and raised his hand to fingerspell "S-A-U-S-A-G-E."

"**SAUSAGE.**" Maria showed him the sign.

Julius, Amy, and Denise sipped their hot chocolate and watched the exchange.

"O-L-I-V-E-S?" Jeremy fingerspelled slowly.

Maria wiggled her fingers. "I just fingerspell that."

"**P-E-P-P-E-R-O-N-I?**"

"I think it's this." Maria used the classifier-F handshape repeated on her left palm. She looked at the others. "What do you think?"

"That's a good question." Denise opened one box and looked at the pizza inside. "Julius and Amy, what sign do you use?"

"Kinda like what Maria does." Julius formed the 'P' handshape and then produced the same classifier combination on his palm as Maria.

"English interference!" Amy interjected. "I don't like it when people just make up signs and go with it as if they have God's authority to dictate how things are signed."

Jeremy paused in the midst of copying Julius's classifier combination with the 'P' handshape and looked at Amy with an expression of total confusion. Maria stepped toward him intentionally.

"Amy…means…to…say." Maria mouthed her words and switched to a slow, English style of signing.

Amy's eyes widened as she watched with the others.

"She…does…not…like…I-N-V-E-N-T-E-D"—Maria paused and showed Jeremy the sign for **INVENTION**—"…invented..signs."

"Oh! I see." Jeremy nodded.

"So…" Julius gently elbowed Amy. "What sign do you suggest for P-E-P-P-E-R-O-N-I?"

"I just think we should consult with others before we—" Amy paused and watched as Maria touched Jeremy lightly on the arm to get his attention.

"Amy"—Maria formed the name sign on her cheek—"is…saying …that—"

"Oh, would you please stop!" Amy stood and interrupted. "He's not going to learn ASL if you keep on interpreting with that Signing Exact English crap!"

Maria's eyes hardened as the two young women looked at each other.

Not again! Julius thought as he recalled their endless arguments and bickering since they were in preschool.

"Uh…girls—" he began, but Amy held up a hand and stood to face Maria.

"Besides"—Amy pointed between Maria and Jeremy—"looks like you have become his interpreter with benefits!"

"**What**!?" Maria stepped toward Amy and held the sign, curling her fingers into a claw handshape.

"Whoa girls!" Denise interjected. "Amy! They just got here and you are already popping off on Maria." She used the **BAWL-OUT** sign. "What's up with you?"

"I just don't like invented signs. Plus, she's breaking the ASL rules by—"Amy rolled her eyes and formed her own name sign—"continuing to sign 'Amy' instead of just pointing to me."

"So…Amy"—Maria rolled her shoulders, sarcastically forming the name sign—"Your Majesty, what sign do YOU suggest for P-E-P-P-E- R-O-N-I?"

"STOP!" Denise stepped between them, holding out her hands like a prize fight referee trying to separate two boxers. "Amy, please sit down next to Julius. Maria and Jeremy, the pizza is getting cold. Can you please go into the kitchen and prepare plates for all of us?"

"Sure." Jeremy picked up the boxes and Maria followed him into the kitchen.

Once again, Denise sat in her easy chair and looked at Amy.

With Amy sitting next to him, her legs touching his, Julius placed a hand on her knee. He could feel the storm of her emotions through the tense muscles and slight shaking of her leg.

She reached down and picked up her purse, opened it, and pulled out a chain necklace attached to a small crucifix. The bottom post protruded in a sharp point, making the pendant resemble a tiny sword. She placed the necklace in her palm and ran a finger over the pendant.

Julius saw that end of the cross piece was smoother and shinier than he had previously noticed. Some of the sharp edges were gone from the time Amy had shown it to him when she was a little girl.

"Amy." Denise waved to get her attention. "I don't think you are really upset with Maria. What's really bothering you? Is it Sybil?"

Julius was glad that Denise chose to use Sybil's name sign instead of 'mother.' He saw the hardness behind the tears that formed in Amy's eyes.

"I HATE my name sign!" Amy formed her name sign on her cheek and stuck out her tongue, screwing her face into an expression of nausea. "Sybil forced it on me when I was a kid." She used the **STICK- TO- HEART** sign and looked at the necklace in her hand. "I do remember what I was called before I ever met that witch."

"Yeah, you told me before." Julius pointed to his ear and shook his thumb. "Hear-Nothing, right?"

Denise frowned. "But that seems such a derogatory, oppressive label for a Deaf person."

"I know, but"—Amy held up the necklace—"when I was on the streets of Mumbai, I got that name from an older girl. She and I were being chased by a cop through a bazaar, and this necklace fell on me." Amy made a stabbing motion with the pendant. "Just before the cop nabbed me, I stabbed him in the leg with this. Then he knocked me out with his club."

"What happened to the girl?" Denise asked.

"She disappeared." Amy looked at the necklace in a moment of recollection. "I think her name was 'Bisha' or something. She called me Hear-Nothing. That's the first time anybody ever cared to call me something, or even give me a name in a way that I recognized."

"Was this Bisha hearing or Deaf?" Denise asked.

"I think hearing. I remember her yelling at the other street kids."

"So, how's 'Hear-Nothing' from Bisha different from 'Amy' from Sybil?"

"It's WHO gave me the name. I know my mother in India called me something. I think it began with an 'S.' She knew I was Deaf but didn't care to come up with something visual so I could recognize my

name. Bisha was the first person who ever CARED"—Amy emphasized the '**cherish**' sign—"to enter my Deaf-world." She paused and looked at the fireplace. "Sybil just came up with the name 'Amy' for me and forced me to use her invented name sign for that. I had no choice but to follow her dictates."

They paused and looked at the fireplace. Denise had not yet turned on the living room lamp. With the fading light outside, the orange flames of the fireplace cast shadowy, flickering patterns across their faces.

Julius picked up Amy's mug from the table and handed it to her. "Your hot chocolate's getting cold."

"Ah! Thanks." She held the mug close to her face and took a deep breath. The warmth and rich aroma seemed to settle her mind.

Denise interrupted their contemplation. "Going back to Maria. She means well—wants Jeremy to understand what's going on. He's new to signing, remember? I think her English signing triggers you because it reminds you of Sybil."

Amy shrugged. "Maybe." She continued sipping her hot chocolate.

Julius shifted in his seat and picked up his own mug from the coffee table. He took a sip and welcomed the fact that his hands were occupied in doing something.

The tempest of emotions stirring within his friend was unsettling. His best-friend she was, and they certainly had developed a deep understanding of each other over the years while they were classmates. But this level of anger and intensity was something new. It wa s a frustrating barrier, preventing him from addressing what he really wanted.

Now he loved her deeply with an affection into which their relationship had evolved. He yearned for something to do so he could express his love, and she could reciprocate and go back to the calmer, happier, and fun-loving Amy he once knew.

"Do you remember at all the name of your birth mother?" he signed with one hand while holding the hot chocolate mug with the other.

Amy took a long sip of hot chocolate and placed the mug on the table. She sat back and looked at the fire as if the flames would draw out the flickering wisps of memory long since faded away. Denise drained her hot chocolate and leaned forward to as she and Julius watched.

"I mostly remember her face. It was long and thin with big brown eyes like mine. She must have been short like me too. I remember not needing to look up at her as much as I did other adults." Amy looked up to the ceiling and shook her head as one memory dissolved. "But no, I never saw her name. Like I said, even though she knew I was Deaf, she never thought to make either her own name or my name visible."

A sudden movement from the kitchen interrupted them.

"Pizza's ready!" Maria announced as she and Jeremy carried in plates with various slices.

Denise held up her hand and gestured. "Put it on the coffee table here. Amy's explaining something."

Amy's eyes narrowed as she watched Maria take a bite of pizza and look at her with a mix of expectation and sarcasm.

Julius saw the slight rise of his friend's shoulders. He knew that Maria would not easily forget the "interpreter with benefits" comment, as the old jealousy-induced female rivalry between these two had never completely disappeared. Indeed, part of him wished Maria weren't there so that Amy could feel free to be herself.

Denise tapped Amy on her leg. "Keep going," she encouraged.

Amy's eyes relaxed and she let down her guard. She raised the necklace and ran a finger over the pendant. "This reminds me of how

Bisha protected me."

"Who's Bisha?" Maria interrupted.

Denise paused in a bite of pizza and gave a warning look.

"Long story. She was the girl who took care of me in Mumbai, India, after my mother abandoned me." Amy held up the pendant, touching the sharp end of the post. "Like this, she was as tough as nails. I saw her really beat up some of the other street kids when they were out of line. She wasn't that way with me." She placed the necklace back into her purse and touched the beaded bracelet on her wrist. "The 'Hear-Nothing' name sign was not given to mock me or put me down. In fact, I think Bisha cared for me. She gave me this bracelet, and I keep it to be reminded of that—how she cherished me."

Maria pointed to her ear and repeated the name sign, look ing quizzically at her hand.

"Hear-Nothing," Julius clarified. "Amy's name sign in India before Sybil took her." He used the **SNATCH-UP** sign from his elbow  in reference to the STEAL sign.

As the others munched their pizza and listened with their eyes, Amy completely ignored the slice on her plate. She nodded and repeated the SNATCH-UP sign Julius had used. "Yes, I was stolen from India." She set her jaw and resolutely shook her head. "Why did my mother abandon me? Was it because I am Deaf? I am confused because I do remember she showed me some love."

Julius pointed at her with his pizza. "If she loved you, I don't think she would have abandoned you."

"That's what confuses me. I want to ask her why. Also, somehow I want to know her name and especially the name she called me when I was little." Amy huffed. "I don't know…I can't get rid of this feeling. And of all people, I had to go get snatched-up by Sybil!" Her shoulders slumped and she looked at the flames.

Julius leaned close and put his arm around her.

Denise finished her pizza slice and put down her plate. "Okay, I got a wild idea. Not sure I should share it with you…"

Maria perked up. "Go ahead!"

"Um…well…" Denise fiddled with her braid. "It seems you really need to go to India and find this out for yourself."

"I was thinking the same thing!" Amy leaned forward, a look of surprise on her face.

"Yes, I have seen you struggling with this for a long time, and it certainly isn't going to resolve itself."

"What do you mean?" Now Julius leaned forward.

"All of these questions you have are very valid." Denise turned to Amy. "Maybe if you actually go to India and find your mother, you might get these answers you are looking for. I have known you since you were a little girl. Ever since preschool, I have seen you struggle with these questions. Back then, they may not have been stated as clearly as they are now, but your actions and behavior certainly showed something was stirring inside of you." Denise used the **STORM** sign  in front of her heart.

"Okay. I think you're right, but how and when were you thinking this could happen?" Amy held the **QUESTION** sign, waiting for Denise's answer.

"And alone?" Julius shook his head. "Amy all by herself in India. I don't think so."

Denise shook her head. "No, not alone. You can go with her."

"What!?" Julius looked at Denise with an incredulous look on his face. "What about my college scholarship? What about her job?"

"We can try to make the trip during the coming summer when you both are on break. You can always come back to your classes and jobs. You both are young and talented. Even if you miss out on something here while you are gone, other opportunities will arise later. For now, this storm in Amy needs to be addressed." Denise stood, slowly nodding her head, appearing to make a decision. "Hold on a sec while I get my laptop." She turned and walked to her bedroom.

This thought had never occurred to Julius. Except for the chaotic time long ago when he was a little child in Seattle and his family was dealing with the loss of his father, Spokane had been his home and the only place he thought to live. Now the notion of throwing everything to the wind and leaving it all to accompany Amy on a wild goose chase to India was like a bucket of cold water thrown at his face.

Julius looked at Amy, whose face was frozen in an expression of expectation, confusion, curiosity, and fear.

Julius thought, *What about my college scholarship? What about my running?* He looked at his brother who was starting to gather the empty plates. *What about Jeremy? Would he be okay without me? Is this really going to help her?*

Julius looked at Amy and nudged her. "What are you thinking?"

Amy's body shuddered as if woken from a trance. "Huh?" She blinked a few times. "What?"

Denise bustled in and knelt on the floor next to the coffee table. She flipped open her laptop and clicked on the internet. "Let's see." She typed on the keyboard. "Zip Quest is a good travel site. Date. Hmm. Let's search for a flight for the two of you five months from now, June."

"Uh, Denise. What are you doing?" Julius waved to get her attention.

Amy rose from the couch and sat on the floor next to Denise. She watched the screen and fiddled with the bracelet on her wrist.

"I see an international flight out of Seattle via a hop-over from Spokane. SEA-Air flight." Denise stroked her chin, narrowed her eyes, and nodded. "Yep. I'll pay for this flight for you both."

Chapter 8

AMY

Late the next morning, the low rising January sun shone bright. Not a cloud in the sky. Due to the steady wind that blew up the valley and over the hill of the SFCC campus, the weather was still cold.

On the very edge of the hill, across the street from the campus, Amy leaned against the Fort George Wright Apartments sign and shivered. "Brrr!" She gathered her fleece coat around her neck. "This cold reminds me of two nights ago."

Julius sat on the hood of his car parked next to the sign. "Which part are you talking about?"

"Sybil's house." Amy shook her head and looked up at the nearby apartments they had just finished touring. A large banner hanging near the entrance announced 'STUDIOS AVAILABLE. STARTING AT $1200 PER MONTH.' "Yeah, Sybil's house," she repeated.

Julius nodded.

She appreciated his understanding that they would never refer to it as her own home.

Julius pointed to an upper window of the building. "What did you think of the studio the manager just showed you?"

"I liked the high ceilings and how it let in a lot of light through the tall windows. It felt warm. Not like the cold stuffiness of Sybil's house." She tucked her coat into the waistband of her pants. "That woman's relentless control is like this wind seeping in and pricking at every part of my life."

Julius stood and placed an arm around her, hugging her close. "Are you warm now?"

"Yes. Thanks!" She looked up at him and smiled, snuggling closer.

"I agree. You definitely need to get out of that house," he signed with his free hand. "The manager said there should be a vacancy April first, two and a half months from now. Think you can be ready by then to move?"

"Wish I could move in today. Don't want to spend any more nights at Sybil's than I need. But yeah, I can wait till April."

"They require first and last month's rent, plus a $300 security deposit." Julius disengaged his arm and counted on his fingers. "That's $300 now and $2400 in a little more than a month. How much do you have in your bank account?"

"You mean the one that Sybil controls? Last time I checked, I have a couple thousand. But I need Sybil's APPROVAL for anything I withdraw."

"I do have some savings, and I am sure Denise can help with the initial costs, but will your salary from your part-time tutoring job at SFCC cover the ongoing rent?"

"I can ask SFCC to increase my hours, but I need to set up a separate bank account that Sybil doesn't control."

Julius walked toward the car. "We can see about doing that at the credit union where I am a member. Come-on!"

Amy stepped back. "I want to talk to you about what Denise brought up last night. India."

"Oh. Okay."

She pointed down the road. "Let's go for a walk."

They joined hands and proceeded to walk along Whistalks Way across from the college. They passed the log construction of a lodge that had been rented as venues for their high school dances and proms. To their right, the hill dropped steeply down to the Peaceful Valley neighborhood where the Spokane River followed a wide curve upriver to the Falls.

Deep in thought, Amy looked over the valley and saw arailroad bridge that spanned the river. Her thoughts swirled like the small rapids below, and this structure stood as a reminder that she yearned for her own bridge across the turbulent waters of her past.

Julius stood next to a metal post and pointed to a small sign. It showed an image of a runner surrounded by lilac flowers and the number four stamped in the middle.

"This is the Bloomsday four-mile marker." He pointed along the road that led downhill to the intersection with Pettit Drive. "Doomsday Hill is that way. During the last Bloomsday race I ran, I remember that is where I pulled ahead of Jeremy." He shook his head. "He sure didn't like that his little brother was able to do that."

Amy followed his gaze down the road and looked at him. "You sure do love your running, don't you?"

Julius shrugged. "I'm not sure I love it. It is a talent that God gave me, and I like being able to do it well, but"—he formed the formed the  **EXHAUSTED** sign—"it sure does demand a huge amount of energy, time, and commitment, especially now that I am on a track scholarship at Gonzaga University."

"Is it all worth it?"

"Well, for me to continue and get the scholarship, I need to perform well in track. Coach said I need to qualify for the NCAA regional championships and post times that qualify for the nationals."

Her eyes widened in a doubtful expression. "That'll be a lot of work."

"Yeah, but if I do, that means I don't have to work to pay for college tuition."

Amy extended her hands and tilted them up and down as if she were balancing a scale. "Work for money versus run for money. Time and energy-wise, pretty much the same thing, huh?"

"Yeah, but I think I enjoy running more than working at a coffee shop or something. It is certainly better than the grunt work I did with Jeremy at the Water Department last summer."

Amy regarded him for a long moment. Surely, she admired his talent, but at this moment, his need to run was the farthest thing from her mind.

She pointed to a flat area near the edge of the hill where the sun had melted the snow to expose a patch of brown grass and weeds. "Come, let's sit."

The cold breeze continued to bend the longer blades of grass, and they located a spot for them to comfortably sit.

"Julius." Amy tilted her head, looking sideways at him. "India?"

Julius plucked a blade of grass, watched it sway in the breeze, then tossed it aside. "Yes, Denise brought that up last night. What are you thinking?"

"Well, since she brought that up, I've been thinking a lot about it." She dropped her shoulders and tears welled in her eyes. "I really don't know myself. I mean. All I know is what Sybil forced on me." She formed her name sign. "My name, everything about me, is White American, like her."

"But what about us? Your real Deaf family? I know you were born in another country, and your real mother, who was hearing and didn't care to make things accessible to you, gave you a name you never heard." Julius rolled his eyes sarcastically at the **LISTENING** sign. "You have us and what we have given you. Is that not enough?"

Amy nodded slowly then shook her head. "Yes, I love you all, especially you, but—" She pointed to her ear and shook her thumb. "I am Hear-Nothing. That is the only thing I know about my true self and where I am from. I need to find out who I really am, not who others determine me to be."

The wind blew a strand of her hair into her face. She brushed it way with a frustrated flick. "Not only did my real mother not care to make things accessible to me, the fact that she abandoned me sure doesn't help me know who I am."

She paused and looked at her shaking thumb handshape. "What does this even mean? In ASL it has no meaning, but in India it obviously means **NOTHING**." She shook her head and emphasized the sign. "Is this who I am. NOTHING?"

"Whoa!" Julius held out his hands. "You are definitely not NOTHING. I mean…" He pointed to the sky and formed the  **SURRENDER** sign. "God created you and you are very special to Him. He is here for you. I mean, when I struggle with something, I surrender it to Jesus and that helps give me peace. Can you do the same?"

Amy shook her head. "Julius, that is what works for you. If I did that, I would just be following what you tell me to do." She raised her eyebrows and formed the **LISTEN** sign next to her eye. "I don't think you are listening to me."

"But will a trip to India really give you what you need?" Julius raised one palm in frustration and placed the other on his chest. "I am here for you. I obviously care for you. Why can't you open your heart and let that be enough for your own peace?"

"I know. I know!" Amy shut her eyes and a tear tracked down her cheek. "Please just listen! Like I said, I NEED to know who I am! Not who that b**ch Sybil forced me to be. Not even who you and my Deaf family know me to be." She opened her eyes and raised her hands, curling her fingers in a pleading expression. "Who am I means what? My original name? This Bisha who gave me my first name sign, my birth mother and what she called me? I especially need to know why she abandoned me?" She vented her frustration with a swear sign.

"Okay!" Julius looked at the college campus across the street. "Okay, I get it but—" He pointed back at the apartments they had just visited. "What about your plans to live on your own? I know Denise mentioned a summer trip to India, but what about you having a job so you can afford the rent at this apartment? How will you do that AND find out all about this India stuff?"

"I don't know. I just know that with your support, and also Denise's support, somehow I can find what I need."

"My support?" Julius leaned forward. "What does that look like?" "Well, Denise said she would buy us plane tickets. So obviously it means we go to India."

"WE go to India?" Julius stood and looked down at Amy, raising his hands to the sky. "You expect me to give up everything I've achieved, everything I've worked for so you can go-on an international wild goose chase that may or may not provide the answers you are looking for?"

"I certainly can't go-on my own. Wouldn't be safe. So, I need you to come with me."

"Amy" — Julius lowered his palms—"calm down. I know I am having a hard time with the communication problems I am facing with the people at Gonzaga University, but you know I have a scholarship commitment to honor."

"I understand, but, if not you, then who would go with me to India? Plus, we plan to go during the summer after your track season is finished. So, what is the problem?"

"The problem is that you don't need to go to India to get what you need." Julius took out his phone and opened the internet app. "You can find out all that information online." He tapped the screen and typed in a word then showed her the phone. "See. I just opened up

Facebook and typed in 'Bisha, India.' Here is a list of people we can check out, narrow down the search, and try contacting her."

Amy watched Julius, giving no reply. She couldn't place this sudden agitation in him. Where was it coming from? What did Julius need from her? Why wasn't he supporting her?

"Plus"—he placed the phone back in his pocket—"I'm pretty sure you need a visitor's visa to travel to India. I think it takes a while to get that."

"Let's apply." Amy defiantly raised her chin. "Like I have been trying to explain but you are too stubborn to listen, I need to see where I am from. Need to find my mother, sit down with her, and find out my name, and learn what possessed her to abandon me like that." She pointed a finger at Julius. "You know something? It seems you love your running more than you love me. You're more interested in being dragged into that hearing world than you are in supporting me."

"Stop!" Julius turned away, facing across the valley.

Immediately her chest tightened from guilt, and she wished she would have controlled what she said.

His hands moved in vague, subtle signs as he gazed across the valley.

She knew he was praying. He lowered his hands and she stepped closer, tapping him on the shoulder. "I'm sorry."

He held up a hand to collect his thoughts before turning to face her. "Fine. I'll start the application for our visitor's visa to India." He raised two fingers to his eye. "But we'll see. I still think you can get what you need online." Pointing up to the sky, he formed the **LET-GO** sign. "I do wish you would give it all to God and let Him answer all your questions in His time."

She grabbed his arm and squeezed. "Thanks, but how do I 'let-go' of a feeling or a need?" She bent over, plucked a clump of dry grass and let go, watching the individual blades float away in the wind. "It's not like I can let-go of it all like this grass." She hugged his torso and he returned the favor with an arm around her shoulder.

"Come-on, I'll take you to Sybil's. I gotta get to track practice."
"Uh, Julius. I really do not want to spend the day in that hell-hole." She grabbed his hand, pleading while signing with the other. "Can I come watch you at practice?"

"Fine."

Silently, they walked hand-in-hand back to the car as their thoughts remained hidden like the unknown origins of the wind.

Chapter 9

JULIUS

During the early evening of that same day, the Spokane river meandered along its course in the area just east of Gonzaga University. At one point along the northern bank, a gaggle of geese exited the river, shook the water from their feathers, and proceeded to walk serenely along the paved Centennial Trail.

A group of male runners passed. Julius led the men through the turnaround point at a park bench about a mile past the Avista Utilities headquarters complex.

Honk! One rather large goose turned, extending its wings with ruffled feathers in defiance.

Julius admired the boldness of this goose and wished it would peck at the legs of his Gonzaga University track teammates as they bantered, moving their mouths with comments.

He looked behind him as he ran. A group of female runn ers followed a couple hundred yards behind.

That gander was puffing its feathers and positioned himself in the middle of the path. On the right of the group of women, the bank dropped to the water's edge, while immediately to their left was an earthen rise about five feet in height. They bunched together and attempted to run to the right of the goose who cut them off and lunged with a full extension of its long neck.

Julius raised his eyebrows and smiled as one of the leading women turned in an attempt to avoid the snapping beak which buried itself into her hamstring just below a buttock. She jumped aside and flailed her arms, mouth open wide in a scream.

The men around Julius sprinted to save their damsel in distress.

Julius slowed to a jog to observe the scene as two male runners chased away the offending goose. The others gathered around to comfort their stricken mate. Julius saw on their faces and mouths the expected reactions of surprise and concern which undoubtedly contained joking comments and perhaps a swear word or two.

But it was all a facade of interactions directed away from him, and he knew the futility of any attempts to gain access, so he continued on his run, resuming the cadence of his steps.

As he ran alone, the wind now at his back, propelling him along the shimmering river back to the Gonzaga University Campus, Julius knew there would be no attempt from the other male runners to catch up to him. Such was his talent as the runner with the highest skill in running. Efforts to catch up with him would be an act of futility.

But he knew his status as a leader was limited to the act of running. The simple fact that he couldn't hear, and the callous attitudes of the other runners, relegated the true leadership roles to others who possessed all their sensory faculties.

He glanced behind and saw the men gather to resume their run. Lifting his knees to increase his pace, Julius ran ahead, for he knew what awaited him at his destination was a far more welcoming, inclusive, and even loving presence. There, his leadership was not limited to a single physical act such as running. The fact that he couldn't hear, and the shared experience of the one who waited for him, qualified him as having great value in his life and those in the community to which they belonged.

Fifteen minutes later, Julius rounded the corner of the Gonzaga University BARC Student Center and stopped to catch his breath.

Amy was sitting and sipping a coffee at an outside table next to the café. Her face brightened. "How was your run?"

"It was fun." Julius plopped on the concrete floor to commence some of his cool-down stretches. "I saw something funny."

As he stretched, he noticed the other male and female runners rounding the corner, stopping to catch their breaths. Apparently, they all decided to finish the run together after the goose fiasco. Because this was an informal, group tempo run, their coach remained in his office for the day.

"Isn't the ground kinda cold?" Amy asked as she observed the other athletes gather in small groups and continue to chat while some of them sat on the ground and engaged in their own stretching.

"After a run, it kinda feels good on sore muscles." Julius waved for Amy to join him. "Come-on down. Join me in some of these stretches."

Amy looked around at the other runners, then down at Julius sitting near her but apart from them. She plopped onto the ground, extending her short legs and grabbing her toes in the same way as Julius. "What's that funny thing you saw?" she signed between stretches.

Julius finished a stretch and turned to Amy. "Have you ever been attacked by a goose?"

"Huh? No, but I've seen a few stubbornly refuse to move as I walk by in the park."

"Well, imagine a big ol' male goose. What do you call it? A gander, but one full of testosterone, all pumped up ready to fight and protect its mate."

"Uh huh?" Amy's eyes were wide in anticipation.

"Back along the path, a huge gander just attacked one of the women runners." Julius pointed to the group. "I don't remember which one it was, but you shoulda seen it! It was like a cartoon. The girl was flailing around and screaming while the goose pecked at her butt."

"Really?" Amy covered her mouth and suppressed a laugh. "What did you all do?"

"A couple of the guys chased the goose away while everyone else tried to console the victim." Julius mimicked holding a phone in front of him. "Woulda been a great video to post."

Julius resumed a stretch. Amy crossed her legs on the pavement near him. They both looked around at the group and saw several mouths moving and eyebrows raised in animated explanations, probably related to the goose incident. Some of the runners rose to perform the final stretch of bending over to touch the toes. Likewise, Julius rose to a standing position. Suddenly, he felt a slap on his leg and looked at Amy.

"Look!" she signed, pointing to one of the women who was bent over, her backside facing them. "She got goosed!" Amy used the **GOOSE** sign with the accompanying handshape representing the fowl  biting a person's legs. Amy clapped her hands.

Julius knew she was laughing out loud. He looked at the woman. Sure enough, there was a small tear in her tights, exposing pale skin just beneath her right buttock. He smiled and joined Amy in laughter. The woman straightened and stiffened as the other people looked with puzzled expressions while Amy and Julius continued to laugh.

Julius saw their stares and noticed their discomfort, but decided he didn't care. In this environment there was only one person with whom he cared to interact. He reached down and grabbed Amy's hand, pulling her up. "Come-on. Let's go get dinner at my dorm."

Chapter 10

JULIUS

Julius placed a bowl of ramen noodles on the small table near the kitchen area of his dorm suite.

"Let me know if this is hot enough," he signed.

"Thanks!" Amy picked up the bowl and took a sip. "It is fine." The four-person suite was a modest two-bedroom, one-bathroom living arrangement on one of the floors designated for freshman men. In one corner of the common area, a couch, loveseat, and coffee table faced a flat screen TV jutting out from the wall. At the other corner, near the door, was a study with two chairs, a desktop computer, and laptop charging station.

Julius brought his own bowl of ramen from the microwave and joined Amy. He took a bite and paused. "Will this be enough dinner for you? I do have some cold, leftover pizza in the fridge. I brought it from the other night at Denise's."

She contemplated a bit then nodded. "One slice of cold pizza would be good."

Julius brought the pizza box from the refrigerator.

They ate in silence for a few minutes.

Because it was a Saturday night when most students were out with their friends partying, drinking, or doing whatever they wanted with their new-found freedom from parental authority, Julius knew they would be alone.

Johnny, his roommate, who only occupied his room about half the time, was probably crashing this evening at his girlfriend's place. Julius didn't mind. The people in the campus housing office obviously assigned him this roommate because Johnny wrote 'American Sign Language' as the only foreign language he had taken in high school. In spite of this token pairing, and the fact that this guy's ASL was not at all fluent, Julius had nothing in common with him.

"So, remember what we talked about?" Amy swept her hand in an arc toward the window that overlooked the lighted buildings and pathways of the campus. "Is this all worth your trouble?"

Julius shrugged. "So-far it has been all right. Classes have been interesting, and they provide good interpreters so I have access." He pointed at his running shoes that were left by the door. "In a couple of weeks, I will have my first college race, and so I am excited to see how I do at this level."

Amy picked up her bowl and drank the rest of the liquid. Then she picked up a single strand of ramen, raising it above her head and sucking it into her mouth with a flourish of the **DELICIOUS** sign. 

"I'm not talking about the academics and athletics of this place," Amy signed. "What I mean is the people here. I watched you today and realize I am the only one you can really communicate with. And I'm not even a student here."

"Yeah, you're right." Julius drained his own bowl. He picked up the last noodle at the bottom and held it aloft while wiggling the fingers of his other hand around it. "Like this little noodle, I feel isolated and lonely in a crowd. It is not fun. Is it all worth it…"

He placed two fingers next to an eye. "We'll see. Here, have a noodle." He held the strand across the table so she could finish it off with a slurp. Then he formed the DELICIOUS sign on his lips, adding the same flourish as Amy had produced. "With my running, perhaps I can finish off all these stupid, ignorant hearing people like this." Amy swallowed, rubbed her belly, and looked at the pizza box.

"Maybe, but I am still—"

The door burst open. In stagger-walked a short man with a disheveled shirt and baggy pants. Unkempt hair drooped over his eyes.

"**Pizza**!" the man signed, with only a partially correct handshape. "Hi, Johnny." Julius greeted his roommate. He smelled alcohol. "What's up?"

"Huh?" Johnny staggered over to the table, repeating the last sign Julius produced. "Mean what?"

"It means—"

Julius was interrupted by Johnny's arm which shot out and flung open the pizza box.

"Ah, **cool**!" Johnny wiggled his fingers sideways on his chest. "Cold pizza." He jabbed at one of the red circles of meat. "How you sign P-E- P-P-E-R-O—?"

"Not again!" Amy interrupted, raising her hands in exasperation. "It's like this." She showed him the classifier handshape for pepperoni.

Johnny took a step back, startled as if he just noticed Amy was in the room. "Who you?" He missed his chin with the **WHO** sign. Julius  pointed to Amy. "This is Amy. I've known her most of my life."

Johnny's eyes widened and he smiled brightly. "Cool!" He looked at Julius, then Amy, and back, pointing at Amy. "Girlfriend?"

"Uh…" Julius looked at Amy and chuckled. "Yes, that's her."

Amy stood and raised her eyebrows. "Darn **right**!" She emphasized the last sign in an announcement.

Johnny's head jerked back with a sudden thought. He looked at the bedroom door then at Julius. "Night you-two sleep where?"

Julius looked sheepishly at Amy. She kept her eyebrows raised and shrugged with an 'I dunno' expression. "I should probably take you back to Sybil's," Julius signed quickly to Amy.

"**No**!" She threw the sign at him. "I'm NOT spending the night  there tonight!"

Johnny's bleary eyes watched them like a movie as Julius and Amy looked at each other in their moment of indecision.

"Fine." Julius pointed at the couch. "You can sleep there tonight."

"Not alone!" Amy shook her head. "A Deaf female sleeping alone in a room with a bunch of drunk guys walking in and out. No way!"

"Okay." Julius looked at the furniture arrangement as Johnny screwed his face into confusion, obviously not following the rapid signing of their conversation. "I will take the loveseat and you take the couch," he signed.

Amy smiled sweetly. "Thank-you, sweetheart!" She pressed him with a half hug.

"So…," Johnny interrupted. "Sleep where?"

"**Couch**." Julius paused to fingerspell. "C-O-U-C-H. She and I  will sleep there."

Once again, Johnny's head jerked back. For a moment, his eyes stared blankly at the ceiling. "Cool!" His face beamed as he held up a finger and pulled out his cell phone. He punched in some numbers and held the phone to his ear. With his slurred speech, Amy and Julius couldn't read his lips.

"Well?" Julius asked when Johnny hung up his phone.

"My girlfriend!" Johnny signed, adding a wink to his large grin.

"Oh. I see!" Julius glanced at Amy with an amused expression.

Johnny's arm shot out, and he grabbed two slices of pizza. "Cold pizza can I have?" he managed to sign one-handed.

"Uh, sure, go-ahead." Julius nodded his head slightly and picked up the remaining two slices, placing them on napkins in front of himself and Amy.

"Gee, thanks!" Johnny signed and took his pizza into the bedroom, shutting the door behind him.

Five minutes later, Julius and Amy were sitting on the couch and finishing up their slices when, once again, the front door flew open. In walked a young woman whom Julius knew to be Johnny's girlfriend.

She strode confidently across the room in her tight-fitting, Saturday-night jeans and accompanying low-cut shirt which didn't leave much to the imagination regarding the ampleness of her breasts. Immediately, the bedroom door flew open and, as Julius and Amy held their pizzas in mid-bite, Johnny rushed up to the woman and planted a prolonged, deep throated kiss on her lips. Then with a smile and a wave, they marched into the bedroom and closed the door.

Julius and Amy looked at each other over their paused pizza bites and laughed.

"No doubt all their clothes have hit the floor by now," Amy commented then stuffed the remaining pizza in her mouth. Their meal done, Amy scooted over to be closer to Julius. He placed his arm around her shoulder and drew her head close. He noticed how nicely her neck fit into the crook of his arm and the comforting smell of her thick, slightly coarse, dark hair. She raised her face, and his hazel-green eyes met the dark brown of hers.

Julius knew that, in spite of their differences, he loved this woman with all of his heart.

Their connection of trust, formed over years of sharing the same life experience as Deaf individuals, forged a deeply rooted belonging that was far more profound than any of the connections being formed by the physical acts in the nearby bedroom. Such was their understanding that the sanctity of their relationship called for such acts to come at a later, more appropriate time.

Julius wondered when would be a good time to take their relationship to the next level. Perhaps he could propose soon, and they could celebrate their engagement during the trip to India.

They drew close, and a tender, lingering kiss affirmed their hearts' connections.

A subtle push signaled Amy's thought. "Uh, Julius."

"Yeah?"

"Do you really want to deal with all THAT?" Amy jerked a thumb in the direction of the bedroom door.

Julius looked at the door, puzzled. "What? The sex?"

"No! Silly!" She slapped him on the chest. "I mean, here at Gonzaga the only person you can kinda communicate with is HIM." She rolled her eyes sarcastically. "Is that the kind of friend you want to be stuck with while you spend all your time and energy at this place?"

Julius looked out the window. Across the way was another dorm building. Through the night view of the windows, he observed several small gatherings and parties. Students were laughing and having a good time.

This was like the script of his life where he saw what he was missing, but the narrative always pointed him back to this little woman who sat next to him and the small Deaf community to which they both belonged.

She is right. God, he prayed, *please let me know what I should do with all this.*

"Okay." Julius freed his arm and turned to face her. "What do you suggest?"

"Uh..." Amy raised her shoulders and looked at him apologetically. "What about India?"

They looked at each other for a long moment, their eyes maintaining that same connection as before.

Finally, he stood and pointed to the computer in the corner of the room. "Okay. Let's look up how to apply for visas to India."

Chapter 11

AMY

Julius pulled up to Sybil's house. "I don't see any lights on in the house.

Amy sat in the passenger seat and fiddled with the crucifix pendant of her necklace. "I do not want to face her now."

"Is she usually awake by now?" He put the car in Park and let it run.

"Oh yeah. She always gets up early."

It was eight o'clock in the morning, and the sun painted the eastern horizon a lighter shade of blue than the surrounding sky. The air possessed that January, early morning bite which caused a plume of exhaust to rise behind Julius's car.

Amy pressed her thumb into the sharp end of the pendant. "I know she's sitting there in the dark, just waiting for me to open the door so she can yell at me about not returning last night."

Julius recognized apprehension, remembering what happened last time they were together with Sybil. "Do you want me to come in with you?"

Amy pressed harder on the pendant, grimaced, and looked out at the dark living room window of the house. "No. I gotta face the witch on my own. I'm not a little schoolgirl anymore. I have a right to live my own life as I please." She placed the necklace into her purse and opened the door.

"Okay," Julius signed. "I'll wait here for you about ten minutes. If things get out of hand, you can come with me and wait while I attend my nine o'clock class at Gonzaga."

As she walked up the path to the house, Amy glanced back and saw Julius's hands moving under the dome light of the car. She knew he was praying for her. She took a deep breath and opened the door.

In the living room, Amy paused to let her eyes adjust to the darkness of the room. Sybil's recliner rocked slowly in the corner. The skeleton- like profile of the woman in her white night gown presented a ghostly outline amid the dark leather of the chair.

The musty smell of the house was enhanced in Amy's nostrils. It was the smell of loneliness; the residue from unmoving countertop objects left to collect dust because there was no sentimental value attached.

In spite of the heat emanating from the floor vents, a chill passed over her. She rubbed her arms and felt goosebumps.

Here was a cold, hard wall she must defy to resist the evil. With her choice to spend the night elsewhere and not inform Sybil, Amy knew she had crossed a line in defiance of Sybil's control.

She didn't care. It was time.

Reaching over, Amy flicked the light switch next to the door. The overhead bulb sprang to life. "Hello." She regarded Sybil with an expression of challenge and almost saluted in sarcasm.

Sybil pushed herself up from the chair. Her nightgown hem fell to her thin ankles and the bony arms bent to place hands on her hips.

"So…," Amy began. "**What's up?**"

"Where…were…you…last…night?" Sybil made sure to form the  'W' on the verb with her Signing Exact English.

Amy tilted her head and extended her thumb toward the front yard where the car remained parked. "With Julius."

"And…did…you…not…think…to…inform…me?"

Amy shrugged. "Yeah. I thought about it."

"I…was…worried…about…you." Sybil leaned forwardand extended a hand toward the door. "I…did…not…know…if…something…happened…to…you…out…there."

Amy smiled and shook her head. "What can happen to me when I am with Julius?"

Sybil stood straight and stiffened. Her face changed from expressionless control to a furrowing of the brow.

Amy saw fear in those gray eyes. This gave Amy the courage to attack. "In fact, both Julius and Denise have taken care of me way better than you ever have." Amy's hands flew in rapid ASL. "I am much safer with them than I have ever been with **YOU!**" She jabbed the pronoun like a knife.

Amy lowered her hands and grabbed the back of the couch which separated her from Sybil. The fingers curled into the fabric then let go. She held up three digits. "Three months. In just three months, I am outa here." The **LEAVING** sign flew in a wide arc. "And there's nothing you can do about it!"

Sybil stepped back as if she had been punched in the face. "Young…lady…you…are…not…ready…for…that!"

"Huh?" Amy screwed her face into the question.

"You…must…prove…to…me…with… your…choices…that… you…are—"

"Prove to you!" Amy interrupted.

Sybil closed her eyes and continued. "—ready…to…be… on…your …own."

Amy grabbed a pillow resting on the arm of the couch and threw it at Sybil, hitting her in the face. "Look at me!" she demanded as Sybil's eyes shot open in surprise.

Sybil's face returned to the expressionless mask. "Because… of… this…and…because…you…did…not…inform…me…last…night…

you…will…lose…privileges.”

“**Fine**!” Amy's thumb flew off her chest. “I don't need any of your privileges!” She formed a swear word and stepped around the couch. “I am done with this!”

“Three…things…you…will…lose.” Sybil held up a finger. “One … you…will…not…get…the…keys…to…the…car.”

“Julius has a car I can use.”

A second bony finger was elevated. “Two…I…will…stop…your …access…to…the… shared… bank… account… so…you…must… get… cash…from…me.”

“Cash,” Amy signed, running her thumb over her fingers. “No problem! Both Julius and Denise have plenty I can use.”

The long middle finger was added to Sybil's skeleton-like digits. “Three…I…will…remove…you…from…the…phone…account.”

“What!” Now it was Amy's turn to step back as if she were slapped in the face. “No way!” She pulled her cell phone out of her purse and held it close to her chest. “You can't cut me off from my friends like that!”

She looked out the window. Julius's car was gone.

Sybil's face changed into a grin of triumph.

Like a mouse forced into a corner and faced with the fangs of a pursuing cat, Amy knew that Sybil was gloating with the knowledge that she found something to control her into staying.

The glare of Amy's dark eyes pierced the expressionless wall and she walked stiffly, silently past into the adjacent hall, slamming the door after she entered her room. The off-white paint peeled and cracked just below the doorknob.

Amy dropped her phone and collapsed on the bed. “*Aargh!*” Hot tears welled in her eyes, and she buried her head in the pillow. *I detest this house. I HATE that woman!*

Curled on her bed, Amy saw a shadow and a glimmer of light.

The rays of the morning sun illuminated the knob of her bedroom door. Like a canyon split apart by an earthquake, the crack below the knob widened as it traversed down to the bottom of the door.

Just over the threshold, Amy saw Sybil's shadow walking through the hall toward her bedroom. Amy saw herself trapped in that canyon, scrambling and clawing her way toward the light of the doorknob.

In a panic, she slapped around on the bed for her phone. She didn't find it.

*Just this very minute, I know that b**ch is calling to disconnect my phone number,* she thought as she sat up to feel around the floor with her feet. Her toes hit the hard plastic of her phone. *There it is.* She picked it up and pressed the video icon next to Julius's number. The screen came alive, showing the dome light of Julius's car.

"Come-on! Show me your face!" Amy signed in frustration.

Fifteen seconds later, the screen shifted to Julius's face as he positioned his phone on the dashboard. "Sorry. I had to pull over." Julius leaned closer with a concerned look. "What happened?"

"Sybil won't even listen to me! She's taking away all my, quote,  privileges! Including my phone!" Amy rolled her eyes with the **QUOTE** sign.

"Wait. If she took away your phone, how come you are using it?"

"No! She didn't snatch it from me." Amy used the **STEAL** sign.  "She's suspending the number on her account."

"Is she doing that because you didn't inform her where you were last night?"

"Yeah. So we gotta quick figure out another way to contact each-other. I know right now she is calling the company to disconnect me."

"Did she only say she'd disconnect your phone? She didn't hit you, did she?" Concern crossed his face.

"No." Amy shook her head. "My phone is not the only thing she will take away."

"What else?"

"She won't let me use her car, and she's freezing my access to the bank account she and I share."

"What!?" Julius's eyebrows shot up. "You can always use my car when I don't need it. I guess I should just give it to you, meaning I can run everywhere I need to go."

"Okay. But what about money?" Amy rolled her eyes and formed the **BROKE** sign. "I will need cash soon and am pretty sure she won't  give me any."

"Well…" Julius paused and looked out the side window. "I think Denise and I will be able to come up with the cash you need."

"Thank-you." Amy wiped her eyes and rubbed her forehead as her emotions stormed. "What do we do about Sybil?"

"Well, we gotta get you out of that house. That's for sure."

"Julius." Amy set her mouth in a hard line. "I want to kill that woman."

PART III

Revenge and Escape

Chapter 12

JULIUS

Wednesday, March, two months later.

Julius sat at the computer table in the common area of his dorm suite and looked out the window. In the courtyard below, a male runner exercised during an early morning workout. Julius recognized him as one of the distance runners preparing for the upcoming races involving the Gonzaga University track team.

His heart tightened as he felt a twinge of regret. *Am I doing the right thing, God? Should I be out there doing that instead?* he prayed, turning his attention back to the frozen screen and Amy.

In her face, he saw the anger of his friend. But he also felt contentment in the comfort of her signing, which was paused in midair due to bad internet connection. Both of her hands were open with middle fingers extended toward each other.

I do wish she would just give it all to you, he continued his prayer.

"Internet speed!" Amy unfroze into the end of her sentence.

"Huh?" Julius leaned closer to the screen.

Amy sighed and continued. "When she took away my phone service, I asked Sybil to increase the internet speed. But you know her." She paused and formed the **HYPOCRITE** sign. "She only does it if she thinks it is important. And since this ZipVid is functioning like it has for the past couple of months, obviously the internet speed is the same." She narrowed her eyes at the paper she had picked up to examine the wording. "How many months does it say we are approved for this India visitor's visa?"

Julius picked up his visa from on top one of the piles next to the computer on the desk. "Here it says six months, single entry," he signed, pointing to the wording on the page.

"Single entry." Amy picked up another sheet of paper and pointed to a dollar amount written on the bottom. "Here's the receipt for visa processing fee." She attached the receipt behind the visa with a paper clip. "We plan to leave in two months, just after our classes are done for spring semester. Do you think it is a good idea for me to get that apartment next month and then leave so soon for a long trip?"

"Now that I think about it, maybe we should reserve that apartment for when we return. I don't think we'll need to be in India that long." Julius flipped through a calendar book on the desk. "Let's see, mid-May to July is two months. We can all tomorrow to see if they have apartments available in August. Technically, we don't need to be back until September when school starts up again for the fall."

Amy held up one finger. "Single entry." She twisted the finger for emphasis. "Means we only have one chance to accomplish it all." She held up four fingers and pointed to the first digit and moved down each finger with each action item she made. "Find a place to stay; locate my birth mother; learn why the hell she abandoned me; and finally, find out the name she called me." Amy rummaged around and picked up a paper. "Do you have your plane ticket?"

Julius produced a similar-looking page. "Yep. Says we take-off Thursday, May 21 at 1:30 p.m. from the Spokane airport. There is a two-hour layover in Seattle, so should be enough time for the international flight check in."

Amy looked at her ticket and snickered, slowly shaking her head. She pointed in the direction of her bedroom door. "I can imagine that witch's face when she realizes I am gone. She has no idea—" Amy paused and shrugged. "Oh well, I'll be long gone by the time she finds out."

"Amy, can you think of anyone whom we can stay with once we land in Mumbai?" Julius asked. "I know we have discussed staying in a hotel or hostel, but that can become expensive. Will be cheaper and more convenient if we can stay with someone."

"Bisha," Amy signed and pointed to the bracelet she had worn since she was a kid. "Something tells me that, if we find this girl—who by now is a woman—she might be able to help us."

Julius shook his head, looking doubtful. "That'll be a stretch. I mean, you don't even know if that is her correct name. Also, are you sure you will be able to find her? You told me you met her on the streets of Mumbai while you were homeless."

Amy shrugged and widened her eyes. "I know, but she's the only one I can think of who might be able to help."

"Okay, let me share-screen." Julius's browser popped up on the left side of the screen. He enlarged Amy's picture so he could see her signing. "Let's try and look her up." He opened up the SearchQuest engine. "What key words should we use?"

"Let's look for 'Bisha-Mumbai,' but—" Amy paused and rubbed her chin. "Tell you what. Why don't you do a SearchQuest and I'll look on Zipbook? That way we can speed up the search."

"Good idea."

"Okay, I'm gonna turn off my video because the ZipVid will go in the background."

Amy's screen went dark as Julius stopped screen-share and typed 'Bisha-Mumbai' in the SearchQuest. A long list of airline flights from Bisha, Saudi Arabia, popped up on his screen. He shook his head and typed 'Bisha-Mumbai-Deaf.' His screen revealed a couple of websites related to the Mumbai Deaf community and a few listings related to the Bisha hotel in Toronto.

Julius sighed. *Okay, God,* he prayed. *Help us find this needle in a haystack. I'll bookmark the sites about the Mumbai Deaf community, but*

I don't remember Amy ever mentioning this 'Bisha' being Deaf. Maybe she became an interpreter.

He typed in 'Bisha-Mumbai-interpreter.' Several listings for interpreting services at the Mumbai Consulate popped up and nothing much else that was useful.

Julius stood. He walked over to the refrigerator and grabbed a Gatorade drink.

Returning to the computer desk, he paused and looked out the window. The morning sun now peeked around the corner of the building and illuminated the path that curved around the trees in the courtyard below. His teammate had returned and was stopped, chatting with a female member of the track team who happened to be running on the same path. They were talking with animated faces, hands gesturing randomly, and were obviously enjoying each other's company. He leaned closer to try and read their lips but, at this distance, it was an act of futility.

Julius sat at the computer and opened the ZipVid app. He read Amy's name on the black screen. Communicating with her was never an act of futility. She valued him and always took the effort to make herself clear. But did she truly know the place she held in his heart?

His calendar book lay open to the month of May with the word 'India' written on the twenty-first day. This took his mind to the possibility of he and Amy having a traditional Indian dinner somewhere in Mumbai. That would be a good place to propose to her.

Soon, I need to get her a ring, he thought as the computer screen came alive and up popped Amy's little brown face with wide, expressive eyes.

"I got nothing but gibberish." Amy wiggled her fingers and twisted her arms and head to indicate the **chaos**. "Just something about Saudi Arabia and Toronto, Canada. What did you find out?"

Julius nodded. "Same. The name Bisha is actually a city in Saudi Arabia and a hotel in Toronto."

"What do we do?"

Through the screen they both stared at each other in confusion.

Suddenly, Amy brightened and snapped her fingers. "Say! Remember that Indian girl on your track team at Shadle Park High School?"

"Yeah?"

"Well, I remember when she won a race and her parents came to congratulate her. The way they said 'victory' was pronounced with a 'B.'"

"Oh. That's right!" Julius brightened. "From my other research, I learned that the way Indian people pronounce words with a 'V' actually looks like a 'B' to us in America."

"So…V-I-S-H-A?" Amy fingerspelled.

"Right." Julius opened the screen-share again and typed 'Visha-Mumbai' in the SearchQuest. Now the screen showed several si tes related to visas and a fashion company in Mumbai.

"Wait!" Amy waved at the screen to get Julius's attention. "Can you scroll down a bit? I recognize what might be a name."

Julius moved the screen down with his mouse.

"There!" Amy hit a finger with the **POW**! sign. "Vishalya!" She  nodded emphatically.

"Okay, but how do we narrow it down?" Julius hovered the mouse over the search bar. "You mentioned she's not Deaf, right?"

"Correct." Amy agreed. "Can I share-screen now? I want to try something with the key word 'interpreter.'"

The screen flipped over to Amy's browser. She typed 'Vishalya-Mumbai-Interpreter.'

"**PAH**!" they both signed simultaneously.

There at the top of the search results was a listing related to the

Mumbai registry of interpreters for the Deaf. Highlighted among the list of names was Vishalya Chatterghee. Amy stared at the screen and shuddered, rubbing her arms.

"Whoa!" she exclaimed. "I got goosebumps! After all these years, the girl stuck in my mind as 'Bisha' is really a woman named Vishalya."

Julius shook his head in amazement. "And to top it off, she is an Indian Sign Language interpreter for the Deaf!"

"Amazing!" Amy shook her head in pleasant surprise.

"God is at work here!" Julius clasped his hands together and looked up.

Amy raised her hands to sign something but stopped. Julius saw that she was at a loss for words.

"We should try and contact her, but first…" Amy shook the 'T' handshape and pointed to the door. "I gotta **pee**." She left the room while her video screen remained on.

Julius looked at the piles of paper on his desk. Visa papers were interspersed with the airline ticket and flight information. He glanced at the screen and clicked the 'stop share' button. On the bottom right and left corners of Amy's screen, he saw two neatly stacked piles of paper. *I should do the same,* he thought, but suddenly, a shadow shrouded the screen. He narrowed his eyes and looked closer.

Behind Amy's chair, Sybil's thin frame emerged and paused. Only her hips and mid-section were visible on the screen.

What's she doing sneaking into Amy's room? Julius thought.

Sybil was still wearing her night gown. A bony hand reached out and picked up a paper. She was examining it.

No! Julius felt helpless to do anything behind the glass screen. With a quick motion, Sybil gathered both piles of paper and left the room.

Julius could do nothing but sit and stare as if he were watching a scary movie on TV.

Less than a minute later, Amy popped into the screen and sat down on her chair. Sensing something amiss, she tensed and looked around her desk. Her eyebrows lowered and she checked the floor area. "Uh, Julius…What happened to the papers?"

"Sybil." Julius formed the name sign and widened his eyes. "While you were in the bathroom, she came in and took your papers."

Amy's face froze. Her eyes narrowed and her lips set in a straight, hard line. Her head turned as she looked at her bedroom door, contemplating what to do. Her mouth curled into a sneer and, with a subtle shake of the head, she held up a finger and looked at Julius. "One second," she signed and left the room.

The silence of the empty screen mocked the storm brewing in Julius's mind. The only thing he knew to do was to pray.

Chapter 13

AMY

During this March morning, the shades remained drawn. The living area of the house was shrouded in darkness.

Pausing at the end of the short hallway just before it opened to the kitchen, Amy saw the faded photo next to the porcelain dolls on the opposite kitchen wall. There Sybil's father posed stiffly beside the rigid posture of her mother. A carbon copy of her parents, five-year-old Sybil stood, unsmiling, staring back at Amy with those expressionless gray eyes.

Right next to Amy, another photo hung on the wall at the end of the hall. An adult Sybil posed in almost the same stance as her father all those years before with five-year-old Amy standing in a slight lean away from her. The woman's arm extended around the little girl's shoulder in a vain attempt to gather her close and present the appearance of affection and belonging.

No other pictures existed in the house. With her parents long since deceased, such was the extent of Sybil's significant relationships.

Amy looked at the picture next to her. She saw her little self staring intently back at her.

Those young, defiant, dark eyes opened the floodgates of memory from the trauma and trials experienced when this stern woman snatched her away from family origins just before this picture was taken.

The memory of being imprisoned on a plane departing from India as Sybil insisted on being called 'mother' etched in Amy's mind. Unable to escape, Amy's insignificance was stamped out by this woman who forced her to be called 'Amy.'

And forcing her to ignore the only name she had known. Hear-Nothing.

Amy paused to collect her thoughts.

She saw Sybil bent over, collecting the garbage under the kitchen sink.

Her travel papers were on the counter next to the sink. "No!"

Amy signed. She lowered her head and took a few quick steps toward the papers.

Sybil stiffened and turned around, placing her body between Amy and the papers. With a quick, strangling motion, her hands tied the garbage bag shut and placed it on the floor.

Amy pointed at the counter. "Those are my papers."

Sybil closed her eyes and slowly nodded her head. "Yes…we…will…talk…about…them." She opened her eyes and looked out the side window which afforded a view down the street.

"What are you looking at?" Amy demanded.

Sybil's eyes turned, but her face remained toward the window.

Amy saw fear in the gray eyes. The same widening of the eyes and expression of fear she saw when she confronted Sybil after spending the night at Julius's dorm. The fear of loss.

Amy stepped forward, raising her chin. "Those are my papers."

Sybil raised her hand to her ear. "I..hear..the…garbage…truck." She pointed out the kitchen window and then to the bag on the floor. "The…truck… is…coming… We…will…talk…after…you…take… this…and…the…bin…to…the…street."

Amy looked at the papers behind Sybil and the garbage bag. She leaned around Sybil and extended her fingers toward the papers.

Sybil pushed the fingers out of the way and pointed to the back door. "Garbage…now!"

Amy glared. She clenched her fists. "Fine!" Her thumb stabbed at her chest. She grabbed the trash bag and exited the back door.

The biting crispness of the cold morning air pricked at her skin as Amy walked toward the garbage bin that stood next to the garage. Like the onerous load on her mind, the week's refuse weighted the bag. The putrid smell reminded her of how she felt.

She flung open the lid of the bin. Envisioning the woman inside the house replacing the bag, she swung it in an overhead arc, causing it to crash at the bottom of the bin. Closing the lid, she felt a rumble and looked down the road.

A white garbage truck was reaching out with its claw to grab the bin of the house next door as the neighbor mowed the front yard.

Out of the corner of her eye, Amy saw the glint of sunlight reflecting off an object lying on the grass just below the shattered window of the garage. It was the broken snow shovel handle she had tossed only a couple of months before.

As she pulled the bin to the curb, she looked at this object. An idea formed in her mind.

The garbage truck pulled up and its claw arms grabbed the bin. Its vibrating rumble permeated Amy's body, encouraging her to become a heartfelt tempest, stirring her into action.

She set her jaw. *Yes, I will do it.*

The claw of the truck deposited the bin with a crash.

She walked straight to the snow shovel handle, picked it up, and marched to the back of the house.

In her blur of rage, the fear and shock in Sybil's gray eyes was the last thing Amy saw as she raised the shovel handle above her head.

• • • • •

The roar of the garbage truck now subsided to a low vibration as it proceeded to the houses down the road. The front door of Sybil's house opened.

Amy stepped into the morning sun. Her face was expressionless as a breeze blew the visa and travel papers she held in her hand. Her purse was slung over a shoulder. She stepped down the path to the street, hesitated, and looked both ways down the street.

Just one image remained in her mind.

She left the door open. She walked down the front path, taking a left at the sidewalk. She did not notice the neighbor pausing in his mowing to observe.

Her mind would not allow it.

Like a zombie with a singular purpose, she marched past the neighbor as he called out to her.

The neighbor received no response. All Amy knew to do was walk.

The image of Sybil's bloody, unconscious face, frozen in fear on the kitchen floor clouded her mind as she walked down the sidewalk in the direction of the only mother she had ever known: Denise.

Chapter 14

JULIUS

Julius fidgeted in his seat during a history class at Gonzaga University.

Being one of the required freshman general education courses, the classroom was a rather large hall. A female interpreter moved her hands and arms down near the podium where a graduate assistant droned out a rather boring lecture.

Julius shifted in his seat, tapping his pencil on his notepad until he caught the annoyed glance of the young woman sitting next to him. He put the pencil down.

I wonder what happened to Amy? he thought as he looked down at the interpreter, whose signs did not register in his mind.

The last image of Amy's face remained stamped on his mind like a tattoo. What he saw on the computer screen early that morning was beyond the usual annoyance, sarcasm, and anger he was used to in Amy's relations with Sybil. It was a mask of rage he had never before seen in her face, a shifting of the eyes into a cold, calculated purpose that meant no good.

He had almost dropped everything to skip this class and hurry over to Sybil's house to make sure Amy was okay. But he said a prayer and remained on campus, trusting that God would bless Amy with some restraint.

Julius stared blankly at the interpreter as the lecture droned on. Suddenly, his cell phone vibrated in his pocket and he pulled it out, recognizing Denise's number.

Denise's serious expression popped onto the video screen. "What's up?" he signed.

"Julius!" Denise paused and glanced to her right. "Amy's in big trouble. You need to come to my house."

"What happened at Sybil's?" Several of the students near Julius glanced at the sudden animation of his signing. He didn't care. "What happened to Amy?"

Denise shook her head. "It's not what happened to her. It's what she did to Sybil."

All sorts of possibilities entered Julius's mind. "I'll come right now. Be there in about fifteen minutes." He hung up the phone and stood, jamming the notebook into his backpack.

He sidled to the end of the row and descended the stairs to the front of the lecture hall. "Gotta go! Emergency!" he signed to the interpreter, no doubt annoying the graduate student history lecturer.

•　•　•　•　•

Traffic was light as he drove on Northwest Boulevard toward the Cochrane/TJ Meenach intersection. Julius hit the steering wheel with his palm. "Ugh! Why can't she control herself?" Worry intermingled with anger as he signed with one hand. A glint of sunlight caught his eye as it reflected off a metal cross which rose above the steeple of a nearby church.

He remembered something. *God,* he began his silent prayer. *Please, please put some sense into Amy. Help her to not be so overwhelmed by things she can't control.*

Julius pressed the brake to stop at a traffic light. *Please take care of Amy and teach her how to surrender all her burdens and worries to you.*

The light turned green. Something prompted him to take a right on Cochrane Street instead of proceeding straight, a more direct route to Denise's house.

He stayed in the right lane and followed the curve of the road to Alberta Street, taking a left on Queen Avenue. Halfway down the street, Sybil's house sat in the midst of unusual activity for the normally quiet block.

An ambulance pulled away from the curb and turned on its lights.

On the narrow road, Julius veered to the right and let the vehicle pass. Law enforcement vehicles were parked directly in front of the house, their lights flashing on the faces of a clump of neighbors standing aside to view the activity. Like the surreal attraction of the dead body of an animal on the side of the road, the scene drew Julius in. He slowed the car to a crawl. His senses heightened, he viewed the details as if watching a slow-motion movie.

A notepad-holding policeman stood in the front yard talking to a man whom Julius recognized as the next-door neighbor. One of the black law enforcement vehicles stood out, the only one without flashing lights. A large star was stamped on the front door with US MARSHAL labeled underneath in large block letters.

The front door of the house was left open, exposing more uniformed officers milling about inside. Just outside the entryway, two officers were conversing. One of these men wore the black uniform of the local Spokane police. The other, a brown-uniformed African American officer, sported a patch on his uniformed chest which matched the star emblem of the US MARSHAL vehicle.

Julius's heart skipped a beat when he noticed what the US marshal was holding in his hands—Amy's laptop with the large SFCC logo stamped on the back.

This US marshal looked up and stared at Julius, a suspicious look in his eyes as the car crawled past.   Perhaps, with the slow pace of the vehicle, this officer sensed something unusual apart from the gawking neighbors.

Julius ripped his gaze away from the US marshal and increased the car's speed. He knew that such men were trained to notice small details, like the suspicious activity of a lone onlooker.

Glancing back in his rear-view mirror, Julius saw that this man continued to observe. I'd better hide this car when I get to Denise's was his only thought.

He sped down the road.

Chapter 15

JULIUS

Julius burst into the front door of Denise's house and entered the living room where Amy sat in Denise's easy chair.

"Am I a murderer?" Amy asked, looking up at him with bloodshot eyes. Several strands of her dark hair stuck out, the ponytail skewed off to the side.

"What happened?" Julius kneeled on the floor next to her. He felt a tap on his shoulder.

"She beat up Sybil." Denise sat on the edge of the couch near the easy chair.

Julius screwed his face into confusion. "Did you kill her?"

Denise patted Julius on the shoulder. "Slow down. Amy, can you try to describe what happened?" Amy stared at the floor.

Julius saw doubt on her face. He had seen her become upset and cry, but this was something different. He gently shook her leg. "Go-on," he encouraged.

She took a deep breath and raised her hands. "Sybil wouldn't give me my papers." Amy shook her head and curled her lips. "So I lost it. I beat her so bad!" There was a hint of surprise and triumph in her eyes, as if she couldn't believe she actually did it.

"How did you beat her, Amy?" Denise prodded.

"Remember that snow shovel I broke last winter? Well, the handle was lying next to the garage." Amy raised an index finger and looked at it with an expression of hatred. "I **whipped** her real good!" She mimicked holding a club, beating her finger again and again.

Julius squeezed Amy's leg. "You did that? What happened to Sybil? How did you leave her?"

"**Blood**…" Amy wiggled her fingers and ran a hand down her face. "Her face was bloody, and I left her lying on the floor."

"Was she conscious?" Denise asked.

"No. Her eyes were closed. I don't know if she was breathing when I walked out of the house."

Julius slumped his shoulders and put a hand on his forehead. *Why?* he thought. *Why does she have to lose control like this? Am I not enough for her that she needs to do stuff like this? God! What do I do?*

He looked up at Amy who resumed staring at the floor with a blank expression. "Did anyone see you?" No response as her eyes remained downcast. "Hey!" Julius tapped her leg. "Answer me!" He felt a firm squeeze on his shoulder.

"Hold on, Julius," Denise interrupted. "No need to get angry now. Amy needs our support. Before you came, she told me that she walked straight here from Sybil's house. I don't know if anyone saw her."

Julius took a deep breath. He looked around the room. On the coffee table was a manila folder containing the packet of Amy's visa and travel papers. His chest tightened as he remembered the US marshal. "We gotta make sure you have all your papers." He pulled out the papers and began flipping through them.

"What are you doing?" Amy asked.

"I got paranoid and drove by Sybil's house on the way here. Saw a US marshal talking with a cop in the front yard." Julius handed the papers to Amy and pointed. "Can you check to make sure you have all the papers?"

"Why?" Amy looked up at him, puzzled.

"The US marshal had your laptop in his hands. He's gonna see all the information about India that we looked up on your compu-

ter yesterday before you beat up Sybil. I want to—"

"Oh **crap**!" Amy interrupted, jamming a thumb into her other hand. "Now the cops have all my personal information from the laptop!"

"They'll eventually figure it all out." Julius pointed again at the papers. "I want to make sure you have all your documents here and didn't leave any at Sybil's so they are alerted about us leaving the country."

Amy looked through one of the paperclipped pages. "Flight information is all here." She flipped through another section of paperclipped pages and nodded. "All the visa paperwork is here." She dropped the papers on the table and slumped on the couch. "But my computer! Now what?"

Julius walked over to the front window. "That's probably what the cops are busy looking at now." He looked out the window, half expecting to see a black vehicle with flashing lights pull up to the curb. "But I just drove by there and don't think they have had time to examine it. Will probably take them a while to bypass your password."

Instinctively, Amy touched the bracelet on her wrist and stroked the smooth beads.

Julius waved to get Amy's attention. "Amy, what—" but she ignored him. "Amy!"

"Julius!" Denise patted the couch next to her. "Please sit down."

Julius sighed and shook his head. He waved a hand toward Amy and looked at Denise. "Why does she always need to react to everything in such an extreme way? I know Sybil is evil, but I've told Amy so many times to just give it to God. He will take care of things."

Denise tilted her head at Amy, who continued to fidget with her bracelet. "I know that is what you believe, but Amy is on her own unique journey. If what you are saying is meant to be, it will happen at the right the right time." Denise nodded and shrugged. "Come-on,

Julius, please sit." Again, she patted the couch, and he complied.

She leaned forward and waved her hand in Amy's field of vision. "Amy, please look at me."

Amy's shoulders rose and slumped. "What?"

"I know you are feeling messed-up." Denise used the **CHAOS**  sign. "But we need to figure out what to do." She pointed in the direction of Sybil's house. "Sometime, probably soon, the cops will figure to check here for you."

"Yeah, and—" Julius began, but Denise squeezed his leg to calm him down.

"All they gotta do is ask around, and they will be pointed straight to this house." Denise paused, stroking her braid as she thought. She looked at Amy. "I suppose you could turn yourself in—"

"No!" Amy's knuckles turned white as she squeezed the bracelet in her fist. "They won't understand!" She raised her fist in the direction of Sybil's house. "They are hearing, just like Sybil! No way will they consider MY perspective!"

Denise got up and kneeled next to Amy. "Please do not panic. I'm only saying that's an option. Not that it is what you should do. Please, let's talk about our options. I know you already have your visas. Looks like we need to change your flight to leave for India ASAP."

Julius shook his head. A suspense movie filled his head with scenes of gun-toting police officers chasing them through the airport. "I don't think we'll make it that far. Now both of us will be arrested."

Denise held up her hand. "Not if we plan it right. You both have all your paperwork, and the only thing the cops know is that Amy has looked online for information about India. Right now, they don't know you are actually flying there." She pointed at Amy. "And the only way I'm okay letting you go is the fact that Julius is with you. No way would you be safe going on your own." Denise stood and took a step toward her bedroom. "Let me go get my laptop so we can change the flight so you leave tomorrow."

"Wait a second!" Julius stood. "What about everything we have planned here? My track season? My scholarship." He pointed to Amy who looked up from the couch with bleary eyes. "What about her job and classes at SFCC? And—"

"Julius," Denise interjected.

Julius ignored Denise and continued, "I know we have been talking about taking the trip to India during the summer. Also, what about Amy moving into an apartment? Just yesterday we discussed that she can do that in August when we return."

"Stop, Julius!" Denise held up a hand. "Look at Amy's situation now. This calls for a change in plans." She placed her hand on Amy's head. "If we waste our time worrying about the future, pretty soon the cops will arrive, and Amy will be behind bars! Then"—Denise twisted her hands in the CHAOS sign—"everything will be even more messed-up than it is now. We need to take care of this first, and then hopefully, things will eventually fall in place with your and Amy's college and living situations."

"Right." Julius looked out the front window to collect his thoughts. His shoulders rose and fell in a sigh. Turning to face the room, he looked at Amy.

Her eyes showed a deep yearning for which he knew he had no answer. It was her need which he alone could not meet.

"If we change the flight so we leave tomorrow, won't that cost a fortune to make the last-minute change?" Julius asked Denise.

"Well, if you let me go get my laptop, I can check to see if that is the case. I am willing to pay the penalty so Amy can get what she needs."

"Okay, so we fly there and land at the Mumbai airport. Then what?" Julius formed the **SLEEP+EAT** signs. "Where do we stay?"

"Yes, you do need a place to stay. That hotel we discussed a while back probably wouldn't work." Denise stroked her braid. "A hotel near the airport would be the first place the authorities looked if they pursued you. Hmm. Where to stay?"

Amy raised her arm and pointed to her bracelet. "V-I-S-H-A," she fingerspelled.

"Huh?" Denise looked at Amy, puzzled. "You mean that 'Bisha' from when you were a kid?"

"We figured it out." Amy nodded at Julius. "I've been spelling it wrong all along. Visha is a nickname for V-I-S-H-A-L-Y-A."

"Yes," Julius interjected. "Before all this chaos happened, we looked it up online. Found that there's a woman named Vishalya Chatterghee from Mumbai." He leaned forward, forming the **IRONY** sign. "In fact, she is actually an India Sign Language interpreter. Imagine that!" 

Denise dropped her braid. Her eyes opened wide. "Really? Then we'd better contact her! I'm gonna go get my laptop." She hurried into her bedroom.

Chapter 16

AMY

Denise entered the room carrying her laptop and wallet, setting them on the coffee table in front of the couch. She sat next to Julius and pointed to the travel papers on top of the coffee table. "Julius, can you hand me Amy's plane ticket? I want to see if your flight can be changed to tomorrow."

Amy pulled at the bracelet on her wrist and rolled one of the beads between her fingers. Sitting at the end of the couch, she saw the computer screen open to the ZipQuest website while Denise typed in the flight information. A sudden feeling of excitement mixed with fear entered her chest as her mind was struck with the immediacy of the trip.

"Yep, I found it." Denise pointed to the screen and then to the ticket in front of her. "The same flight arrangement starting tomorrow at the Spokane airport. Has you leaving at 1:30 p.m. with a layover at Seattle. Then a couple hours later, you take-off on an international SEA-Air flight to Mumbai."

"What is the penalty for changing the flight?" Julius asked. "This last-minute flight change will cost me $500." Denise pulled a credit card from her wallet and held it up. "That's okay. I'll pay for it. We need to get Amy to where she needs to go."

After booking the flight and paying the penalty, Denise waved to Amy. "Come"—she patted the couch next to her—"sit next to me while we look up this Visha person who might be able to provide you a place to stay."

Amy moved to sit next to Denise so that she could view the SearchQuest screen along with Julius.

"Okay, so Vishalya." Denise paused and looked at Amy. "How do you spell her last name?"

There was no response from Amy. Here was the real possibility of meeting a person that existed primarily in the nether reaches of a dream- like memory. What if it all fell apart and this person wanted nothing to do with her?

Then again, here was a potential friend who could help connect with her long-lost origins and clarify some of the questions that burned in her mind.

All of that, coupled with the dread of being arrested, created a drug-like cocktail of emotions, feelings, and thoughts that shrouded her physical senses.

"Amy?" Denise tapped her on the thigh.

Julius elbowed Denise. "C-H-A-T-T-E-R-G-H-E-E is the spelling." He fingerspelled the name slowly.

"I will add 'Mumbai interpreter' to the search." Denise typed into the computer.

A list of names, businesses, and services popped onto the screen. Denise scrolled down. "What is the Hindi word for 'Deaf'?" she asked.

Julius picked up his phone and typed some words. "Try 'bahara.'"

"Let's see…" Denise scrolled down some more. "Let's try this one, 'Mumbai bahara.' It shows a list of names." She opened the website and clicked on a link labeled 'providers.' "Let's scroll down a bit more. Aha! Vishalya Chatterghee!" Denise clicked on the name.

On the screen emerged the picture of an attractive, smiling Indian woman who looked to be a bit older than Julius and Amy. She had shoulder-length brown hair, prominent cheek bones, and broad shoulders. Her brow contained the typical Indian darkening around the eyes.

Leaning forward, Amy shuddered. There were the eyes! Those intense eyes that stared across the cold train platform so many years before. In those eyes was the same hint of coldness: a tough, hard edge which could only be formed from a life lived on the streets of Mumbai.

"That's her," Amy announced.

Both Julius and Denise looked at her. "Are you sure?" Julius asked.

"I'll never forget those eyes." Amy pointed at the woman. "Those are the exact same eyes I remember. Plus, the same facial features, and it seems she is tall." Amy formed the **CORRECT** sign. "So, yes, this is Visha."

"Okay." Denise gathered herself up as if about to do something important. "On this website is a link we can click for a live video-chat. You ready?"

Amy shook her head and stood. "Wait! What are we going to do? Just talk to her? Ask questions? What do we ask? What if—"

Denise grabbed Amy's wrist and gently pulled her to a sitting position. She pointed between Julius and herself. "We will support you. Maybe this woman can help you when you get to Mumbai. Perhaps find a place you can stay where the cops won't easily find you."

Julius added, "But don't tell her right away about your current situation with the cops. We don't want to scare her away so she won't help us."

"Agreed." Denise hovered the mouse over the video call link. "Are you ready?"

Amy took a deep breath and nodded.

Denise clicked the link and a small video screen popped up. After a few seconds, a dark-skinned woman appeared.

It was not Visha. On her head she wore a headphone with a thin microphone protruding in front of her mouth. The mouth moved in a language none of them recognized.

"She's probably speaking Hindi," Denise signed and paused, not sure how to proceed with the conversation.

The woman flipped her microphone above her forehead and moved her hands in a foreign sign language.

In the living room, the three of them looked at each other.

"I-S-L," Julius fingerspelled. "I think that's Indian Sign Language."

The woman moved her hands some more.

"I think she said 'phone' or 'call,'" Julius signed, looking at Denise. "Plus, it looks like she's using their two-handed alphabet system. You know the British Sign Language alphabet, right? I think it is similar to the manual alphabet of Indian Sign Language, ISL."

"Yes. Let me try." Denise shifted forward. "WE CALL." She code- switched, using the same 'call' sign they observed the woman use. Both of Denise's hands raised to produce the alphabet. "V-I-S-H-A-L—"

The woman on the screen raised her hands. Her eyes widened and she nodded in recognition. "V-I-S-H-A?" She spelled slowly so they recognized it.

"Yes!" Both Denise and Julius replied

Amy leaned forward with a look of anticipation.

Suddenly, the little video screen went blank. "What—?"

Denise signed, but the screen came to life.

"Hello," a woman signed. "My name V-I-S-H-A."

In the living room, all three of them froze, not sure how to begin.

"Hello?" Visha tried again, a puzzled look on her face.

Denise grabbed her braid and stroked once. She gently elbowed

Julius, and the two of them slid to the side. Reaching out, Denise touched Amy's arm and beckoned her to scoot into the full view of the video.

Slowly, Amy shifted so that her face filled the self-view screen. She looked into the eyes of Visha. That ghost-like memory returned, transposing her mind to the cold concrete of the train platform as she sat alone, her only comfort long-ago found in those same intense eyes that stared back at her now in this very moment.

Visha moved her hands, and Amy recognized a sign that could mean 'help.' There was a look of concern on Visha's face.

Amy pointed to herself. "I'm A"—she paused her hand, looking at it as she began forming her name sign. She shook her head and tried again, pointing to her ear and shaking her hand.

Visha's face went blank. Her eyes narrowed then suddenly shot wide open in recognition of the same long-buried memory. "Hear-Nothing?" she signed. Her jaw dropped in an incredulous expression.

Amy very slowly nodded her head. From the pit of her belly, she felt a sudden rush of feelings and emotions. Like a storm drain gushing from a flooded sewer, all of the buried memories and recollection of her origins came bursting forth, overwhelming her mind.

Amy closed her eyes. Tears welled then flowed freely. Her shoulders shook in deep sobs.

An arm reached out. Denise scooted into the screen, hugging Amy. Julius shifted close to Amy so he, too could be in the screen. He placed a hand on Amy's shoulder, which continued to shake.

Having recovered a bit, Amy wiped her eyes. Visha watched in surprise and confusion.

"I didn't understand, either," Amy said, looking at Denise and Julius, then Visha. "What do we do? How do we explain to her what is going on?"

Denise began but hesitated. She seemed not sure how to negotiate the language difference. "My name is Deni—" she paused during the one-handed ASL fingerspelling and shifted to both hands. "D-E-N-I-S-E–me." She pointed to Julius. "J-U-L-I-U-S–he. Two-us friend her." Denise pointed to Amy and looked at the screen to see if Visha understood.

Visha nodded. "I—partner—past," she signed.

Denise and Julius looked at each other, both shaking their heads.

"I got an idea." Denise held up a finger then imitated typing on a keyboard. She opened the chat box on the screen and typed. "Hello, Visha, my name is Denise. This is Julius. Hear-Nothing has a given American name of Amy. Do you understand this typed English text?"

Visha leaned forward to type on her computer. "Yes, I understand English. I am shocked to see Amy after all these years. How did she know to contact me here?"

"It was a lucky guess," Denise typed. "Amy remembers you being the first person to ever communicate with her visually. She assumed you might have become an interpreter. That led us to contact this place."

"Yes, I am a video relay interpreter here. I just happened to be working today. I don't work here every day, so am glad you called." Visha paused and craned her neck to look at Amy, who now sat halfway out of the screen. Visha looked down to type. "Can Amy type in English?"

Denise nodded and scooted aside. "Amy, you can chat with her now," she signed.

"Hi," Amy typed.

"I am shocked to see you," Visha responded. "I didn't recognize you at first, but when you signed 'Hear-Nothing,' I remembered. In fact, you are the reason I learned sign language and became an interpreter. Several years after you disappeared, I began learning India Sign Language, and it eventually led me here." Visha looked up from the keyboard.

With this direct eye contact, Amy recognized that same concerned observation she experienced during that rainy day on the train platform seventeen years earlier. Visha's expression gave her hope.

Backed by the two people she loved most in life, Amy felt a temporary respite from the surrounding dangers. However, neither Julius nor Denise had any tangible connection to her past, her origins, or even to the name she was called by those who had brought her into this world.

For the first time since Sybil snatched her away, through the eyes of this woman who faced her, Amy saw a destination which could potentially grant the answers she sought.

"I want to show you something," Amy typed. She held up her wrist and pointed to the bracelet.

Visha's eyes narrowed slightly. Slowly, her head shook and a tear welled, tracking down one cheek. "Wow!" she signed and looked down to type. "You kept my bracelet!"

"Yes," Amy typed. "It's always with me."

Visha wiped the tear from her face. She shook her shoulders as if to compose herself. "So, tell me about yourself, Amy. Where are you living after all these years? Did you go to school? Who is your family? I have so many questions!" Visha looked up for the response.

Amy held up a finger and nodded. "I'm coming to India," she typed.

"Oh!" they read on Visha's lips as her expression changed from wonderment to surprise. "Then let me know what you need!" she typed and beckoned with a sign they all knew to mean 'Come-on over!'

Chapter 17

JULIUS

Julius opened his small carry-on backpack. *I have the visa travel papers, my wallet, the money I withdrew from the bank, water bottle, and passport.*

During the previous day after his morning class, his plan was to spend the day finding out about apartment availability for Amy in August. A secret side trip to a nearby jewelry store to check out engagement rings was also on his agenda.

But no. Amy had to go and mess everything up by assaulting Sybil, making herself a fugitive from the law, and now him an accessory to her crime.

He yawned and looked around Denise's living room, his mind in a sleep-deprived fog from having to spend almost the entire previous night packing in his dorm room.

I can't believe I'm doing this! God, be with me, he thought and zipped up his backpack.

"Here, try this one on." Denise held up one of her sweaters and showed it to Amy. "I know it may be hot and humid in Mumbai, but you'll probably need this on the trip over."

Amy grabbed the purple, knitted sweater and pulled it over her head. Like the quills of a porcupine, strands of her hair stood up from the material's static electricity. She walked over to the full-length mirror behind Denise's propped open bedroom door. She observed as most of her body disappeared into the sweater, which was made to accommodate Denise's wider frame. "This makes me look like a fat grape."

"That's all I got." Denise patted her wide hips. "I don't have anything smaller to fit you better."

Amy pulled off the sweater and folded it, placing it in the open suitcase which Denise provided. "I wish I could go get my clothes from Sybil's house. They fit me better." She waved to get Julius's attention. "Do you think you could run over-there and sneak in to grab some of my clothes?"

"No way!" Julius shook his head. "I'm sure the cops have that place staked out. I'm not gonna put myself in a position to be interrogated." He smiled, pointing to the sweater in the suitcase. "Plus, you look kinda cute in that. Like a plump, juicy, delicious grape I could eat up!" He imitated holding a bunch of grapes, tilting his head back and depositing them in his mouth, punctuating it with a flourish of the DELICIOUS sign.

"Shut up!" Amy picked up a blouse from a pile and threw it at him.

He held up the black and white checker-patterned blouse and examined it. "Why don't you wear this for the trip?" He tossed the blouse back to Amy.

"Yes, try that on. Plus, here are some jeans that can go with it." Denise handed Amy a pair of faded blue jeans.

Amy stripped to her bra and panties, which she hadn't changed since the previous morning. She put on the blouse, which billowed out to the side and pulled up the jeans, holding them up with one hand. "Want me to travel like this?" she asked and let go of the pants, her skinny brown legs exposed as the jeans crumpled to a heap at her ankles.

Both Julius and Denise laughed.

Denise hurried into her room to grab a belt.

Julius smiled as he looked at Amy standing there with her messed-up hair, baggy blouse, and legs sticking out into her crumpled up jeans on the floor. The scene reminded him of a toothpick doll he once constructed, jamming it into a marshmallow so it could stand up.

In spite of Amy's emotional shenanigans, she was his best-friend. He couldn't imagine his life without her. What about the marriage proposal? What about the engagement ring?

He sighed and shook his head as he placed his backpack near the back door of the house. In all this chaos, when would he ever have a chance to show Amy his true feelings so she could respond in the way he wanted?

"Here you go." Denise laughed and pulled up the jeans, threading the belt through the loops and pulling the buckle tight. She tucked half of the blouse into the hips of the jeans and stood back to observe. "There. Now you will fit in with all the other girls in the latest fashion of half-tucked blouses and baggy jeans!"

"Okay, fine!" Amy folded the donated clothes and placed them in the suitcase.

Julius picked up Amy's updated flight itinerary from the stack of papers next to her purple carry-on backpack, another donated item from Denise. "We did inform Visha what time to pick us up from the Mumbai airport, right?" he asked.

"Yeah. Last night we told her about the Seattle-to-Mumbai flight," Denise answered. "She'll pick you up when you arrive and take you to her place."

"What was it she called her place?" Amy asked. "Her flat? Why did she call it that?"

Julius shrugged. "I think she meant her single-floor apartment. Maybe that's why they call it a 'flat'?"

Amy paused, tilting her eyes up to recall a memory. "Oh yes. I remember those high-rise buildings from when I was a kid." She shook

her head and shrugged. "'Course, I was one of those kids stuck on the streets with no access to these buildings." She used the **DEMOTE** sign to make her point.

Denise looked at her watch. "It is now nine o'clock a.m. We gotta get you to the airport before noon." She looked out the front window. "I thought Jeremy was supposed to be here by now. Even though we are taking my car parked out in the back alley, he is coming along to help drop you at the airport, right?"

Julius looked at his phone. "He texted me. He's on the way." Realizing something, Julius reached into his pocket, pulling out his car keys and handing them to Denise. "That reminds me to give these to you. Won't be needing these for a while." He jerked a thumb toward the garage at the back alley behind the house. "My car is parked in your garage. Make sure you drive it once a week while I am gone so the battery doesn't die."

Denise grabbed the keys. "Okay. First, we gotta get some breakfast in you. Let me cook up some eggs and toast." She started for the kitchen but stopped, reaching in a pocket and pulling out a wad of money. "Amy, take this. This morning before you woke up, I withdrew one-thousand dollars from the ZTM, all in twenty-dollar bills. Use it wisely."

Denise walked into the kitchen as Amy folded the cash and placed it securely in her backpack.

Fifteen minutes later, after all their bags were deposited next to the back door, Julius, Amy, and Denise ate their eggs and toast at the dining room table, when Julius saw his brother's jeep pull up in the front of the house.

Jeremy got out and entered the front door. On this cool, spring morning he wore the mottled brown and green fatigue jacket from his days in the military.

"Come. Have some breakfast." Denise beckoned to the seat next to Julius.

"Hi, everyone." Jeremy sat and helped himself to some eggs.

Julius turned to his brother. "I stopped by Mom's house early this morning—"

"Slow down," Jeremy interrupted. "You're signing too fast. I don't understand."

Julius pulled out his phone and opened the Notes app.

"Stopped by Mom's house this a.m. Explained what's happening and said goodbye," he texted and handed Jeremy the phone.

"Okay. I will keep in touch with you and let you know how she is doing. You know she doesn't text much and isn't that good with tech stuff on the phone," Jeremy typed and handed the phone to Julius.

"Thanks. Also, let her know how I am doing in India."

Jeremy looked at his brother then grabbed the phone. "How are you doing now?"

Julius read the note, took a bite of toast and looked at Amy. "What?" She returned his look with a puzzled expression. "Nothing," Julius signed and returned to the phone. "I hope I am doing the right thing," he typed. "I have decided to leave everything in Spokane and support Amy during her trip to India. This morning at Gonzaga U, I put in a formal leave of absence request. I hope it gets approved and I don't lose my scholarship." He handed the phone to Jeremy.

"I hope so, too," Jeremy typed. "What about Amy at SFCC? Will she lose her job?"

"Denise will take care of that after we leave. Hopefully that all works out for her, and she can return back to normal after this mess is taken care of." Julius paused his texting to take a bite of eggs. "I can't believe this is all happening. I mean, suddenly to drop everything and escape on a plane while the cops are after Amy is surreal. I really want her to find out what she needs, and it looks like we have a place to stay with a woman named Visha in Mumbai. But I can't believe I am doing this."

Jeremy took a bite of eggs, looked at the phone, and nodded. "This is what you've always done." He handed the phone back to Julius.

"What do you mean?" Julius texted.

"Well, remember after I lost my hearing from the chemical attack in the military? You were there for me, supporting me, helping me to recover and adjust to being Deaf. Now you are doing the same thing for Amy. Supporting her."

Julius looked at the phone and put down his eating utensils. "You're right. I hope it all works out. But I don't know what else to do." He handed the phone to Jeremy and stood to pick up his plate to return it to the kitchen.

A flash of light as the sun reflected off something out in the street.

Julius looked out the window, put down his plate, and instinctively grabbed his brother's shoulder, squeezing hard.

A dark sedan pulled up and parked behind Jeremy's jeep. Stamped on the front passenger door was the US MARSHAL emblem. The driver's door opened and out stepped the same officer Julius saw standing in Sybil's yard the previous day.

Julius waved his hand to get the others' attention and pointed out the window.

"Sh*t!" Amy signed and stood.

Jeremy grabbed and pulled her down. He put his finger in front of his lips. "Shh…"

Julius knew that his brother's years of military experience taught him to stay low when danger approached.

Jeremy pointed to Julius then Amy and motioned them toward the suitcases near the back door. "Go!" Jeremy signed. "You drive." He pointed to Denise. "She, I stay. Talk to cop."

As Julius and Amy crawled on the floor to the back door, Denise stood slowly, reached into her pocket and removed a key from Julius's chain. She tossed the key and it slid on the floor, stopping near the suitcases. Julius paused and glanced back.

"Here's your car key," Denise signed low and discrete under the view of the front windows. "I have the spare key. Text me where you leave the car at the airport. I'll come pick it up later." She sent them off with an ILY sign.

Julius nodded and touched Amy's shoulder. "Let's go. Quietly! Grab the bags. We go to the garage."

The living room lights flashed from the front doorbell ringing.

Julius and Amy picked up their bags.

Julius opened the back door. He knew that a closing door made a click. Taking no chances, he turned the knob, softly closed the door, and slowly released the knob. Their backpacks and suitcases swinging crazily, he and Amy sprinted over the grass to the garage.

●　●　●　●　●

Just behind the front door, out of sight from the officer, Jeremy watched Denise open the front door.

"Hello," she signed.

In the back-lighted entryway, standing a foot taller than Denise, the officer presented himself. The neatly trimmed curls of closely cropped dark hair identified him as African American descent. Dark glasses, which reflected Denise's face, rested on his nose. His mouth moved as he craned his neck in an attempt to see who else was in the room.

Behind the door, Jeremy raised a foot to step forward, hesitated, and glanced out the back window of the house.

Julius backed his car out of the garage, closed the garage door, and drove away.

Straightening and stiffening out of habit when present in front of authority, Jeremy stepped into the officer's view.

On a lapel pinned to the opposite chest from the US MARSHAL badge, 'Officer Raymond "Ray" Steele' was etched in black lettering. He opened his mouth and said something.

Denise shook her head and pointed to an ear.

Officer Steele took off his glasses and folded them carefully. Reaching next to his gun, he snapped open a case on his holster, and deposited the glasses. He straightened and looked at the Border Patrol patch on Jeremy's jacket, stepped forward, and said something to him.

Now it was Jeremy's turn to point to an ear and shake his head. Officer Steele stepped into the room and looked around. He said nothing while it appeared he was taking in details. His gaze paused at the dining table with four plates, three of them containing half eaten eggs and pieces of toast. He pulled out a notepad from another pouch in his belt and seemed to slightly shake his head in annoyance. As an introduction to his name, he pointed to his lapel then wrote on the pad. He handed the pad to Jeremy, but Denise grabbed it, holding out her hand for the pen. "I am looking for Amy Mattson. Do you know where she is?"

"We do not know where she is," Denise wrote, handing back the pad.

"Okay. Do you have any idea where she might have gone?" Steele wrote.

Denise looked at the pad and then at Jeremy. She held up a finger and wrote. "Hold on. I think we need a sign language interpreter here to help with communication before we proceed."

Officer Steele read the message, shaking his head in obvious frustration. Leaning his head to the side, he pressed a button on a coiled wire and spoke into the microphone on his shoulder. After a minute, he let go of the button and returned to his writing pad. "Okay. We will wait for an interpreter to arrive. Meanwhile, can I have a look around for a bit?"

"Sure, help yourself," Denise wrote on the pad and handed it back to the officer. Then she walked to the table, cleared the dishes, and busied herself in the kitchen.

Jeremy watched as Officer Steele walked across the living room. Their eyes met in the uncomfortable silence of their communication barrier. There was, however, a slight nod of respect between them, an acknowledgment of their status as keepers of the peace.

Steele continued walking and paused to examine a picture collage Denise kept on the fireplace mantle. It contained various photos of Denise with both Amy and Julius throughout the years.

Jeremy realized it would be a long wait for an interpreter to be available, so he took out his phone and sat in the easy chair.

The officer entered Denise's bedroom and moved about like a uniformed ghost.

Jeremy feigned a focus on a game app, his mind far away regarding his brother and companion on their journey to the other side of the world.

Chapter 18

AMY

It was early evening at the Seattle-Tacoma airport. From the boarding lineup, their plane sat, shiny and white, the onramp attached to it like a leech. The woman smiled and scanned their boarding passes.

Amy held Julius's hand as they headed down the tube hallway toward the plane's entrance. She grabbed his arm as they stopped at the back of the line that waited to enter the plane.

"What's wrong?" Julius asked in ASL.

"I'm not sure." She looked nervously at the cave-like entrance. "I got this weird feeling all of a sudden."

"I'm with you. We will be okay." Julius patted her hand reassuringly.

As they waited, Amy noticed the narrow windows that lined the cream-colored walls of the tube. A memory flooded into her consciousness. In her mind's eye she saw a similar tube many years before and felt the vise-like grip of Sybil dragging her to an unknown destination.

With a sharp intake of breath, Amy jerked her hands away from Julius and balled both fists, holding them close to her chest.

"What now?" Julius asked.

"I just felt Sybil's ghost!"

"What do you mean?"

"It was weird. I remember when we boarded the flight to come to

America, we were in an onramp just like this. She was holding my hand." Amy shuddered, opened her hands, and gathered Denise's donated purple sweater around her. "I just felt her cold, hard hands, not yours."

Julius examined his hand that just held Amy's. "You were definitely holding my hand and not hers. But—wow. Such a strong memory!"

Amy grabbed Julius's arm. "Do you think I killed Sybil? Maybe her ghost is here to haunt me."

Julius placed an arm around her shoulder. "God will take care of us. I've been praying a lot since this happened. I believe Sybil's spirit can't do much against the power of Jesus."

Amy looked nervously behind her. "Don't they have air marshals that can arrest us?"

"We'll be fine." Julius looked behind them but didn't seem convinced.

"If we—" Amy began, but the line moved forward. The carry-on of the passenger behind them brushed her shoulder. "Oh! Sorry!" she voiced.

Amy and Julius entered the plane and passed the threshold of their journey's point of no return.

The touch of Sybil's ghost remained as a lingering effect on Amy's hand while they deposited their backpacks in an overhead bin and occupied two seats near a window in the center of the plane.

A pleasant smell wafted into her nostrils as one of the flight attendants passed. Amy's chest tightened, and her breath quickened as this smell had an opposite effect from its intent. It was very similar to that fragrance she remembered from the attendant on the original flight with Sybil. That alternate environment settled into her memory.

Amy reached out her hand and intertwined her fingers with those of Julius. The warmth of Julius's hand negated Sybil's ghostly presence and brought Amy more into a present state of being.

Another passenger settled into the aisle seat next to Julius. Thankfully, this passenger sported a pair of headphones and closed his eyes, head slightly swaying to music. No threat of strained communication or interaction there.

Amy looked out the little oval window next to her. Outside was the usual bustle of airline workers doing their jobs so this plane could arrive at its destination. She placed her head on Julius's shoulder.

There was a vibration. Julius grabbed his cell phone from his pocket. He clicked the screen.

Amy saw Denise's face pop up.

"How is everything going on your trip so-far?" Denise asked.

"Up till now, good," Julius responded. "Like a normal trip. Haven't been any issues yet."

"Let me see Amy."

Julius gave the phone to Amy.

"How are you doing?" Denise looked concerned. "Are you feeling safer now?"

"Doing better." Amy patted Julius's arm. "I got him here to protect me. We are just sitting here, waiting for the plane to take-off."

Outside the window, Amy saw the service trucks move out of view as they backed away from the gate.

"Let me talk to Denise." Julius grabbed the phone. "What happened with the US marshal?"

"I tried delaying him as much as possible." Denise stuck out her

tongue, exaggerating the **DELAY** sign. "Insisted on waiting for an interpreter so you could make your escape." She held up a finger and added the **WARNING** sign. "I gotta warn you, though. You don't want to mess with this guy. His name is Officer Raymond Steele." She slowed down the fingerspelling so they could catch his name. "I think he goes by 'Steele.'"

Julius furrowed his brow. "What do you mean, 'warn us'?" he asked.

Amy leaned closer to the screen.

"Well first of all, he informed us—meaning Jeremy and I—that Sybil is not dead. She is in the intensive care unit at Sacred Heart Hospital."

"Whew!" Amy placed a palm on her brow. "I am not a murderer!"

"No, Amy, you are not a murderer, but this officer is pretty serious about finding you. He asked a few questions about why you would be interested in India and the Mumbai interpreter services. We all know he got this information from your laptop."

Amy covered her mouth. "That's right!" She formed a swear sign on her hands. "The last internet search on that laptop was related to Visha!"

"Yes," Denise continued. "So I think we gotta assume Officer Steele knows about Visha, and either plans to pursue you, or will flag your passport and alert the authorities in India."

Now Julius formed his own swear word. "Probably both." He looked out the window as the plane taxied down the runway. "We can't just jump out of this plane to escape. I hope we don't have half the Mumbai police force greeting us at the airport."

Denise shook her head. "I don't think he knows you are actually on a flight right now. He doesn't have your visa and flight information, and I don't think Sybil is conscious yet to tell him anything—"

"Visha," Amy interrupted. "Right now, all she knows is that we are visiting India and trying to track down my mother. She has no idea about the cops."

"Right," Julius agreed. "We gotta figure out a way to tell her so she will support us and not freak out. Hopefully she doesn't get a visit from the Mumbai cops before we arrive. That would be bad!"

Suddenly their seats vibrated.

"Whoops!" Julius exclaimed. "Gotta go. The plane's about to take-off."

"Okay. Please be safe." Denise formed the **ILY** sign. "Call me when you get to Mumbai. Godspeed!"

The screen went blank as the seats of Amy and Julius pressed into their backs. Outside, the ground disappeared as they lifted off and soared over the suburbs surrounding the Sea-Tac airport.

Amy fiddled with the beads on her bracelet. Settling into her seat, she looked out the window. This was her second time ever on a plane, and she observed with awe the view that only birds could access in all of God's creation.

The plane rose and banked left. Into the window emerged the snow-capped peak of Mt. Rainier, its western face glowing blue in the twilight of the setting sun.

From her perch high in the sky, Amy saw the majesty of this natural wonder. She also saw the shadow the mountain cast beyond its eastern slopes. In this shadow were the twinkling lights of houses and neighborhoods. It reminded her of the dark actions performed in that little house in Spokane.

This God's eye view of the little lights brought some comfort to the turmoil of her mind. It was the bolstered hope from the fact that at least she was doing something and rapidly moving toward answers to the questions which plagued her existence. Was it a spirit that compelled her forward? She wasn't sure. All she knew was that she must progress in this direction to unknown events in the obscure consequences toward which she and Julius hurtled.

Amy observed the mountain slowly recede out of the window's view and settled against Julius's shoulder. She recalled the previous flight those many years ago, and the wall she immediately knew to build between herself and that rigid woman who insisted on being called 'mother.'

As a little girl, she had looked out the plane window in trepidation, yearning for the fleeting comfort in the eyes of her real mother. Now, as a young woman, she observed the world outside the window, pensively settled in the presence of the person she loved the most.

She looked forward with hope that she would find her mother and finally clear the fog of angst and confusion around her identity, name, and origins.

PART IV

The Return to Dharavi

Chapter 19

JULIUS

Julius sighed as both he and Amy joined what was hopefully the last long line of their long journey.

With the exception of the crowds of brown-skinned people that looked like Amy, the Mumbai airport seemed no different from the large international hubs of the Seattle and Amsterdam airports through which they passed. Here, placards written in English and the squiggly lines of Hindi directed them to present their travel documents, passports, and visas at the glass-surrounded enclosures ahead.

Julius felt a squeeze on his arm. "**What's up?**" he signed, tired, and flicking his middle finger on his chest while looking down at his companion.

Amy pointed to the expressionless face of the agent behind the glass wall at the front of their line. "How will we understand him when we get up there?" she signed and pointed past the agent to a hallway containing a row of doors. "And what happens if they suspect us and throw us into one of those rooms over-there?"

Julius placed a hand over hers and squeezed it. He wished she wouldn't complicate matters by obsessing on paranoid thoughts about things they couldn't control. He brought out a cell phone from his pocket. "We'll text with this. Hopefully he understands English."

At the beginning of the line, Julius observed the agent speaking with a mixed-race couple as they handed their documents through the small opening in the glass. The man was Indian and the woman was Caucasian.

"I think this guy speaks English. Seems he is doing that with this couple," Julius signed. "I want to try and read his lips." Julius lowered his right eyebrow in an effort to lipread the agent. He shook his head and pointed to his phone. "Looks like we're gonna need to text. With the Hindi accent, I can't read his lips in English."

Ten minutes later it was their turn. Amy raised herself on her toes so she could see the man. Julius saw that the agent's eyes were as expressionless as his face. The man extended his hand for their documents. First, he scanned Julius's documents and did an eye-scan of his face while holding up his passport picture.

Julius watched for any hint of concern or alarm. None came.

Next, the agent scanned Amy's passport.

Julius collected his breath as it seemed the man took a bit longer to look at the information that presented on the computer screen in front of him. Julius knew that any flagged information would likely be related to Amy.

His heart skipped a beat as the agent checked her face with the passport picture and looked back at the computer screen.

He didn't do that with me, Julius thought.

Amy stood as tall as her short stature allowed. It seemed she was trying to appear as pleasant and relaxed on the outside, but he knew she was feeling exactly the opposite inside. Julius sent a silent prayer that the agent would be oblivious to Amy's act.

The man nodded slightly as he pressed and held both passports open with one hand while holding what Julius assumed was a visa stamp in the other. The agent's mouth moved in an apparent question.

Julius shot Amy a quick glance and shook his head while pointing to his ear. He held up his cell phone and typed, then held it up to the glass.

Amy pulled at Julius's sleeve. "What's it say?" She pointed to her mouth with the sign.

When the agent finished reading, Julius showed her the phone's text, "We both are Deaf. Can you write down your questions for us please?"

The man watched their exchange and seemed to sigh. As it was heading toward evening, he must have had a long day and was tired. He opened a drawer and pulled out a note pad, scribbling on it with a pen and then placed the pad up to the glass. "What is your purpose for visiting India?" the note asked in neatly formed English letters.

Julius typed into his phone and showed it to Amy. "We are here to see her mother and visit family." He raised his eyebrow in a question seeking her approval.

"Yes, go-ahead," she signed, and nodded as Julius showed his phone to the agent.

The man read the text. "Okay. Velcome to India." Julius read the Hindi-influenced English on the agent's lips as he stamped both passports, handed back their documents, and waved them through the border.

A dozen steps past the customs area, the room narrowed. They encountered a sliding glass door and hallway wide enough for only a single person to pass through.

Julius looked up and noticed the motion sensor was on the outside of the door, only admitting people one way. "You go first."

He followed Amy through the hallway to a similar sliding glass door that opened to two very stern-looking military personnel holding rifles. Their eyes made it clear that nobody should even think of trying to turn around and go back the way from which they came. It occurred to Julius that these very same rifles could be pointed at he and Amy the moment a message about a mixed-race Deaf couple came through the two-way communication devices attached to the shoulders of these guards.

They found themselves in an expansive, high-ceilinged arena

where a mass of brown-skinned humanity pressed in a chaotic swarm around several baggage carousels that shuttled the passengers' luggage in a continuous loop. Both Julius and Amy stopped to take in the sight.

In this crowd, Julius saw several other Caucasian people who stuck out like single dandelions in a field of grass. He realized that he, likewise, was one of these flowers.

"Let's go see if our bags made it." He pointed to a carousel marked by a digital display that flashed their flight number.

Amy grabbed his arm. "Do you think Visha is in this crowd?"

Julius observed several people grab their luggage and exit through the large sliding glass doors that marked the exit. Outside was an equally dense crowd of people kept at bay by two armed guards standing sentry on both sides of the doorway.

 "I don't think the general public is allowed to enter this area," Julius replied with the 'L' handshape for the **BANNED** sign. "She's probably waiting for us in that crowd outside."

Amy held out her hand. "Can you give me your phone so I can text her?" She nodded her head in the direction of the carousel. "You can get our bags."

"Okay." Julius handed her his phone. "You stay right here." Julius took a deep breath, dove into the gap between two men, and elbowed his way through several rows of people. There, among the piles of similar-looking black luggage bags were the two with the red ribbons Denise had tied for easy identification. He grabbed each bag with a hand and heaved, knocking people aside, and plowed through the mass of humanity to pop out in the clearing next to Amy.

 Julius dropped the bags. "Whew! Too many people here!" He exaggerated the **SILLY** sign in front of his nose. "Did you get ahold of Visha?"

"I texted her, but no response yet." Amy handed the phone back to Julius. "Seems like we got a good signal here, but maybe it is blocked on her end." She pointed to the exit. "Let's see if she is waiting outside."

Hitching the small backpacks onto their shoulders, they extended the suitcase handles then headed toward the door, pulling the wheeled luggage behind. Exiting the climate-controlled building, the first thing Julius noticed was the heat-laden humidity wafting past his face. It was accompanied by a slight burning smell. He stopped and observed a quagmire of vehicles behind the waiting crowd of people. Autos, buses, taxicabs, plus those green and gold three-wheeled vehicles called rickshaws crammed, maneuvered, and scooted every which way in a chaotic mess of movement.

"I don't see Visha," Julius signed with the 'V' handshape touching twice near an eye, the **name sign** had showed them during the video  call several days before.

"What do we do?" Amy asked, a worried look on her face.

"Just wait." Aware of his 'dandelion' status in this field of brown grass, Julius waved a hand in the air. "Hopefully she recognizes me, one of the only White people here."

A man popped out from the wall of people and approached, grabbing their luggage.

Instinctively, Julius yanked both pieces of luggage back and stood over them, glaring at the man. "What you do?" Julius asked in what he hoped was a clear voice.

The man bowed slightly and leaned forward. He tilted his head toward the street. "Taxi," Julius read on his lips.

Julius shook his head. "No need," he voiced and waved his hand dismissively.

The man stepped forward. "But how you go—" he started protesting in English, but suddenly was elbowed out of the way by a tall woman.

"Visha?" Julius signed as the woman bent toward Amy.

The hug in which this woman enveloped his little friend confirmed that it was indeed Visha.

Chapter 20

AMY

The first thing Amy noticed was the warmth of the embrace. It was different from the heat of the humid Mumbai air. This was an envelope of affection like the hugs Denise gave when her support was most needed.

Amy was surprised at the strength of the arms in the embrace. When it was released, she looked up. Right in front of her were the eyes of Visha; those same intense eyes that had observed her across that train platform in the cold so many years before.

Visha's hands remained on Amy's shoulders, and she held Amy at arm's length as if she was a photo of cherished memories. She let go and tilted her head in a way that seemed to say 'okay.' "Hi! You, he fine?" Visha pointed to Amy and Julius with a curious, questioning expression, and held her thumb up in a question.

"Yes, we are fine." Amy used the same thumbs-up sign. "A bit tired, but we are happy to be here."

Visha's face changed to a puzzled expression, and she repeated the **TIRED** and **HAPPY** signs Amy used.

"You know, tired like—" Julius closed his eyes and stuck out his tongue, tilting his head to the side.

Visha smiled slightly but kept the same puzzled expression. She glanced at Amy and then at the taxi driver.

"Okay." Amy held up two fingers and pointed them at herself. "Watch-me." She pointed to an airplane parked nearby and extended her arms, swaying in a flying motion. Then she formed the **AIRPLANE** handshape and descended it slowly to the palm of her other hand. This was finished up with Amy crossing her arms in the **RESTING** sign accented by closed eyes and a tilted head, without the extended tongue Julius had produced.

Visha smiled and nodded, forming what appeared to be the Indian Sign Language (ISL) version of OH-I-SEE, which resembled the ASL sign for **UNDERSTAND**.

In the pause as Visha picked her luggage to give to the taxi driver, my saw that Visha's shoulder-length hair was a shade lighter than her own jet-black hair. It was a surreal experience as she stared at the woman who was the girl in the vague memories of her past. In her heart, Amy wanted to bond right away, but her mind told her to wait and observe. Was Visha as fluent in sign language as she appeared? Did she really understand Deaf people?

Visha's light fuchsia shalwar-kameez was matched with a green sari draped around her neck and shoulder.

Amy glanced down at her own clothes. *I gotta get out of these and into something like what she is wearing*, she thought, glancing in the direction of the armed guards at the airport's entrance. *That way I can blend in better and escape notice.*

"Come." Visha waved them in the direction of the taxi driver who placed their luggage in the trunk of his car. Visha spoke to the driver using either the national language of Hindi or the local Marathi dialect. After a series of head-wagging agreements and gestures, Visha faced them. "Come," she signed again and mimicked the steering wheel of a car.

Visha entered the front passenger seat. The driver opened the rear doors. Julius entered directly behind Visha while Amy occupied the seat behind the driver on the right side of the car, opposite from that experienced in America.

Like a rock thrown into the roiling rapids of a river, the car plunged into the Mumbai traffic. As Visha gave verbal instructions to the driver, Amy looked out the side window and was reminded of the street scene she knew as a little girl.

There were the squat-nosed industrial trucks and multicolored buses with metal tassels hanging from the sides. The little rickshaws scooted and twisted among the much larger vehicles in a never-ending hurry to gain a space in the road ahead. At both sides of the road, rickety bicycles, appearing to almost fall apart, proceeded slowly, their owners peacefully pedaling as if on a country ride but mere inches from the passing vehicles. One cycle veered to pass a black, cud-chewing buffalo, cutting off the path of an on-rushing truck.

Amy collected her breath as the truck's driver suddenly braked, slowing within inches of the cycle's back wheel. This truck driver waved his hand out the window and no doubt uttered some swear words to no effect on the cyclist, who ignored the outburst and continued his country ride.

Up ahead, the traffic snarled into a chaotic, congested mess at a roundabout-style intersection with a single traffic light poking up in the middle of an island. As they hurtled toward this intersection, Amy thought that they were headed for a definite collision.

The taxi slowed abruptly and scooted between a truck and a vegetable-laden cart pushed by a vendor. As they rounded the island, Amy saw a single cop standing, waving his arms, and bulging his cheeks as he blew a whistle in a vain attempt to direct the traffic according to the blinking light on the pole. Just behind the police officer, a thin, brown dog stretched and yawned as if it was settling down for its evening nap on a deserted island in the middle of the ocean.

Looking at Julius, Amy saw that Julius, too, was observing the scene outside the window. She poked him in the shoulder. "A chaotic mess out there, huh?" she commented, crossing her hands and wiggling her fingers to represent the mass of vehicles.

Julius formed the exaggerated **SILLY** sign in front of his nose. "Yeah. Interesting. It's amazing how there are no accidents."

From the front seat, Visha glanced back at them, smiled, and and nodded. She pointed out the window and formed what Amy recognized as classifier handshapes for vehicles. Visha's extended tongue with back and forth hand movements confirmed her understanding of their conversation.

"Yes! Wow!" Amy responded, nodding her head emphatically.

As Visha turned to face the front, Amy noticed Julius lowering his right eyebrow and staring at the back of the woman's head. "What's wrong?" Amy asked.

"I wonder how much she can understand if we sign in ASL at our normal pace?" He used the repeated opening and closing of the hands sign for **fluent ASL**.

"I'm not sure. "Amy glanced at Visha to make sure she wasn't watching them. "She seems to understand ISL pretty well. But I don't think she has had any exposure to ASL. Why do you ask?"

"Well, sooner or later, we gotta tell her about our trouble." Julius glanced to make sure Visha wasn't observing them through the rearview mirror. "I don't think we will be able to keep it a secret that we have a US marshal on our tail."

Now his eyebrow scrunched really low. Amy knew he was worried.

"Do you think we can trust her?" Julius continued. "I mean, if we tell her the truth, will she report us to the Indian authorities?"

"Just a sec. Let me think." Amy held up her finger and looked at Visha. From her side view in the back seat, she saw the firmly set jaw and strong, square shoulders of this woman. A memory popped into her mind of this same jaw and the way a much younger Visha had muscled her way into a stern rebuke of the harassment that Amy had suffered from the spiky-haired boy as they begged on the streets of Mumbai.

Amy's eyes confirmed what her mind's eye saw; that this woman was their only ally amid the danger they faced. She joined her hands together in the **ALLY** sign. "We have no choice but to trust her."

"Okay. We'll **follow your gut.**" Julius poked his belly with the sign.

It was dark by now, and the taxi pulled into a circular drive in front of a high-rise building. Pale yellow lights under a canopy illuminated the entrance to this residential complex as a brown-uniformed watchman stirred and yawned, adjusting his brown and black hat. He rose from a chair.

From the front seat, Visha turned to face them. She smiled and pointed to the upper part of the building. "My F-L-A-T," she fingerspelled with the single-handed letters of ASL.

Amy wiggled her fingers. "You can fingerspell in ASL?"

"Ha," Amy read on Visha's lips, which was confirmed by the universal YES sign.

Maybe she understands more ASL than she is letting on, Amy thought as the taxi driver was paid.

They wheeled their bags toward the entry.

The watchman approached and conversed with Visha, tilting his head and extending a hand in the direction of Amy and Julius.

Visha pointed at the watchman. "D______," they read on her lips as she fingerspelled "D-I-N-E-S-H." Visha moved her hand in the direction of the watchman, inviting them to introduce themselves.

Julius put a hand on Amy's shoulder. "Is it wise to disclose our names?" he asked Amy in rapid ASL. "I mean, if there is an announcement for them to be on the lookout for a mixed-race Deaf couple from America, we are pretty much **sitting ducks.**" He used the

animal classifier handshape and shot it with his other hand. "If we tell this guy our names, chances are he will report us to the cop."

Amy saw that Visha was looking at them with a puzzled expression.

Julius held up a finger and smiled then turned back to Amy. "We need to be careful and keep quiet." He used the index finger on his lips for **SAY-NOTHING**.

"I think we should—" Amy began but was interrupted by Visha's shrug and obvious verbal introduction of their names.

The watchman smiled, pressed his hands together, and bowed slightly in a welcome gesture. He escorted them into the building and pulled out a set of keys, unlocking the operation of the elevator buttons. He tilted his head goodbye and resumed his position in the chair outside.

When the elevator doors opened, they entered the building. Visha pushed the button for the eighth floor.

As the pressure increased at her feet from the rising elevator, Amy saw a nod and slight smile on Visha's face. The eyes, however, were hardened in a question that showed the same expression of concern, harkening back to those many years before when these very same eyes made the connection with her during the isolation, anguish, and misery Amy had experienced when her mother abandoned her on the train platform.

Chapter 21

AMY

That evening the cool spray of water, slightly heated in a small tank attached to the wall, brought relief from the humid air. Amy recalled the last time she had taken a shower in this country of her birth. Back then she was surrounded by similar-looking white, floor-matching tile as she showered in the orphanage just prior to being snatched away by Sybil.

As she turned off the water and stepped out of the shower to grab a towel in the small bathroom of Visha's flat, Amy remembered the rough texture of the over-used, orphanage-issued towel that was thrown at her seventeen years ago, the last time she took a shower in India. Now the towel was soft and inviting. As she toweled off, Amy wondered if the rest of this journey would be as welcoming and accessible as Visha's hospitality. She didn't think so.

But she was hungry, and smelled something good. She put these thoughts out of her mind and dressed in Visha's donated tee shirt with NEW YORK printed on the front in pink letters. She tied the waist string on the also donated shalwar, baggy pants, which extended way past her ankles. She bent over to roll up the cuffs before exiting the bathroom.

"Hi, guys!" Amy waved a hand and approached the small round table near the kitchen.

Visha and Julius sat at this table in front of a steaming bowl of spicy-smelling rice.

Visha raised her hand, extended her thumb, and produced a pouring motion above her head. "Shower good?" She kept the extended-thumb handshape.

"Yes! Ahhh! I am clean." Amy smiled, scrubbing her torso in a bathing motion.

Amy took a few steps toward the table, but Visha put out her hand for her to stop. She suppressed a giggle then pointed at Amy's ankles.

"Different pants." Visha used a sign Amy and Julius didn't recognize.

"**Huh**?" Amy curved a finger in a question mark.

Visha pointed out the window. "Shopping," they deduced from the sign. Then Visha pointed at Amy's clothes. "Ve go," they read on her lips.

Amy looked down at her clothes. "Yes, I agree," she signed and joined them at the table.

"C-H-I-C-K-E-N B-I-R-I-Y-A-N-I," Visha fingerspelled in ASL and waved for them to help themselves.

After a few bites of the delicious rice dish, Amy saw Julius pause his meal and look at her shirt. "What's up?" she signed.

"I don't think it's a good idea for you to wear that shirt." Julius shook his head and lowered his eyebrow. "We shouldn't wear anything that draws attention to the fact that we are from America."

Amy glanced down at the stylistic NEW YORK letters printed on her shirt. "Okay. I agree but"—she formed the **HONORIFIC-YOU**  sign— "you are very white." She exaggerated the **WHITE-PERSON** sign in front of her face. "Does this mean you will color your face brown so you blend in better?"

Julius placed his pale hand next to Amy's dark brown arm. "Yeah, I hadn't thought about that."

Amy saw Visha pause her eating. Her eyes had that same hard, puzzled expression from their recent interaction with the watchman.

Visha put down her fork and picked up her cell phone. She typed and handed the phone to Amy.

"Let's communicate this way for now," the message read in English. "It seems you two are discussing something serious when you were down there being introduced to the watchman. Would you mind letting me know what that is?"

Amy grabbed the phone and began typing. She paused and looked at Julius. "I'm not sure how much we should tell her." She used the **INFORM** sign.

Visha's eyes narrowed.

Julius looked at Visha whose face had an expression which demanded a reply. "Okay, go-ahead and tell her all," Julius signed.

Amy took a minute to type into the phone and handed it to Visha. Now the eyes showed concern. Visha typed a reply.

"I am sorry your mother was so controlling. I understand your anger. I am glad she is okay. Do you think the US marshal has already arrived in India and is working with the Mumbai police to track you down?"

"No!" Amy signed, shuddering while shaking her head. She typed into Visha's phone. "Sybil is NOT my mother. Yes, she adopted me, but really, she snatched me away so she can have something in her life to control. She used me for her own selfish purposes and doesn't deserve to be called my mother. We are here to track down and find my birth mother. I need to find out the name she called me and ask her some questions."

Visha looked at the phone and slowly shook her head, forming a sign that looked like LET-GO. She typed into the phone. "But your birth mother **abandoned** you in the middle of the night on a train platform. From my perspective, she also doesn't deserve to be called your mother. Are you sure it is worth the effort to try and track her down?"

Amy read the message. She placed the phone on the table. Visha made a good point. Amy had never thought of it this way and wasn't sure how to answer Visha's question. She wondered if she actually met her birth mother, would she know if the woman deserved to be called her mother? Perhaps she would find out.

A thought occurred. Amy held up a finger. "Hold on a sec," she signed, pulling off the bracelet from her wrist and handed it to Visha.

Visha examined the multicolored beads. The same fingers that crafted the original bracelet touched the knots Amy had tied to expand the leather strap over the years. "Yes, I know." Amy lipread her Hindi- influenced English pronunciation as 'remember.' "This ____ ok you." Visha continued, pointing to the middle finger of one hand then forming the universal 'OK' sign.

Amy wrinkled her nose and repeated the finger-pointing-OK sign combination. "What does this mean?"

"**I-M-P-O-R-T-A-N-T**," Visha fingerspelled.

"Yes, it is. Let me get something else." Amy walked over to her small backpack near her suitcase and pulled out her purse. Back at the table, she reached into the purse and grabbed the crucifix necklace,  depositing it on the table. The rays of the overhead light glinted off its sharp edges as she deposited it on the table. "This too I kept."

Visha handed back the bracelet and picked up the necklace, examining it as the pendant swung on the chain. "I remember this," she signed. "You got when police ___ us." She used the two-handed index finger sign, which Amy deduced as '**CHASE**.'

Visha placed the necklace in Amy's palm and cupped her hand over it. As the older woman's eyes looked into hers, Amy recognized a softness, as if these eyes were searching for something, a connection or relation that was long-ago lost. In these eyes and the subtle squeeze of the hand that held hers, Amy knew that her information was safe with Visha. She recognized that this woman was more than an ally—

she was the sister she had lost all those years ago and now had the opportunity to reconnect.

Visha picked up the phone and typed. "That same shop where you got this is still there at the entrance to the bazaar just down the road from here. Some things never change. They are still selling these very same religious items." She pointed in the southerly direction of the road outside and then typed some more. "Back to your mother. Why the need to track her down?"

Amy read the message. "My I-D," she fingerspelled. "It is my I-D-E-N-T-I-T-Y I need to find." She formed the 'A' handshape name sign on her cheek and signed THROW-UP with a gagging reflex.

Visha wiggled her fingers and brought them to her forehead with a clenched fist. She tilted her head in understanding.

Amy pointed to Visha and then to her own ear, finishing with a wiggled thumbs-up in the formation of the 'Hear-Nothing' name sign used long ago. She shook her head. "Okay, SO-SO," Amy signed and picked up the phone. "I hate the name sign that Sybil gave me. It represents the American hearing identity she has tried to force on me practically my whole life. I remember my birth mother calling me a name. But it was all verbal, I never really knew what it was. You were the first person who ever thought or even cared to identify me in a visual way."

Tears welled in Amy's eyes. "My hope is to find my birth mother and learn the name she called me. I also need to find out from her own mouth why she chose to abandon me like that. Was it because I am Deaf?"

Visha read the message. "I help you," she signed.

Amy and Julius looked at each other and nodded, pleasantly surprised that the ISL sign for **HELP** was the same in ASL.

Visha typed some more. She placed the phone where they both could see. "Tell me more about this US marshal. What are the chances

that he will come looking for you here in this flat?"

Julius picked up the phone and typed. "We know Amy is being pursued. Denise, whom you met on the video-chat from America, tells us the name of the US marshal is Officer Raymond Steele. From Amy's computer and other sources, he will eventually figure out that we have come to India and connected with you."

Visha read the message, then looked out the window of a sliding glass door that opened to her balcony. Her jaw tightened and her broad shoulders rose in tension. She looked at the cell phone and typed. "How soon do you think this officer will be here?" She handed the phone to Julius.

Julius typed. "We have no idea when. I think we need to assume that he is on his way here now."

Visha read the message and froze.

Amy saw the same hard eyes Visha possessed long ago on the tough streets of Mumbai when she directed the begging actions of the kids. There was a metamorphosis in this woman, as if the pleasantly decorated flat and welcoming meal no longer existed. Now she became that tough street kid whose primary purpose was to preserve and protect those whom she called her own.

As Amy and Julius glanced at each other with puzzled expressions, Visha stood and marched purposefully to the door of the porch. She flung it open and stepped out onto the balcony. Amy and Julius followed her, the warm, humid air wafting over them as they peered over the balcony. It was a dark night, and the half-moon tilted just over the horizon above the Arabian Sea. If there were stars, Amy couldn't see them because of the bright lights from the surrounding buildings.

From this eighth floor perch, Amy observed the night scene of the city as it spread out before her. Just to the southwest, below the high-rise buildings standing here and there, the landscape's most prominent feature was the river of blue from the tarped roofs of the huts within the nearby slum. A few blocks away, this river was illuminated bright blue from the floodlights of the nearby buildings. Further away, the the cerulean hue darkened and finally became black as the river receded in the distance beyond the reach of electricity.

Amy's eyes followed this river and peered into the darkness. *Will I find my mother there?* she wondered. *Are there people out there who may remember my name?*

In spite of the warm air, she felt a chill in her heart; a fear that highlighted her isolation. Instinctively, she reached for Julius and pulled herself close. His arm around her shoulder touching on the skin of her neck provided a refuge from the fear.

Amy looked at Visha, who remained poised, both hands on the railing, staring intently at the courtyard below. Just under the edge of the canopy over the building's entrance, Dinesh, the watchman, sat dozing in the otherwise empty courtyard.

Why is Visha looking at him like that? Amy wondered.

Visha straightened and nodded, pointing down at the watchman. "Yes—" she formed the two-handed 'D' letter in ISL and separated her hands in a sign that looked like FEAR.

"Sorry. I don't understand," Amy signed.

"**D-A-N-G-E-R**," Visha fingerspelled and resumed pointing  down to the watchman. "Police he tell," she signed in a sentence almost identical to ASL.

Amy's arm tightened around Julius's waist. "Are they coming now?"

"How do you know?" Julius signed to Visha as he took his arm from Amy's shoulder. "Has the watchman done something to show you he will go to the police?"

"No, just feeling I have." Visha replied and faced Amy. She flipped her extended finger in what appeared to be a sign for 'then.'

"We pay, get clothes," she signed, finishing up with a gesture that looked like 'scarf.'

"S-A-L-W-A-R K-A-M-E-E-Z," Visha fingerspelled in ASL then pointed in the direction of the slum. "We tell Q your ___." Visha produced what appeared to be the ISL letter for 'Q' and pointed to her nose.

Amy pointed to her own nose. "What's this?" she asked.

"**M-O-T-H-E-R**," Visha fingerspelled.

"I see," Amy signed.

"We gotta learn some ISL," Julius commented.

Amy looked out over the balcony. She felt exposed. The bright, surrounding floodlights illuminated her amid the shining metal and windows of this residential complex. She had an urge to dive into the dark river of tarp that snaked off into the distance. No doubt people were going about their nightly routines. She saw moving, twinkling lights that indicated the use of candles or oil lanterns in the areas of less electrical power. Perhaps it was in this darkness where she would find the answers she so desperately sought.

Chapter 22

JULIUS

Julius opened his eyes and stretched, propping up on his elbows. The thin mattress of the couch on which he slept was much harder than the cushy ones he was used to back in America.

A strong, nutty, slightly burning smell entered his nostrils. He glanced around to locate the source. On the countertop gas-burning stove, a medium-sized pot sat over a low flame. A smaller pot steamed next to it. Rising to investigate, Julius saw that the small pot percolated with boiling chai. The other pot contained a sticky-looking, dark brown, grainy substance. He noticed an added sweet aroma now that he was closer.

As there was no one in the living area of the flat, Julius opened the porch door and stepped out onto the balcony. The air had a unique combination of staleness and humidity left over from the overnight heat with a freshness blowing in from the nearby sea. He also sensed the woody smell of fires and looked toward the street below.

Little plumes of smoke rose from wood-burning, cooking flames in carts manned by vendors at various locations on the curb. Hand-drawn carts piled high with various wares, vegetables, fruits, and a couple containing bulging bags of grain lined the road. One cart, pulled slowly by a black buffalo, meandered at the edge of the crowded street. Various auto parts cluttered the cart. Julius wondered if this was the Indian version of the delivery service that supplied the auto parts stores in America.

There was a movement down in the courtyard. Julius saw Dinesh, the watchman, saunter slowly to the entry gate to admit one of the resident's cars. Julius leaned forward and shook his head while grabbing the cold metal of the balcony railing.

What am I doing here? he thought, scanning the street for any sign of a police presence. *I'm in trouble because I am now considered by them as an accessory to Amy's crime. Is this all worth it to support and protect her like this?* He looked out over the horizon where the sea met the sky. He prayed, *What should I do, God?*

His cell phone buzzed in his pocket and he pulled it out. It was a text notification from Jeremy that flashed on his screen. *I should update Jeremy when I get a chance,* he thought, but hesitated, hovering his finger over the Holy Bible app next to the Messages app on his phone.

What is that verse about laying down one's life for friends? he wondered and tapped the app then clicked on the book of John. Julius started reading John chapter 15, verses 12 to 13: *This is my commandment: Love each other in the same way I have loved you. There is no greater love than to lay down one's life for one's friends.*

Julius stared at the words.

Am I laying down my life for Amy? he wondered, rereading the verses. *Help me, God!* He sighed, shaking his head as he prayed.

A hand tapped his shoulder. "C-H-A-I," Visha fingerspelled and handed him a cup and saucer of the steaming brown liquid.

"Thanks!" Julius pocketed his phone, accepted the drink, and took a sip. The coffee-like taste pleasantly complemented his other senses.

"L-A-P-A-I." Visha pointed to a small table on the side of the balcony where three small bowls of the sticky-brown substance waited.

The patio door opened. "Ah! Breakfast!" Amy signed one-handed while holding her own chai in the other. Her hair was tousled to one side, and the pink NEW YORK shirt remained wrinkled since her recent rise from sharing Visha's queen-size bed in the only bedroom of the flat.

They sat at the small chairs and partook of the simple breakfast with the tiny spoons Visha provided. As the table was very near the railing, Julius could see the courtyard below where Dinesh paced and continued opening the gate to admit the residents' cars.

"Doesn't he ever go home and sleep?" Julius pointed below and tilted his head on his hands to indicate sleep.

Visha produced a disinterested glance below and shrugged. "Night he bother," she signed.

Amy paused a sip of chai, puzzled. "The sign 'bother' mean what?" she asked.

"**W-O-R-K**," Visha clarified.

"Oh! I get it!" Amy turned to Julius. "I guess the ISL for 'work' is the same-as our ASL sign 'bother.'"

"Down he go home," Visha continued.

"Okay, so 'down' in ISL probably means '**now' or 'soon**.'" Amy nodded and took a bite of lapai.

Visha picked up her phone and typed. "After breakfast, I think we should go down to the bazaar and shop for some clothes. Let's get you out of these American clothes."

Amy read the message. "Yes, I want a colorful combination," she typed. "Fuchsia and something that goes with it."

Visha looked at the phone and tilted her head in partial agreement. "The more colorful you are, the more you will be noticed. We'll pick something that is neutral so you can blend in with what most other people are wearing." She handed the phone over and looked at Julius. "You same," she signed.

Julius looked down at his American clothes and nodded. "**Same**, yes." He joined his hands in the ASL sign then grabbed the phone to type. "What about Amy's mother? What will we do today to accomplish that?"

Visha pointed to the river of tarp which now gleamed bright blue in the morning sun. "D-H-A-R-A-V-I," she fingerspelled.

"So that's what it was called!" Amy slowly nodded and stared at the vast expanse of huts. She formed a circle with her index finger and thumb in front of her forehead. "I had **no idea** the name of even the place where I lived when I was a kid."

Julius took a moment to observe the slum. From this elevated view, it was difficult to see the details of the street scene between the blue tarps. The hectic movements of people and vehicles at a few intersections or open clearings told him that this area was no different from the chaotic street scene below. He wondered if the Mumbai cops had a strong presence in that area as well.

Julius nudged Amy. "Now that you have found out the name of the place where you grew up, maybe soon you will be able to add your own given name to that list of things you will learn."

Visha continued typing. "Just after I started learning ISL, I got to know some Deaf residents in Dharavi. I still see them once in a while. Perhaps you should meet them."

Julius and Amy read the message. Julius grabbed the phone and typed, "Yes, that would be nice, but will they know how we can find Amy's mother?"

Visha looked at the phone and pondered. "Perhaps not. I do know about one man who has lived a long time in the same area where your mother abandoned you. I assume your mother has lived close to that. I think his name is Nasir. He is an elder in that neighborhood. I have a friend named Iftikar. We all call him 'Ifty.' He should know how to find this man. Today, I will track down Ifty."

As Amy and Julius read the message, Visha pointed at their food. "Food cold eat," she signed.

Julius took a bite of lapai and smiled. It eased his mind that many of the ISL signs were similar to that of ASL. During this pause in their conversation, he felt the slight breeze blowing in from the sea. The humidity carried a heaviness that covered him like a warm blanket. Looking out over the balcony, his eye caught a movement below. Dinesh was opening the gate.

Julius tensed and grabbed Amy's arm.

A tan jeep entered the courtyard, the word POLICE stamped in English letters on the front doors.

"Oh **sh*t!**" Amy extended her thumb into the circle of her other  hand.

Visha's chai cup paused in mid-sip.

A brown-uniformed Mumbai police officer exited the driver's side of the jeep. The front passenger door opened. Out stepped another brown-uniformed officer.

Julius shifted in his seat for a better view of the scene below. The other officer walked around the front of the vehicle and joined the Mumbai cop. Julius froze, recognizing the US MARSHAL patch on this man's chest.

"Officer S-T-E-E-L-E!" Julius fingerspelled and pointed.

Julius's heart raced as he observed the African American officer who looked around the courtyard behind the same dark glasses he wore in Spokane just a few days prior. The immediacy of their crisis placed front and center in his mind, Julius glanced at the patio door. His only thought was to escape.

Slowly, Visha put down her cup and narrowed her eyes as the two officers conversed with Dinesh. With both hands, Visha reached out and pulled Amy and Julius away from the railing. They all crouched behind the table and peered over the floor of the balcony, observing the conversation below.

Dinesh extended his finger and began raising his arm to point up. With a rough movement, Visha grabbed Amy and Julius, pulling them into the flat. "Go!" She pointed at their suitcases. "Clothes second."

"Huh?" Julius signed.

Visha tightened her lips in frustration. She pointed at his pajama bottoms. "Off!" she commanded then produced a sign that looked like ALL, but he knew to mean **HURRY**.

Julius grabbed his jeans and quickly changed in the bathroom. The women entered Visha's bedroom. When they emerged, Amy wore Denise's jeans and Visha remained in her pajamas.

Visha picked up her purse from a table next to the front door, pulled out her wallet, and pointed. "Get yours," Visha directed and opened the door. "Go! Backpacks guide," she commanded.

"You mean **B-R-I-N-G**?" Amy clarified.

Visha nodded, guiding Amy with a small push toward the backpack near her luggage. "Hurry!"

Julius grabbed his backpack and saw Amy put her purse in her own backpack. "Where do we go?" he asked, using the same **GO-AWAY** sign Visha produced.

Visha pointed into Amy's purse at the crucifix necklace. "Necklace marry over-there." She pointed in the direction of the Dharavi slum. Amy joined her hands repeatedly with the **MARRY** sign. She looked at Julius, puzzled.

Julius widened his eyes, shaking his head profusely.

Frustrated, Visha pushed them into the hall. "Necklace **S-T-O-R-E** go! Police I stay here meet!" She pointed down the hall in the opposite direction from the elevator. "Store you stop. There I **meet** you," she finished with a sign that looked like two vehicles crashing together and shut the door.

Julius and Amy rushed to the end of a hall and opened a small door under an EXIT sign written in English. They found themselves at a landing of stairs.

"Hold on a sec." Julius held up a finger and crouched low, cracking open the door to peer back into the hall. He felt Amy press up against him to peer over his head.

In the dimly lit hallway, he saw a yellowish spreading light as the elevator door opened. Out stepped the watchman, followed by the Mumbai cop and Officer Steele. The cop seemed incredibly thin next to the thick, heavyset frame of the US marshal. Even in the dim hallway, both officers wore their dark glasses.

They stopped in front of Visha's door and the watchman knocked. Her door opened, and the morning sun beamed into the hallw ay, illuminating the details of the guns on the belts of the officers. After a few words, the three men entered Visha's flat.

Julius closed the exit door. "Let's go down." He beckoned for Amy to follow.

They descended the stairs. The stairs ended at another small door. They exited into a back alley.

Julius looked both ways to make sure there were no other cops waiting for them. "Let's go down to the street," he signed as they entered the alley which ended at a curve in the same busy road that passed in front of the residential building.

"She told us to find that shop at the bazaar entrance." Amy pointed down the bustling street. "I think it is that way. We will wait for her there."

They disappeared into the street-side crowd, scurrying in the direction of the tarp-covered slum.

Ten minutes later, Amy and Julius stopped at the entrance of another alley. Immediately to their right was a shop. To the left of the door was a cart containing various sized statues of Ganesh, the Hindu, elephant-headed god.

There, hanging on a jewelry display to the right of this shop's doorway, was a collection of the exact same necklace Amy carried in her purse.

Amy pointed at this jewelry display. "There is my necklace! I remember crashing into that same cart while Visha and I were being chased by the cop." She reached in and partially pulled out her own necklace. "Somehow I ended up with this wrapped around my neck."

Julius pushed her hand back into the purse. "We don't want the shopkeeper thinking you have stolen that necklace." He waved her in the direction of the shop. "Come. Visha told us to wait in front of this store."

As they waited, Julius looked around at the scene. Farther into the alley, various other stores lined either side of the narrow lane. People's faces carried nonchalant, almost bored looks as they scurried about their morning routines in the organized chaos of the bazaar. Just beyond the shops, Julius recognized the blue-tarped roofs of the slum.

On the opposite curb from where they stood, he saw a small group of dirty, raggedly clothed street kids holding up their palms, poking and prodding the adults passing by.

He touched Amy's shoulder and pointed at the kids. "Long-ago, that was you."

Amy grabbed Julius, shoving him behind the jewelry cart so the kids couldn't see him. "Hide your white-face! The moment they see you, they will think, Ka-ching!"—Amy pulled the arm of an imaginary slot machine—"Rich American, and will swarm around you. Perfect advertisement for the cops!"

Out of the street kids' line of sight, they had a good view down the street in the direction from which they came. Off in the distance where the line of high-rise residential and office buildings ended, Julius saw the wall protecting the city from the Arabian Sea. The water was a blue backdrop to the city-scene.

From the shifting crowd, the multicolored hues of their clothes shimmering like leaves fluttering on a fall day, Visha's tall frame emerged, wearing a light green kameez over a tan salwar.

Visha looked at the necklace display. "Same necklace you find," she signed. "Two-you okay?" Concerned, she glanced quickly behind her.

Julius held up a thumb. "We are good." He glanced down the street. "What happened with the cops?"

Visha raised her hands to begin signing but hesitated. With a furtive glance around, she pulled out her phone and typed for a minute and showed them the phone. "That Officer Steele is one tough man! I sure hope he doesn't catch you. Both the Mumbai policeman, named Officer Manish, and Officer Steele asked a lot of questions about you. Obviously, your suitcases were there right in front of them, so I couldn't hide the fact that you were visiting."

Julius grabbed the phone and typed. "Okay, so now they know we are here and are staying with you. What did you tell them?" He handed the phone back.

"Come," Visha waved for them to follow. "More S-A-F-E inside."

They followed her into the store and waited as she typed some more.

"I fooled them. Acted completely surprised that you are in trouble with the law and are being pursued by the police. They wanted to know why you were in India and where you went from my flat. I told them Amy was trying to find out more about her origins and that you went to visit the orphanage from where you were adopted. I don't know which orphanage that is, but they will figure it out. Hopefully it will divert them. I said nothing about your mother."

Amy and Julius read the message.

Julius looked out the side window of the shop and down the street. He typed into the phone. "Now that your flat is staked out by the cops, are you sure you were not followed here?"

Visha hardened her eyes and texted. "I know these streets way better than any of those cops, especially a US marshal who has no experience in Mumbai. Remember, I grew up on these streets. I snuck out from the basement maintenance area of my building and made doubly sure I wasn't followed."

She reached into her purse and pulled out a small business card, handing it to Julius. It contained a star in one corner with 'Officer Raymond Steele' printed in bold letters. Under the name was 'United States Marshal Service' along with email and phone contact information. Visha texted and handed her phone to Julius. "Officer Steele gave this to me with instructions to contact him as soon as you returned to my flat."

Amy stood squarely in front of Visha. "You will protect us?" It was a command with a questioning expression.

Visha nodded, softened her eyes, and nodded. "I promise," she signed and pointed into the alley. "D-H-A-R-A-V-I," she fingerspelled. "Come, clothes we shop." Checking down the street to make sure they were not pursued, Visha left the store with the other two following.

Julius stayed out of the street kids' line of sight as they disappeared into the crowd. *Will Amy find the answers she is looking for in this chaotic place?*

Chapter 23

AMY

Amy entered a side alley entirely lined with the narrow openings of clothes stores. *How do these shops compete?*

She was used to the American style of store placement with retail outlets spaced so that vendors did not sell their wares in the same proximity. Here, there were at least ten clothing stores lined right next to each other like books on a shelf. Even in the midst of this narrow alley, barely wide enough for two people to pass abreast, cyclists pedaled by, carrying various items on the racks over their rear wheels. An occasional rickshaw scooted and paused, turning to avoid running over the people in front who meandered peacefully here and there as if on a leisurely walk along the street.

Stepping over two high cement steps in front of a clothes shop, Visha beckoned to follow. "Come, this store good," she signed.

The narrow, ten-by-twenty-foot shop displayed women's salwar-kameez along one wall while men's kurtas hung on the opposite. On a far wall, various sarees were draped on a rod.

Two shopkeepers stepped forward and clasped their hands together, bowing slightly in greeting. Amy guessed that the older man was probably the owner and his look-alike son the assistant.

Visha's mouth moved rapidly in the local Marathi dialect as she conversed with the two men. She pointed at both Amy and Julius. The owner waved his hand along a row of colorful kameez. Visha shook her head and stepped close to the plain-colored clothes near the back wall.

"Come, **try on**," Visha signed with a movement that resembled the ASL sign for CHALLENGE.

The owner beckoned Amy closer while his son guided Julius to the other wall.

Amy held up a light salmon-colored kameez. It had a nice white embroidered pattern along the collar. The owner handed her a pair of white salwar and said something, tilting his head in the direction of a small doorway in the back wall.

"Try for fit," Visha interpreted, intertwining her fingers in a sign for **MATCH**.

Amy entered a tiny room with a hole in one corner of the floor. A spigot protruded over a nearby pot already filled with water. There was a mirror attached to the door and nothing on the walls.

I guess one of these days I'll have to squat over a hole like this, she thought, remembering the days when she participated in communal squats over similar holes in the various outhouses along the streets in the slum. She changed and deposited her American clothes into her backpack then exited the bathroom.

Standing with his own new clothes draped over an arm, Julius looked Amy up and down. He smiled and nodded, holding up the 'F' handshape. "Nice! **Beautiful!**" he signed and entered the bathroom.

Visha placed her hands on Amy's shoulders, held her at arms' length, and looked her over. Visha nodded and pointed out into the alley. "Yes, now you can gather."

Amy understood the sign to mean **MINGLE**. She looked out to the street and saw another similarly attired woman walk by. This short woman could have passed as an older version of Amy, an observation which eased her mind.

The bathroom door opened and out stepped Julius, wearing a light tan kurta over matching, colored salwar. It made him look tall and thin, plus a bit more refined than his previous clothes.

"Oooh! Nice!" Amy circled her fingers, closing and kissing them in front of her face with a flourish. "Beautiful!"

"Thanks. Now what?" He held up his hands with the question.

Visha herded Amy next to Julius and handed her phone to the owner of the shop. "Picture," she signed and stood next to Amy, kneeling slightly so she wouldn't appear so tall.

The owner clicked the picture and handed back the phone. He pointed to the walls and said a few words.

Visha nodded and touched Amy's kameez. "Fits yes?" she signed and pointed to the walls. "Now pick one more, we go."

Amy and Julius chose their second sets of clothes then folded and placed them in their backpacks.

"Now pay." Visha produced a movement similar to the ASL sign for **SPEND-MONEY**.

Julius pulled his wallet from a back pocket and opened it. "American dollars?" He showed the bills to Visha.

"Oh! Money you not change?" Visha crossed her hands with the ISL sign.

Julius copied the sign. "What's this?"

"**E-X-C-H-A-N-G-E**," Visha fingerspelled and pointed outside. "Over-there airport?"

"Oh! Sorry." Julius closed his wallet and looked at Amy. "Crap! We forgot about that in our rush to leave the airport."

Amy hit her forehead with her palm. "We've been so busy worrying about the cops that we forgot basic things like exchanging our American dollars for Indian rupees."

"Oh! Okay." Visha understood enough. "I pay now." She reached in her purse and produced her wallet. "Later clean we go." Seeing the puzzled looks on Julius and Amy's faces, "**B-A-N-K**," she fingerspelled, and paid the shopkeepers.

"I guess this sign for 'clean' in ASL means 'bank' in ISL," Amy commented to Julius as they left the shop. She turned to Visha. "Thank -you so much! You didn't need to do that." Seeing Visha's blank face, Amy clarified, "Later we pay," she used the ISL sign she just observed Visha use.

Visha waved her hand and dismissively shook her head. "I-F-T-Y we go find now. Maybe he help find N-A-S-I-R."

They stepped off the curb and turned in the direction of the blue tarp-covered shanties. Visha led them through the crowd along the portion of the bazaar that contained a row of shoe vendors.

Amy noted the retrospective sense of belonging through the comfort provided by the loose fit of her salwar-kameez. She was now back with her people. This allowed the fear to loosen its grip, and she relaxed in observation as they moved along the narrow street.

True, as they maneuvered through tight spaces, there were the head-wagging, hand-waving mannerisms she was accustomed to as a little girl and the chaos of too many people in no hurry. This she understood. But the moving mouths in a language she never had access to learn set her apart as different. Plus, the fact that she had a blazing, white-skinned companion at her side further enhanced her separation from the crowd.

Instinctively, she grabbed Julius's arm. In spite of his physical difference, he was her flowering dandelion, supporting and protecting her in the midst of this grassy field.

Suddenly, Visha veered to the side and grabbed the arm of a man on a bicycle. The cycle jerked sideways, almost spilling the pile of grain bags on top of the rear rack.

The man lowered jet-black eyebrows under a shock of spiked, black hair protruding from his head. An assumed swear word emanated from this man's mouth.

Visha reacted with a stern look and a mock slap to the face.

Amy's mouth dropped. Visha's action brought back a memory—

This was the spiky-haired boy who had bullied her! Would the mock slap now transform into a real one and cause this man to tumble backward, just like he did when Visha slapped him during the time when Amy was known as Hear-Nothing?

Visha's face softened as she said a few words to this man. She pointed to her ear and shook her thumb. "Hear-Nothing, remember?" Visha signed in ISL as she spoke Marathi.

Amy recognized her given American name on Visha's lips as Visha pointed and Spiky Hair looked. *Would he remember that she was the cause of the abuse he previously suffered from the hands of Visha?* Hesitantly, Amy nodded in greeting and made eye contact with the man.

The man smiled and his eyes softened. He placed a palm on his chest, bowing slightly. "Ifty," he pronounced, extending his hand in greeting.

Amy copied the head bow and shook his hand. She pointed at Julius. "My boyfriend," she voiced the name as the men shook hands.

To Amy's great relief, there was no indication that Ifty remembered the abuse. There were a few slaps on the shoulder as Ifty appeared to tease Visha. Perhaps they were reminiscing about the old times, but Amy did see the word 'Nasir' produced on Visha's lips, along with a palms-up, questioning look.

Julius poked Amy's shoulder. "I think he's giving directions to Nasir's house," he remarked as Ifty extended his hand down the alley in the direction of the slum. His hand twisted and turned, an obvious indicator of direction giving.

Visha's head twisted and tilted in understanding. "Ha," she pronounced. "He help us," she signed.

Ifty pressed his hands together in the 'namaste' goodbye and cycled off.

"Hope Nasir help find your mother. First, bank we go." Visha rubbed fingers together on a hand. "Money we exchange." She crossed her hands with the sign and indicated for them to follow.

A few minutes later, they approached a building just down the street from the entrance to the bazaar. Thick steel bars covering the doors and windows marked it as a place of heightened security. Big, block English letters over curving Hindi script identified it as the Bank of India.

Visha put out her arm and stopped them. She raised a finger and pulled two hands toward herself with a questioning expression as she observed the entrance of the bank.

Amy copied the sign. "What?" she asked.

"**S-E-C-U-R-I-T-Y** where?" Visha clarified.

Amy and Julius looked at the entrance. True, there was not the usual, brown-uniformed security personnel guarding the entrance. At another bank a few doors down, Amy saw one guard, a black hand gun prominently displayed on his belt.

Visha extended a pinkie finger and shook it. "Bathroom he go maybe." She shrugged.

Suddenly, around the far corner of the bank stepped a brown-attired man with a pistol on his belt. Amy saw his eyes check them out as he approached the entryway. She also saw a blue star-shaped patch with GREATER MUMBAI POLICE within a red circle displayed on his left shoulder.

Discretely, Amy pulled Visha's sleeve and jerked a thumb in the direction of the cop.

Visha stiffened and stepped in front of Julius to block the officer's view of him.

"Come, careful," she signed quickly and herded them into the bank.

Chapter 24

JULIUS

Compared to the soft American dollars which Julius just exchanged, the small stack of rupee notes in his hand felt like thin pieces of plastic. As he walked toward the exit of the bank, he glanced at the top note and saw the smiling face of Gandhi welcoming him to participate in the Indian economy.

Visha pulled at his sleeve. She pointed to the money, then at the wallet in his back pocket. Inserting one hand into the other, sandwich-like, she pointed to Julius's backpack and imitated **placing the wallet into it**. "Keep safe," she signed and stepped toward the exit, beckoning  Julius and Amy to follow.

On the sidewalk they paused and, out of the corner of his eye, Julius caught a brown hue. He looked and found himself face-to-face with the Mumbai police officer who now stood guarding the entrance of the bank.

The officer's disinterested observation of the street scene now became the hardened suspicion of surveillance. He observed this white man accompanied by two Indian women.

I dare not sign. That'll be a sure give away, Julius thought. *This cop has probably seen pictures of Amy and me as international fugitives.* He tore his eyes away from the officer and subtly shook his head in warning at Amy, who also looked at the officer.

Not knowing what else to do, they both looked at Visha.

Softly closing her eyes and tilting her head in an indication for them to follow, Visha started walking toward the nearby entrance of the crowded bazaar.

As they rounded the corner to enter the bazaar, Julius noticed the officer following them a few steps behind.

Did he call out to us and become suspicious because we didn't answer? Julius wondered, watching Visha who gave no indication that she heard the cop.

Visha turned and placed a firm hand on a shoulder of each of them. "Follow!" she commanded.

They followed her into the crowd.

Visha moved between a walk and a run. She sidestepped and angled with surprising ease between a clump of people, rickshaws, and bicycles, narrowly avoiding a collision with a bicycle overloaded with enormous baskets.

Julius and Amy followed closely, knowing that if they lost contact with Visha, they would be clamped in the bear-like grip of the pursuing cop.

Past the shops, Visha veered left into a narrow alley. Seeing the blue tarps on top of the shanties lining this way, Julius knew they were now in the bowels of the Dharavi slum. Visha glanced behind. Julius followed suit, seeing the cop turn into this alley, also proceeding between a walk and a run.

Now they ran, Julius holding tight to Amy's hand. The thinning crowd of the alley afforded less obstacles.

Visha's strong shoulders swayed as she led them to a sharp turn.

She skidded into a dye factory.

Dripping wet multicolored cloths hung from above-head ropes.

Julius and Amy both slapped into a row of red-colored cloth as they maneuvered into a center aisle.

Startled workers paused and watched.

"Hurry!" Visha signed frantically. She held open the back door of the factory.

They were now in another alley. Visha turned right and continued in a run. They ran along the twisting curves of this alley. Chickens scattered as they leaped over them. The reeking, open sewage drain in the middle was sidestepped.

Amy teetered. Julius grabbed her, jerking her to the side as she narrowly avoided falling into a large muddy pothole.

The alley straightened.

Visha stopped before an open clearing.

Julius saw the heaving chests of both Visha and Amy as they tried to catch their breaths.

Out in the clearing, a group of young boys stopped playing cricket around a set of makeshift wickets, and stared at the intruders.

Julius looked behind him, saw no cop, and quickly recovered his breath. He observed their guide.

Although Visha's body was the same, this was not the warm and pleasant host he saw in her flat this morning. Surrounded by the dilapidated wooden shanties of the slum with several women and children pausing in their activities to observe, Visha doubled over with hands on her knees to catch her breath. Her eyes shifted here and there, checking down the alley and looking at the dark entrances of side alleys for any sign of danger.

None came and, apparently satisfied that they were safe for the time being, Visha straightened and frowned. Her eyes became narrow slits as she observed the nearby shanties.

Amy glanced at her newly purchased clothes and then at Julius. She swore with the circle-thumb sign. "Our clothes got ruined when we ran through that dye factory!"

Julius saw a red splotch on Amy's shoulder and looked at his shirt, spotting a similar stain on his chest. "Great! Now we are marked and easily recognizable." He pointed to the gawking onlookers. "When the cops come, these people will tell them to look for the mixed-race couple with red dye on their clothes!"

"Thank God we bought another set of clothes. We'll have to change at Nasir's house."

Julius noticed Visha observing them, narrow eyes and a scowl still registered on her face.

"Are we lost?" Julius asked in ASL, not sure how to act out the concept.

Visha's eyes shifted to him and the scowl remained. "Kya?" she pronounced, not understanding the question.

"**L-O-S-T**?" Julius fingerspelled. He slowed his signing. "N-A-S-I- R house where?"

Visha extended her thumb downward. "Lost, no," she signed.

"Okay, what—" Julius questioned.

Visha held out her hand, closing her eyes. "No talk," she commanded and tilted her head back the way they came. "Follow!" She turned and strode purposefully toward the entrance of a nearby side alley.

"Is she mad at us?" Julius asked Amy.

Amy looked at the back of the woman. "I don't think so. I remember she was like this long ago when I was with her on these streets. I think it is a survival instinct." Amy gestured her hand at the dirty street and cluttered huts that surrounded them. "You know, this isn't exactly a safe place."

"But can we trust her?" Julius lowered his right eyebrow and looked at Visha.

Amy shrugged. "It's not like we have a choice, is it?"

As they progressed through the cluttered alley, it became narrow to the point where one could almost touch the residences on both sides with arms outstretched. The overhanging eaves overlapped, darkening the alley.

A door opened, and Julius bumped into a lady stepping out of her house.

"Sorry," he pronounced in English.

It was too dark to see her facial reaction. He sighed and shook his head as they continued along the narrow passageway. *Do we just continue to blindly follow this woman who is so hard to understand?* he thought, glancing at Amy whose face registered not a hint of suspicion. *Doesn't Amy have questions, too? Why does she so easily trust?*

Julius saw Visha pull ahead. Her purposeful steps exuded confidence.

He realized that he, too, must learn to trust. *I do trust you, God,* Julius prayed. *Help me. What is that verse? John 15:13. "There is no greater love than to lay down one's life for one's friends."* He quickened his steps to catch up to Visha. *Protect us, God, as we trust this woman,* he concluded his prayer.

Visha stopped in front of a narrow door to one of the shanties in the alley.

"This must be Nasir's house," Amy commented.

Visha rapped on the door with her knuckles.

The door opened. An elderly man with a pleasant face and salt-and-pepper hair stepped out to greet them. One leg swung awkwardly out, and he put his weight on the other, keeping his hand on the door for balance.

Visha said some words and pointed at Amy and Julius. It seemed at one point, she pronounced the word 'mama' on her lips.

The man listened, nodded, and turned to the two of them, clasping his hands together in greeting.

"N-A-S-I-R," Visha fingerspelled.

Nasir opened the door wide and waved for them to enter. They stepped into a small, sparsely furnished front room. A single, low-wattage bulb illuminated the red area rug and matching fabric of the couch and two arm chairs which lined the wall.

Julius edged closer to Amy and peered into the adjacent room. Metal pots and pans lining the back wall of the residence indicated that this room functioned as a kitchen. A single overhead bulb shone on the jet-black, waist-length hair of a woman who lit the gas cooker. She appeared quite a bit younger than Nasir.

Perhaps she is his daughter, Julius thought as he glanced around and saw no other rooms in the residence. For their safety, he hoped Nasir and this woman were the only occupants.

The less people knew about them, the better.

Chapter 25

AMY

"Chai?" Amy read on Nasir's lips as he mimicked drinking from a cup.

She looked at Julius and they both nodded.

Nasir waved them to one of couches against the living room wall opposite from the front door. A golden-framed picture of an attractive elderly woman hung on the wall above the couch. A string of white garland strung across the top corners of this picture, signifying her passing.

This must be Nasir's wife, Amy thought as she settled on the couch, watching him speak some orders into the cooking area of the residence.

Nasir sat on the arm chair at the end of a low coffee table placed in front of the couch. He spoke some Marathi words to Visha. She bowed her head and responded. This seemed to be a gesture of respect.

Amy watched, surprised at Visha's chameleon-like change from the shifty-eyed, paranoid, and protective street guide to now this poised and respectable interpreter.

Visha responded to Nasir and waved for him to speak to Amy and Julius.

Nasir stiffened, shifting his body to face them. His mouth moved.

This is probably the first time he's ever talked with Deaf people, Amy thought.

"You come to India why?" Visha interpreted.

"We are looking for my mother." Amy pointed to her nose with the concept she remembered Visha signing in ISL.

Visha's mouth moved in interpretation. She nodded 'go-on' when done.

"She abandoned me at the train station near here when I was a kid. I need to find her." Amy paused, hoping Visha was able to catch everything she signed.

Apparently, Visha understood enough. Her mouth continued to move. Her face maintained the blank, verbal translation, facial expression mode.

Nasir asked a question but was interrupted by the woman from the other room who entered, carrying a tray holding cups of chai.

The woman looked at the guests and nodded shyly then placed the drinks in front of them.

Nasir spoke, nodding in the direction of this woman.

Visha pointed to her nose and made a gesture meaning 'small.' "**Daughter** name P-R-I-Y-N-A," Visha interpreted and made some gestures which Amy could not understand.

The woman produced a quick bow and scooted out of the room. Amy wanted to ask her some questions and clarify what Visha just explained about her, but Nasir spoke up.

"Find your mother why?" Visha interpreted. "She left you. You move to America. Have good life. Why you need your mother?"

Amy looked at Julius, who shrugged for her to answer. "It's complicated." Amy was sure Visha didn't understand this ASL sign. "My I-D-E-N-T-I-T-Y," Amy fingerspelled. "I need to find out what name she called me." She pointed at Visha. "Long-ago, Hear-Nothing, she called me, but I also need to find out why—"

Nasir took his eyes off Amy and turned to Visha, asking a question.

Visha glanced between the Deaf couple and Nasir, then shifted to face Nasir. She spoke a long sentence in Marathi. She and Nasir had a dialogue.

Amy and Julius watched them like a movie without captions.

Amy saw Julius's right eyebrow lower. His fingertips dug into his legs.

Subtly, Amy placed a hand on his leg and squeezed. "It's okay," she signed as Visha continued talking with Nasir.

"Does she understand enough to explain on her own about all of this?" Julius's signs were tense but, except for his lowered eyebrow, he kept his facial expression pleasant. "I mean, shouldn't she be letting you explain all this instead of taking over and doing it herself?"

Amy closed her eyes softly, also maintaining a pleasant facial expression. "The more Visha explains, the better Nasir will be able to help us find my mother. Remember, we have no choice. We gotta trust her."

"But I hate being left out like this. What if she lets it slip that we are in trouble?"

Amy raised a hand to respond but paused, noticing that Visha and Nasir were looking at them.

"Yes?" Amy signed, smiling sweetly. "Continue."

"So, Nasir remember woman—" Visha paused. She held up a finger and pulled out her phone to begin typing.

As they waited for Visha to finish the message, Amy observed Nasir. In the face, creased by years of living in this environment, she saw a man who experienced what she only knew as a vague and distant memory.

He looked at her and smiled, an indicator that the message Visha typed contained good news. Behind these dark eyes, Amy saw the life which she lost; that of existing in the familiarity of her original given name and rising to a belonging with her people. It was a trajectory parallel to Visha's journey out of these slums.

Julius's leg brushed Amy's as he shifted his weight. His presence diverted her mind to a realization that her belonging also resided with him and the Deaf people he represented.

The front door opened. A crack of light spread across the packed dirt floor. A man entered the room. He had a face similar to Nasir's and appeared to be about the same age as Visha.

Nasir raised his hand toward the man and spoke, apparently explaining about the presence of the new people in the room. He then spoke to Visha.

"His son M-A-D-A-N," Visha introduced and spoke to him in Marathi.

Amy saw her name and Julius's pronounced on Visha's lips.

The younger man pressed his hands together in greeting, then sat in the remaining chair next to the outside wall.

"What did Nasir say?" Julius asked, pointing at the old man while emphasizing the **TELL-US** sign.

Visha handed over the phone, which Amy and Julius read. "Nasir tells me that he never knew your mother, but he does remember a story he heard long ago, around the time when you were a little girl. There was a woman who was homeless near the train station. She had a Deaf daughter whom suddenly she lost one day. Nasir assumes this woman was your mother."

Amy looked up and frowned. "She lied! I was not lost. I was abandoned!"

Visha looked confused. She copied the **LIE** sign.

"L-I-E," Amy fingerspelled and turned to the phone to type. "I was abandoned and not lost. I need to find her and ask her why she did that. Does Nasir know where she is living so we can find her?"

Visha read the message and asked Nasir the question. They spoke in rapid Marathi sentences. Madan joined the conversation with various head wags, nods, and gestures interspersed between them.

"Okay," Visha spoke and then typed into her phone. She handed the phone to Amy. "Nasir doesn't know the name of the woman whom he assumes is your mother. He does know that this woman got into a relationship with a man who lived near the train station. She moved into his house, and eventually they moved away to another place. Nasir doesn't know where."

Amy read the message and scowled. "But how will we find out this information? I was abandoned seventeen years ago," she signed. "Are there still people around that might know where my mother moved?"

Visha gestured for the phone to be returned. She held up her hand, nodded her head, and pointed at Madan before resuming the text. "Tonight, Madan will go to the area around the train station and inquire about your mother. He will ask the people in the beggar community. Hopefully at least one person remembers your mother."

Amy pointed to the picture of the elderly woman on the wall. "I wish I had a photo of my mother which Madan can show people. She probably was around the same age as this woman."

Visha seemed to understand. She nodded and continued typing. "Nasir can't go because of his handicap. Hopefully, by tomorrow morning, Madan will know about your mother and will let us know her name and the place to where she moved."

Sitting close so they could read the text together, Amy and Julius looked at each other. "Okay with you?" Amy asked him.

Julius looked around the room, pausing at Nasir. Amy saw a look of concern on the old man's face. "Okay, go-ahead," Julius signed, and Amy nodded in agreement.

After a few instructions from Nasir, Madan rose and clasped his hands together. He said a few Marathi words, bowed slightly, and exited out the front door.

Nasir stood and walked into the back room.

Julius grabbed the phone from Amy and typed. "You didn't tell them about our trouble with the police, did you?" He handed the phone to Visha.

"I didn't tell them," Visha typed. "Eventually, everyone around here will know the police is looking for you. Just the fact that a mixed-race couple like you arrived in this part of Dharavi is known by the neighbors. We will need to move fast." She handed the phone to Julius.

Julius typed, "Do you think Nasir and his son will tell the police where we went?"

Nasir entered the room and spoke to Visha. She responded with a few words and silently read Julius's message.

Thank God Nasir can't read English! Amy thought. It seemed strange that Nasir was standing there, smiling politely and completely unaware that they were talking about him.

Visha finished reading the message, typed, and handed the phone back. "Eventually the police will be able to get the information about you from Nasir and Madan." As she read the message, Amy noticed Visha returning to her conversation with Nasir. "They have their ways of forcing confessions," the message read. "So we need to move on from here quickly."

Amy saw Julius's hand tense on his lap as they watched the conversation between Visha and Nasir. Julius's hand waved in the direction of Visha. "Hey! What are you talking about?" he demanded. Amy knew he was getting tired of being left out.

"Dinner." Visha produced a sign that looked like SLEEP+FOOD. "He wants—" Visha continued, but Nasir interrupted her. She held up a finger in front of Julius and Amy, returning to her conversation with Nasir.

Nasir's face showed concern. He gestured and waved his arms as if he were arguing with a vendor in the bazaar.

Now Julius's eyebrow scrunched low. "She'd better not be telling him about our troubles," he signed small and discrete to Amy.

Amy nodded. "I hope not. Let's wait and see what she says."

As she watched Visha and Nasir talk, Amy felt a twinge of paranoia. Besides Julius sitting next to her and Denise back home, there were no other people she trusted. She knew that if Visha couldn't be trusted, they were diving into an unimaginable predicament.

Finally, the conversation stopped.

Visha turned to them. "He D-E-M-A-N-D we have dinner. But— " She glanced at the door as if expecting the cops to burst through any time. "I tell him no." She sighed and looked at her hands, shaking her head in frustration. "Interpreting difficult," she signed.

Glancing at her watch, Visha picked up the phone and typed. "I am sorry I can't sign this clearly with you and need to depend on text. Nasir really wants us to stay for dinner, but I have a better idea. I know a Deaf couple who lives nearby. Their names are Jayesh and Saima. It is less likely that the police will find us there, so I think we should have dinner with them. Plus, my flat is probably being staked out. We will need to spend the night at their house."

Amy and Julius read the phone and looked at each other.

"Why is she making all the decisions for us without asking?" Amy signed in rapid ASL.

"Good question," Julius responded. "I need to clarify something." He typed into the phone. "So, you didn't tell Nasir about us being pursued by the police? Also, won't it be rude to all of a sudden crash at the place of strangers?"

Visha read the message and looked up, puzzled. "C-R-A-S-H?" she fingerspelled.

Julius closed both fists in a **GRAB** sign. "Arrive, interrupt their 
lives," he signed slowly.

Visha typed into the phone. "I did not tell Nasir where we are going. That way he can't tell the cops even if they try to force it out of him."

Visha waved for Amy and Julius to look at her. "Here in India, people welcome openly." She formed 'velcome' on her lips as she produced a sign that looked like BRING-HERE. " They will happy **welcome** you their home." She stood, pointed to her watch, and motioned for them to stand. "Hurry! Clothes you change now. Soon we go."

Amy and Julius glanced down at their red dye-stained clothes, stood, and grabbed their backpacks. They stepped toward the back room. In the corner of the room opposite from the kitchen, a curtain was drawn, hanging from a rope attached to two walls.

Visha opened the curtain and nudged Amy into this area. "You change," Visha signed and closed the curtain. She pressed a hand on Julius's chest. "You wait. She done, you change. We go meet J-A-Y-E-S-H!"

Chapter 26

JULIUS

A group of slim boys played cricket, blocking the way in the narrow alley. One boy ran crazily, flailing his arms before hurling the ball in an overhead arch, straight at the little batsman who swung will all his might. The bat smacked the ball, and Julius jumped as it veered straight toward his legs. The ball plopped into an adjacent puddle, spraying brown droplets over the legs of his new salwar.

"Whoops!" Julius signed and wiped off his pants, then picked up the dripping wet ball.

Dropping his bat, the batsman ran up to Julius. "Sorry!" he signed with one hand while extending the other for the ball.

"Wait!" Julius leaned forward with a start. "You know sign language?" The boy opened his mouth in a toothy smile and continued holding out his hand.

Julius handed him the ball. "But how—" Julius continued, but the boy giggled, signed "thank-you," and ran to resume the game with his friends.

"Is he Deaf?" Amy asked Visha.

"No, he…ah…how do you say C-O-D-A." She pointed down the alley to where a man sorted vegetables on a cart in front of his shack. "Boy he J-A-Y-E-S-H son."

They walked past the boys who paused their game and stared. Visha poked the shoulder of the short man sorting vegetables.

"Hi, Visha"—he formed her name sign and looked at the newcomers with a surprised expression. "Who they?"

"They Deaf friends from America," Visha explained in ISL then looked at Amy and Julius. "Go-ahead, introduce yourselves."

"Hi! My name Amy," Amy showed her name sign and pointed to her thumb. "A…how do you do the ISL for 'M' and 'Y'?"

Visha placed three fingers on her palm for the 'M' and made a 'Y' with the index finger and thumb of one hand while pointing to it with the other.

"Ah! **A-M-Y**." Jayesh copied the ISL fingerspelling and then pointed to Julius. "And you?"

Visha raised her hand to assist but paused and nodded for Julius to try.

"My name J—" he began with the ASL letter while Jayesh demonstrated with the inverted, bent index finger of the ISL letter. "Okay, J-U-L-I-U-S," Julius continued with Jayesh demonstrating each letter in his own language.

"Again," Jayesh signed with an encouraging smile.

"**J-U-L-I-U-S**," Julius slowly produced each letter in ISL. "My name sign Julius." He demonstrated the 'J' on his right eyebrow.

The man straightened as if making an announcement. "My name sign **Jayesh**." He placed an open hand shape next to his eye and wiggled his fingers, apparently in reference to the wrinkles from his perpetually smiling eyes. He opened his mouth and made a sound,  waving in the direction of his cricket-playing son.

The little boy tossed his bat to a friend and scrambled over. "He little Jayesh." The man formed the same name sign, finishing with the ISL sign for **CHILD**. The boy smiled and giggled.

His father opened the door to their shack, welcoming them inside.

A thin woman greeted them just inside the door. Her white teeth shone as her dark face brightened in a smile. Clasping her hands together, she nodded a greeting, revealing a long braid that reached her knees.

"S-A-I-M-A," Visha fingerspelled. "She and Jayesh I met long ago. They help me learn sign language."

From behind the woman, a young girl peeked out. This girl's teeth also gleamed as she smiled shyly.

Julius noticed that this girl resembled the woman much more than little Jayesh resembled his father. *I wonder if her name is Little Saima?* Julius wondered.

"Me name sign **Saima**," the woman introduced, closing her hand and extending it down as if stroking her braid. She nudged the girl forward. "My daughter **D-I-L-N-A-V-A-Z**," Saima fingerspelled. "Her name sign this"—she formed the ISL letter for 'D,' changing one hand to the same descending, clasped hand as her own name sign. 

Julius and Amy introduced themselves.

Visha used rapid ISL to explain the purpose of their visit.

Julius observed the residence.

Like the home of Nasir a few alleys away, this hut was sparsely furnished. Unlike that other residence which contained two rooms, this one was but a single room. In one corner a hand-pumped cooking stove propped on the floor in front of a simple shelf containing metal bowls, plates, and cups plus a few cooking utensils. Stacked next to the opposite wall were three of the six-foot-long, woven cots which Julius understood to be the family's beds. As there were no couches and chairs in the room, a fourth cot stood near the cooking area. A small, green- colored blanket draped over one end of the cot with a cutting board, knife, and partly chopped vegetables announced that the visitors had interrupted the family's dinner preparations. The only light was a single bulb hanging from the ceiling and a shard of orange color from the setting sun as it peeked through the threshold crack of the back door.

Saima signed something which Julius recognized as 'clean.'

Dilnavaz transferred the blanket and cutting board to the floor.

Jayesh lifted a cot from the stack and deposited it in an angle next to the other. "Come sit," he insisted.

Julius and Amy sat on one cot while Visha and Jayesh occupied the other. Saima squatted over a bowl and washed some vegetables near a spigot in the wall while her daughter sat on the blanket and cut vegetables. Little Jayesh sat on the packed dirt floor and flicked a cricket ball up and down as he watched the adults.

"You come here India ___?" Jayesh formed the last sign with a questioning expression.

"We look for my mother." Amy touched her nose as she switched to a gesture-sign hybrid of ASL and ISL. "Long ago I live here." She  pointed toward the front door. "Out there street I live. I very small. My mother **abandon** me." She used the ASL sign for DROP. "Why?" Amy shook her head and raised her arms. "I need know why. Also, my name she call me."

Jayesh's smiling eyes changed to a quizzical look. "Name, your mother call-you…why…" He looked at his hands as if not sure how to translate his thoughts.

Saima paused her washing and looked closely at Amy. In her observation, Julius recognized a connection: an act of being present to deeply understand as only two Deaf women born in this slum could experience. Saima placed a gourd-like vegetable in a bowl and waved a hand to get Amy's attention.

"Your mother, she ___?" Saima produced a sign next to her ear that resembled EXPLOSION in ASL. "What?" Amy repeated the sign.

Visha leaned forward and produced the same sign.

"**Normal**," Amy read on Visha's lips. Confused, she looked at Julius.

Visha raised her hands and leaned forward to be of assistance, but Saima lifted a hand and nodded with a stern expression. The hand lowered, indicating that Visha should sit back and watch.

Saima stood and pointed to her nose. "Your mother talk, hear correct?"

"Yes," Amy affirmed.

"She beg?" Saima pointed out the single window in the house.

"Yes." Amy nodded. "My mother beggar."

"Ah! Hearing beggar." Saima stepped closer to Amy and placed two hands on her head, slowly stroking down in a blessing.

Amy's eyes widened, and her shoulders hunched slightly during the action.

Saima finished the blessing and observed Amy with a deep look. "You Deaf, your mother troubled." Saima used a one-handed sign, pressing down on Amy's shoulder. "She hearing. What she do?"

"Abandoned me," Amy responded.

"Yes, abandon you." Saima nodded slowly as the two Deaf women connected in understanding. "Your long-ago name you need find out," Saima confirmed, tilting her head slightly in agreement. "I understand."

Jayesh waved his hand. "Your mother, how will you find?"

All the adults looked at Amy.

Little Jayesh, apparently bored with this adult talk, shifted to the side of the room and bounced the ball against the wall. His sister went back to cutting the vegetables.

Amy looked at her bracelet and started stroking the beads. Julius watched her as she ran her fingers over the smooth beads. He knew she was deep in thought. He wanted to help her with her answers, but knew to let her think.

"Tomorrow morning, Nasir's son Madan will come," Julius explained in slow ASL. "He will explain what he finds out about Amy's mother."

Jayesh and Saima looked at him with blank expressions. "Could you go-ahead and explain to them in ISL?" Julius asked Visha.

As Visha explained their plans to Saima and Jayesh, Julius placed a hand on Amy's leg. There was no response as she continued stroking the bracelet.

He knew she had a lot to process, but he wanted to hurry things along so she could get the answers she needed. Once she got those answers, perhaps then she could free her mind to focus on him and the relationship he wanted with her.

Julius sighed as he remembered his original plans to propose to Amy on their summer 'vacation' to India. *No chance for that now,* he thought.

Julius squeezed her leg, shaking it a bit. "Are you okay?" he asked.

Amy's head turned slowly as if she woke from a trance. "I'm okay, I guess. When Saima said I was abandoned"—she hit a finger with her other hand—"that hit me hard. Up until now, that has always been something that happened to me"—she formed the sign for quotes—"way over-there."

Amy swept a hand around the room. "Now that I am here, and told by another Deaf woman that I was abandoned—" She jerked her head back while doing the same with a clenched fist. "POW! Like a punch in the face. I mean, like me, she probably was born on these same streets, but I bet her mother loved her enough not to abandon her."

Amy lowered her eyebrows and shot a quick glance at the others, shaking her head slightly with a realization. "Even though she is obviously poor, Saima seems to have everything she needs. But what is it about me that caused my real mother to abandon me so that the witch, Sybil, could adopt me and mess up my life? I bet Saima didn't have to deal with that."

Julius's heart felt heavy. He placed a hand on her shoulder and pointed around the room. "But you are cherished by us." He closed his eyes as he emphasized the CHERISH sign.

"I know." Amy slumped her shoulders. "I need to know why I wasn't cherished by the mothers in my life." The introspective look reappeared on her face.

Seeing extended head wags across the room and signs indicating agreement from the others, Julius recognized the conclusion of the other conversation.

In this tiny space where the majority of the family's life occurred, two separate languages prevailed. With this lack of comprehension regarding the other party, there was no animosity in the mind of Julius.

The bond between the people in this room, forged by their common life experience, sparked a deep trust in his heart toward these people who shared his same culture as a Deaf person.

Jayesh's smiling eyes turned to Julius. "Dinner special tonight." His face brightened as he stood and beckoned for him to follow. "Chicken," he signed and finished with an axe handshape decapitating an imaginary head.

Chapter 27

JULIUS

An hour later the pleasant smell of a steaming, spicy chicken-curry dish filled the room. Everyone sat in a circle around the green blanket spread on the floor.

Julius observed the steaming dish placed before them and recalled the cute little black fowl that recently scrambled in the chicken-wire enclosure just outside the back door during a vain attempt to escape Jayesh's gleaming hatchet. This gave Julius pause, but his pangs of hunger superseded any aversion to this offering of fresh meat.

With a wooden spoon, Saima dished portions of rice, vegetables, and the curry onto the metal plates of her guests. A plate of stacked chapati sat in the middle of the table.

All except Julius grabbed a round, flat chapati and ripped portions using a deft, one-handed finger push-and-pull motion.

Julius saw Amy perform the chapati hand dipping and mixing along with the others as if she had done it all her life.

Saima paused the mixing of her food and looked at Julius. "You not hungry?" Saima signed.

Julius had not yet touched his food. "Okay, I will try." He grabbed a chapati and, using two hands, ripped off a small piece.

"Oh!" Saima smacked her head with a palm. "You American! I forget." She looked at the shelf where she kept her utensils. "No forks, only spoons. Want to try spoon?"

"No. Thank-you." Julius held up the piece of chapati and smiled. "I'll try eating your way."

Jayesh and Saima tilted their heads in agreement as they all dug into their food.

"Saima." Amy waved to get her attention and licked her fingers so she could sign without flicking curry all over the place. "Your mother, father: they Deaf or hearing?"

"My mother, father hearing," Saima responded. "Why you ask?"

"Well, the two of you and your family seem happy." Amy pointed to the kids as they dug into their food. "You know how to love them, cherish them. Your mother teach you that?"

It seemed that Visha understood Amy more readily than did Saima and Jayesh. "Tell her about your parents," Visha addressed Jayesh.

"My mother, father they Deaf," Jayesh explained. "Saima, me grow up same street. Our fathers work together in clothes-dye factory."

Julius wondered if it was the same factory they ran through earlier that day and spoiled their new clothes.

"Yes, long ago I little girl." Saima lowered her palm near the ground. "His father teach my father sign. They become good friends. My mother learn sign, too, but my father sign fluent. Mother sign so-so." Saima ripped a piece of chapati with her right hand and pointed to Amy with her left. "Your parents over-there America sign?"

Amy shook her head. "I wouldn't call what I have in America a 'parent.'"

Saima and Jayesh glanced at each other. It seemed they were confused.

"What I mean," Amy continued. "Woman A-D-O-P-T me," she spelled in ISL. "She sign same-as robot. She use sign English. Very awkward. Gross!" Amy finished with the **PUKE** sign. "Father none. No man would marry her."

"Ah!" Saima acknowledged and scooped up some food.

Julius tried to wrap his brain around a hearing father who signed fluently and a mother who didn't.   He hoped someday to meet this father of Saima. From his experience with the other Deaf students with whom he and Amy grew up, Julius knew that it was the other way around; usually it was the mothers who signed with various levels of fluency and the fathers mostly fingerspelled and produced a few awkward signs. Of course, his own father was a faded memory, evaporating with the smoke of the Seattle bombing when he was a boy.

Little Jayesh licked his fingers and started to stand.

His sister said something in Marathi, and the boy frowned, retorting something back.

Saima grabbed the boy's arm, pulling him down and held a hand out in the direction of the girl. "Sign it!" Saima demanded.

"Sorry," the boy glanced apologetically at the guests. "I finished. Can I get up?" he signed as his sister made a snide face and twisted her head at him.

"Yes, go!" Saima shooed him away and looked at her guests. "Sorry. His sister bossy."

Amy smiled and scooped the rest of her food off her plate. "They cute." She looked at Saima and Jayesh. "You-two do a good job raising them."

"Yes, they normal kids," Visha interjected. "Their first language ISL correct?"

"Of course," Jayesh continued and looked at his wife as this information was the most normal thing in the world.

"I will clean up," Saima announced and collected their plates.

Amy poked Visha. "Let's help her."

The women gathered the dinner items and moved to the kitchen-corner of the room.

Jayesh held up a finger in front of Julius. "Cart outside I move now. You stay." He exited the front door.

As Julius settled on a cot to wait, he watched the activates in the room. The women in the corner were cleaning dishes. Dilnavaz busied herself with folding the blanket.

In the dim light of the room, Julius watched Amy as she crouched in that Indian way and rinsed a bowl in the flowing water of the spigot, a strand of her long, dark hair partly covering her nose. Her face was relaxed, and her eyes observed the tasks with a peaceful focus.

He had rarely before seen such serenity in her face. His heart softened for this soul whom he loved more than anyone else in the world. It struck him that she would not find such peace in his America, but in a totally opposite part of the world and surrounded by a completely foreign way of living. There was no communication as the women focused on their tasks. Such was not needed, for the very act of existing within the same space was sufficient for their tranquility. The culture forged by the similar life experience of the two Deaf women became a testament to this fact.

But what of me? Julius's mind left the women in their collective space as he thought of himself. *God,* he formed a silent prayer, *it seems Amy is finding her answers. But will this destroy me and whatever chance I have for a good life in the future? When and if she does find these answers, will Amy have the space in her mind and heart for what I want?*

Julius watched Amy's dark hands scrub a plate in the sudsy water of a metal bowl. He imagined a flash of gold on her left hand. *Yes, a ring would look good on that finger,* he thought and felt the empty ring finger on his own left hand.

But when will I ever get a chance to give her what I want? He sighed and looked out the back window at the dilapidated door of the residence across the aisle. *Certainly not in this place!*

A person walked past the outside window. Julius's mind diverted as he considered where Officer Steele and his cronies where settling for the night. Were they staying in a flat above the Mumbai jail? Or were they taking advantage of the late evening hours to scout the location of

Julius and Amy and narrow their search to this section of the Dharavi slum?

Should I sleep tonight? Julius wondered. *Or should I stay awake and keep watch?*

By this time, Little Jayesh had come back inside. Both he and Julius set up the cots for sleeping.

A vision entered Julius's mind of cops bursting into the hut, catching the sleeping Deaf people completely off guard. Julius stood. He had to do something, anything to move him and Amy away from these predators. *God, please protect us*, he prayed.

Chapter 28

AMY

Amy sat on a cot with her back to the wall. "So much has happened today." She patted the cot. "Come sit here."

Julius plugged his phone into a nearby outlet so the light they were using to communicate in the dark room wouldn't drain the battery. He scooted close to Amy. "Yes, it has been a whirlwind. I can't believe we are here."

Amy looked along the adjacent wall at the cot which contained the sleeping mother and daughter. "I really like Saima. She reminds me of myself. She is Deaf like me and was born in this same place but, even though she lives in this tiny hut, she seems very happy." Amy touched Julius's leg. "Do you think that if Sybil had not snatched me away from all this, then I would be happy?"

"Happy? I am not sure what it will take for you to be truly happy. I see that you are enjoying your time here with this family, and hopefully, tomorrow we will find out where we can locate your mother. Do you really think that finding her will bring you this happiness you are looking for?"

Amy's eyes turned, unfocused, to the light of the phone as she collected her thoughts. *Happiness,* she thought. *Have I ever really been happy? Can I ever experience the bonds this family has? Will I find this happiness when I see my mother?*

She took a deep breath and shrugged, raising her palms. "To be honest, I don't know what I will find. Since we arrived here, I've just been following Visha, doing whatever I need to get where I'm going."

"Get where you're going…" Julius paused and seemed to consider what to say.

"Yes, that is just it. Get to where I am going." Amy pointed out the window near the back door. "I have no idea where I am going. All I know is that who I meet and what I find out from them will hopefully bring me more peace than I have experienced my whole life up-till-now."

"Well, I do hope that Nasir's son Madan comes tomorrow morning and gives us news about your mother's whereabouts." Julius grasped Amy's hand and squeezed it. "But in the meantime, can you possibly consider what you already have? Can that not be enough for your happiness?" With his other hand he reached up and grabbed something imaginary above his head. "You know, Jesus is available for you. Can you think about that?"

Amy saw their intertwined hands and felt a pang of guilt. She looked at Julius's eyes. "I know you are with me." She patted his hand. "I feel you here. I am thankful for that." Reaching up her hand, Amy copied Julius's grasping at an imaginary object. She looked up at her hand and shook her head while wiggling her fingers in the **EVAPORATE** sign. "Jesus…God…I am sorry. I don't feel it."

She swept her hand around the room. "I don't see it." She placed her hand back on Julius's and squeezed. "I do see you and these people here with me, supporting me. But, yes, I will think about what you have told me."

"Okay." Julius nodded and squirmed on the cot. "Hey, I'll be right back. I gotta pee in the outhouse behind the house."

"Okay, come back soon." Amy grabbed Julius's phone as he exited out the back door.

Suddenly alone on the cot, the dim light of the phone cast a cocoon, enveloping Amy's thoughts and providing a focus. She looked at the screen in confusion. Julius's questions had scrambled her mind, and she wasn't sure what she needed. Like she observed with Saima and her children, Amy did know she wanted the protective, reassuring presence of a mother. Propping the phone on her purse, she clicked the number of the only person who came to mind. Denise.

Denise's face popped into the screen. Her hair was disheveled, not yet twisted into the usual braid. "Hi, Amy! I have been worried about you all day! Tell me everything that happened since you arrived in India."

A few minutes later, after explaining most of what happened the previous couple of days, Amy felt a tap on her arm.

"Who are you talking to?" Julius asked.

"It is Denise," Amy explained. "I called to catch her up on what has happened so-far."

"Oh! Hi, Denise, what's up?" Julius settled on the cot next to Amy.

"Hi, Julius." Denise smiled through the screen. "Yes, Amy just explained most of what has happened. How are you doing?"

"I am fine. For the time being, we are safe. Tomorrow we will find out what we can about Amy's mother." Julius shot a quick glance at Amy then back at the phone. "Speaking of—quote—'mothers,' what have you found out about Sybil?"

Denise's face turned serious. "Well, she is recovering but still at the hospital. You really did a lot of physical damage to her, Amy. Sybil will press charges against both of you. I got a visit yesterday from a local police officer who is helping with the investigation. This time the cops had the wisdom to come with an interpreter. He told me Sybil will be hiring a lawyer so we all need to prepare for a big legal battle in the future. I have been very careful not to disclose anything about you, but eventually they will figure it all out and catch up to you."

The peace shattered on Amy's face. Her hopeful, more tranquil eyes from a few minutes ago were replaced by a hard, narrow stare above the line of a tense mouth. She was happy to be talking with their cherished mentor from back home and could taste the answers within her grasp. But, like water from a small crack in a dam, the reality of their situation spurted forth as a premonition of her impending doom.

"I am assuming Officer Steele has figured out you are in India and is on his way there." Denise's eyes widened in concern. "Are you prepared for that?"

"Actually, we have seen him. He is pursuing us." Julius swept his hand in the direction of the room. "He doesn't know we are here in this hut, but we have seen him and a Mumbai cop who is helping him. I don't think they have seen us, but they do know we are here in Mumbai. Soon they will figure out we are in the Dharavi slum."

"Please be careful you-two!" Denise pleaded. "You know I love you both and want to support you the best I can."

"We love you, too, Denise." Amy tried to smile, but fear elevated her heartbeat and quickened her breath. "You are our true mother You  know that, right? She needed the verification and emphasized the **TRUE+BIZ** sign.

Denise nodded slowly, softly closing her eyes for a second. "Yes, and I will always be there for you. I am glad you-two are together to navigate this situation. I know it is very late for you, so better let you get some sleep."

"Good night." They both sent her off with the ILY sign.

Amy heaved a sigh and made sure Julius's phone was plugged in. "I am exhausted. Need to sleep." She looked around the room. "No one is watching. Quick! Give me a kiss." She grabbed Julius. Their lips met briefly. "Good night."

Julius smiled brightly and pulled Amy closer to prolong the kiss.

"Hold on a sec." Gently, she pushed his chest and held him at arm's length. "Sleep now," she pleaded then curled into a ball.

Chapter 29

AMY

The next morning, after a breakfast of eggs and chapati for them all, the kids were off to school.

Amy, Julius, and Visha stood at the open front door of the hut.

Saima stood at the door to say goodbye to the visitors.

Jayesh lowered a palm to indicate they should wait. "Cart I get." He walked to the back of the hut and exited the alley door to get his cart.

"Here, take." Saima handed a metal tiffin to Amy. "Eat later."

"Thank-you." Amy accepted the food and gave it to Julius to free her hands for signing. "But not needed," she signed to Saima. "We will buy food later."

Saima shook her head and closed her eyes softly. "Tiffin you return later." She opened her eyes and brought the tips of her hands together. "That way we meet again."

Saima lifted her arms to rest the palms of her hands upon Amy's head. Slowly, the hands moved down the side of Amy's head then pressed together in a 'namaste' blessing.

Amy's shoulders dropped and her mind calmed. Now she was ready for the journey ahead.

"Challo." Visha's lips moved as she tilted her head in the direction of Jayesh, who was beckoning for them to follow as he stood next to his cart where the back alley intersected with the street.

"Oh! I almost forgot!" Visha fished a small piece of paper out of her purse. "M-A-D-A-N." Amy recognized the ISL fingerspelled name of Nasir's son. "This paper give to him." Visha gave the paper to Saima, pointed down the alley, and signed something rapidly, which included the signs MEET and **CHAI**.

We will meet Madan at the chai shop, Amy thought. She vaguely remembered a chai shop near the entrance to the bazaar.

They said goodbye to Saima and followed Jayesh through the maze of alleys in the slum.

At one intersection, Jayesh stopped and looked back, smiling brightly. "This way short-cut. Follow."

As Jayesh pushed his cart overloaded with various vegetables, Amy noticed the surprising ease at which he pushed and maneuvered the two-wheeled cart through the crowds of people, donkeys, dogs, and buffalo as well as the rickshaws and small autos that fit in the alleys. His

lower calf muscles bulged as he turned the cart at a sharp curve just before the main entrance to the bazaar.

"Chai shop here!" Jayesh pointed and cheerfully produced the pinky-extended sign for drink. He shook Julius's hand and pressed together his hands in goodbye to the women, then pushed his cart to disappear in the chaos of the main street outside of the bazaar.

The three of them sat at a small table with Julius occupying the street-side chair.

"Tin chai," Visha called out, holding up three fingers.

A chai walla appeared and produced three metal saucers holding small cups of the brown liquid.

"We wait for Madan." Visha nodded her head and pointed to the chai. "You take."

Amy lifted the cup. The sweet, nutty smell of chai entered her nostrils.

She settled into the hectic complacency of the scene on the street before her. There was never a still moment. Near a corner of the shop, a brown, female *pariah* dog lay stretched out, dozing, as a litter of recently born pups suckled at her teats. A group of young men sat along the curb of the street, arms draped over each other, cigarettes hanging from their mouths. They stared at the pretty female shoppers who passed their way.

Near this group of men, outside the same shop where she acquired her crucifix necklace, Amy noticed a commotion. A group of street kids pulled and prodded the western clothes of a white man browsing a hat rack.

"Julius!" Amy grabbed his arm. "Switch seats with me." She stood to give him her seat.

"Why?" His eyebrow scrunched low.

"I don't want those kids over-there to notice you." Amy pointed across the alley. "They'll spotlight you to the cops for sure."

Julius sat in Amy's vacant chair near the wall of the shop as she strategically seated herself to block the view between him and the kids.

"We gotta get something to cover your head." Amy grabbed a lock of his auburn hair. "This is an announcement for everyone to stare."

Julius covered his head with his hands. "We will go buy a hat," he began, but was interrupted by Visha's sudden turn to a man who approached their table.

Nasir's son Madan said a few Marathi words to Visha.

Amy scooted forward in her chair, closely watching a few turns in their head-wagging conversation.

Visha turned to face Amy and Julius. "Madan find your mother's information. She lives in K-A-L-Y-A-N—"

Amy's eyes shot open wide. "Where is that?" she interrupted, taking a quick breath. She held out a hand. "Julius, give me your phone so I can look it up on the map."

"Hold on," Visha signed. "I explain." On the palm of her hand, she pointed to the middle, as if it were the center of a **map**. "Here Mumbai." Then she pointed to the pinky finger part of the hand. "Kalyan out here. Not far. One-hour train ride."

Amy looked at Visha's pinky, then looked at Madan and Visha. "Did he tell you my mother's name?"

Visha asked Madan something. Apparently, it was to clarify about the name. "Your mother name P-O-O-N-A-M."

Here, presented in front of her, was a tangible hard fact about her own birth mother. Poonam, the name of her mother, the one who brought her into the world.

This news of her mother was like a new, attractive bead she found and could add to her childhood bracelet.

Amy's heart quickened. She needed to know more. "Where in Kalyan does she live?" she signed to Madan.

His confused face turned to Visha for help, and she posed the question in Marathi. The shrug and half turn of the head in Madan's response were enough for Amy to recognize that he didn't know.

"He not know," Visha said.

Amy interrupted. "What about her last name?"

Visha copied the signs at the end of Amy's sentence. "Mean what?" Her face was puzzled.

"Umm…S-U-R-N-A-M-E," Amy fingerspelled.

"Madan not know," Visha answered. "Her given name, all he know. And place near Mumbai where she move before."

"Oh." Amy's chest tightened. Her mind twisted and turned, and she twisted her bracelet, feeling each of the worn beads. She wanted to add more beads to this bracelet—the news of her birth mother and finally meeting her birth mother.

Her birth mother, Poonam, was in this same city as she was. They had to find her.

Amy's hope mixed with annoyance that this man didn't care enough to ask for more details and thus be better able to help them out. Even Visha's matter-of-fact expression as she interpreted the sparse message piqued Amy's agitation.

I wish I could run over to the people Madan talked to and ask them myself, she thought and turned to Julius, raising her arms in frustration. "What do we do now?"

Julius set his eyebrows in contemplation. "We will figure it out."

Her fingers fiddled furiously with the beads on her bracelet.

Madan's awkward smile betrayed his discomfort with Amy's intense questions. He edged away, saying goodbye to Visha, and left the chai shop.

They sipped their chai.

A sudden movement near the corner of the shop diverted their attention as another dog approached too close to the mother's pups. The mother dog rose with bared fangs, hair bristling at the shoulders. The pups turned their heads, rooting around together. One stubborn pup refused to let go and hung from a teat. The other dog slunk away, and the mother once again settled into her duty.

Amy drained her chai. "Why couldn't my own mother do that with me?" she signed, pointing to the mother dog.

"Do you mean protect you?" Julius asked.

"Yeah. We just saw this dog fight. The mother protect her pups. I know there's absolutely no way she would even think to abandon them."

Julius, Amy, and Visha observed the squirming mass of pups. One little pup lost its place in the row and scrambled to push its way back in. The others wouldn't budge, and the little pup's mouth opened in a cry for help.

Visha pointed to the pup. "Weak"—she formed a sign that resembled chopping off one's arms—"often dogs abandon them.

Sometimes kill."

Julius repeated the arm-chopping sign. "Do you mean **handicapped**?"

"Yes," Visha responded. "Make room for other normal ones to

grow."

*There's that word, '**normal**,'* Amy thought. *Does that mean I am abnormal?*

"So, I really need to find my mother," she signed and shook her head. "This dog fights so hard for her pups. Why didn't my human mother fight for me?" She looked at Visha. "Did she abandon me because I am not—quote—normal?" Amy used the ISL sign for the last word.

Visha looked out at the street, dismissing Amy's direct question.

"We should go." She circled her hands in an obvious sign for **LOCOMOTIVE**. "M-A-H-I-M train station over-there." She pointed down the street.

Amy's head swiveled. "Hold on a sec." Seeing the street kids down the alley, she placed a hand on Julius's leg. "We need to get something to cover your head. You stay here while I go across the street and buy you a hat."

"Okay," Julius replied, pushing his chair back into the shadow of the overhanging eave of the shop. "I'll wait here with Visha."

In the security of blending in, Amy approached the hat rack in front of the store. It was next to the same display of religious artifacts and crucifixes that she had bumped into as a child. The White man had moved on so the street kids had no reason to be in the immediate area. She picked up a navy-blue hat with a bill, a logo of the Mumbai Indians cricket team emblazoned on the front. She approached the checkout stand just inside the door.

As she handed over the rupee notes for the purchase, the clerk suddenly looked at the entrance of the store.

Amy glanced in the same direction and froze.

A brown police jeep stopped at the curb.

Amy forced the money into the hand of the clerk.

He gave her the change and placed the hat in a bag.

Amy felt the hair on the back of her head rise. Without showing her face, she walked to the entrance and stopped behind the crucifix display.

But she had to look.

Peeking around the display, she saw the brown US Marshal-emblazoned uniform of Officer Steele. Next to him stood the same Mumbai police officer she observed the previous morning in front of Visha's doorway.

Instinctively, Amy grabbed one of the larger crucifixes from the display rack. Her thumb felt the prick on the sharp end of its post. Her fist tightened around the object as she watched.

The Mumbai cop introduced Officer Steele to the clerk.

From her hiding spot, Amy saw the name MANISH GILL stamped upon a name tag pinned to the chest of the cop. Steele held up two small pictures to show the clerk.

Amy's heart skipped a beat. She realized they were probably snapshots of her and Julius.

The clerk nodded his head and pointed to the same direction from which Amy and her friends had come.

"Nasir," she read on the lips of the clerk.

How in the hell did he know that? Amy forced a walk as casually as she could away from the entrance of the shop.

Chapter 30

AMY

"Whew! You're okay!" Julius pulled Amy to the interior of the chai shop. "We thought for sure the cops nabbed you."

"Come." Visha placed her arms around them both to herd them away.

"Hold on!" Amy took the blue hat out of the bag. "Put this on."

Julius put on the hat while Amy tucked strands of his auburn hair inside the hat.

"CHALLO!" Visha gritted her teeth and jerked at both of their arms. Her eyes darted suspiciously to the empty jeep parked across the street.

The three of them exited the bazaar at a brisk walk and crossed the street. A couple of darting rickshaws narrowly missed them. Visha cut through another alley. Julius and Amy followed her through a maze of streets.

The end of one alley opened to a shop-lined avenue with high curbs. On the other side was an elevated platform. The words MAHIM STATION in prominent English and Marathi letters announced the place on an overhead sign.

"Come, we buy train tickets." Visha marched across the street.

They ascended the old metal stairs to the side of the platform and passed a group of street kids lounging near a back wall of the station.

Instinctively, Amy stepped to the side of Julius to block any kids view of him. She and Julius followed Visha to the small glass-enclosed ticket office in the middle of the platform.

Visha stepped to the back of a small line as a bored-looking station master accepted people's money and handed out tickets in the booth.

"What's that?" Julius pointed to Amy's hand as they waited at the side of the line near the rear of the ticket office.

"Oh!" Amy opened her hand which displayed the large crucifix pendant with the chain draping between her fingers. She held it up and turned it around, observing the sharp metal angles as the bright overhead light glinted off the edges. "Oops! I guess I stole this from the shop back there."

"But why?" Julius pointed at her purse. "Don't you already have one in there from when you were a kid?"

Amy reached into her purse and pulled out the smaller necklace. She held up both items to compare. Except for the size, they were exactly the same. She held up the larger one. "I grabbed this to protect myself from the cops." She looked at the smaller crucifix. "Same," she signed with a stiff motion.

Slowly, her eyes turned to the back of the ticket office. Her eyes remained on the shiny concrete spot on the floor, and her mind froze in remembrance. She turned her head, pausing at the crowd of people waiting for the Kalyan train to arrive.

With a quick intake of breath, Amy turned her body in the direction of the lounging street kids near the exit stairs. Her chest tightened and tears welled in her eyes. "Yes, same," she signed, and placed two fingers near an eye in the **LOOK-PAST** sign.

Julius touched her shoulder. "Are you okay?"

"I remember this place!" She stepped next to the back wall of the ticket booth. "I am standing in the exact spot where my mother abandoned me!"

Like the flashback in a movie, Amy's mind transported to that dark rainy day those many years before. Panic gripped her chest. She grabbed Julius's arm, pulling him close. Here she was, a little girl abandoned on the cold, concrete platform. She felt the warmth of Julius's arm, but her mind remained in that prison from which there was no escape; being alone in a crowd with absolutely no access to understanding or communication.

Julius's arms hugged her close. "I'm here for you." He looked at her face and pointed to Visha who was handing over the money for the tickets. "I am with you. We are with you."

Amy looked across the platform and saw the street kids sitting in a circle. It seemed they had just awakened and were discussing what they would do that day. Their dirty clothes and disheveled hair reminded her that she, too, was once one of them.

"Tum___ ho?" Visha stepped into Amy's view with a concerned expression.

Protected within Julius's embrace but her eyes wide with shock, Amy pointed to the street kids. "Before same," she signed to Visha.

Puzzled, Visha looked across the platform. Her mouth went slack and her eyes opened wide then narrowed.

Within Visha's intense eyes, Amy remembered seventeen years ago and saw the eyes of the girl who stared across this very same platform as she strung beads on a bracelet. That moment of mutual understanding provided the only escape little five-year-old Hear-Nothing knew in the time before she was given a name by the strange white woman named Sybil. Now, Amy remembered cowering next to this same wall as the tall girl with the bracelet leaned forward and moved her mouth.

Stepping out of Julius's embrace, Amy placed a hand in Visha's and pointed to her ear. "Hear-Nothing," she signed. "Remember?"

Yes," Visha replied and buried Amy in an embrace. "I forget this place same where you, me met." She looked around. "Wow! Now life different, correct?"

Amy shrugged, looked around, and nodded her head. "Yes, life different. But past and now same thing happen. I remain abandoned." She hoped Visha understood what she was trying to say.

Visha tapped Amy's hand, which still held both crucifix necklaces. "Maybe put that in purse," she suggested. Her shoulders hunched and eyes narrowed with intensity as she looked up the train tracks, pointing to her ear. "Hear train. Come!"

As she and Julius followed Visha to the waiting crowd, Amy realized that the memory of this place also transported Visha back to that time when she too must survive. Then as now, the woman in front of her morphed into that tough street kid who fought against anything and everything that threatened those whom she was trying to protect.

The platform vibrated as the train approached. People bunched together as it slowed to a stop. Like a can of sardines, the train was already packed with people. Regardless, the three friends pushed with others as the doors opened.

Amy found herself sandwiched between Julius and another tall woman. The woman raised her arm to grab an overhead handle bar. The strong smell of her armpit entered Amy's nostrils, so she turned her head away.

As the train lurched forward, Visha jostled her shoulders and turned to face Amy and Julius. "That American police. What's his name again?" she signed.

"Officer S-T-E-E-L-E," Julius answered.

Visha tilted her head at Amy. "What you see in shop back there?"

"I saw shopkeeper say name N-A-S-I-R." Amy fingerspelled the name. "He point up street same way we came. He knew where we came from."

Visha formed what appeared to be a swear sign. Her narrowed eyes looked around as if many Officer Steeles surrounded them. "They probably beat confession from Nasir now. Will find out your mother name P-O-O-N-A-M. Also find out she live in Kalyan."

The train rounded a curve, and Julius reached up to grab a stabilizing bar. "We need to assume they will follow us to Kalyan," he signed one-handed to Amy. "Too risky. Maybe we should drop our plans to find your mother."

"No!" Amy scowled up at him. "I MUST find out my name." She jerked a thumb in the direction behind the train. "Plus, I WILL ask my mother what possessed her to abandon me back there!"

Julius slowly nodded his head.

The three of them swayed with the jostling of the train.

Too short to reach the overhead bar, Amy pushed between two people and grabbed a vertical bar near the door. She tightened her grip around the cold, hard steel of this post. It was the only solid thing upon which she could grab as she hurtled toward a dubious future.

Part V

Surrender

Chapter 31

JULIUS

During late afternoon of the same day, Julius stood at the large third-floor window of his room at the OYO Divine Hotel in Kalyan, India.

After the rickshaw ride from the train station, he, Amy, and Visha checked into this hotel and decided to book separate rooms, one for the women and one for himself. Doing so would attract less attention from the prying eyes of other tenants who might snub their noses at two young Indian women sharing a suite with a White American man.

Julius noticed the two-story residential buildings with flat terraces on their tops. It was not the sprawling jumble of huts, buildings, and high-rise towers they had just left in Mumbai thirty-five miles to the southwest. Here, the buildings ended just before the dirty-brown waters of a river with trees and vegetation blanketing the rural hills beyond.

Julius watched the street below. The perpetual crowd of people and vehicles went about their daily routines like scurrying ants in a line. A brown-uniformed police officer wearing a black, beany-style hat stood in a traffic circle, waving his arms in a vain attempt at directing the vehicles. This was one person to avoid in the quest to find Amy's mother.

A street marker announcing Gauripada Road caught his eye. He followed the snaking pathway of the street through the buildings across the way. Finding Amy's mother was like the search for a needle in a haystack.

Julius's phone vibrated in his pocket and he pulled it out.

"Meet in the hall," read Visha's text. "We go to dinner now."

Out in the hall, Visha and Amy were alr0eady waiting for him. Visha pointed in the direction of the floor. "C-A-F-E downstairs we go."

"Good! I'm hungry," Amy signed as they entered the small lift that took them to the ground floor.

He smiled at Amy. She looked cute.

Inside the café, they were seated at a small table in the center of the room just past the entrance of the hotel. The few other customers appeared to enjoy their early evening chai. Along one wall, glass panels overhung a variety of dishes steaming with the smells of biryani, tikka masala, naan, and other buffet items. From the screen of an overhead TV, scenes flashed the shocked faces of actors as they responded to an insult in a soap opera serial.

The swinging door to the kitchen area opened, and a male server wearing a white kameez approached. He pointed to the open menu on the table. "Vat you like?" Julius read his lips.

Visha nodded her head toward the wall. "B-U-F-F-E-T you want?" she signed to Julius and Amy.

"Sure," they both agreed and got up to fill metal plates with ample portions from the buffet. They returned to sit at the table.

"How will we find your mother?" Julius asked Amy between bites of palak paneer and naan.

"I suppose we should ask around." She looked around the café. "Wonder if anyone around here might know her?"

"I doubt it." Julius ripped off a piece of naan and waved it in the direction of the outside window. "I'm not sure what is the population of this city, but there are probably many Poonams that live here. How do you figure we will find her in this mass of people?"

Some of the other customers paused in their conversations and stared.

"Why are they all staring at us?" Julius asked Visha, lowering his eyebrow.

"They not see signing before," Visha explained. "Plus, you American."

"I feel like an animal in a zoo." Julius turned his head and returned the stare.

"Ignore them." Visha looked in the corner of the café where a neatly attired man sat behind a counter on top of which stood a cash register. "I call O-W-N-E-R here to ask him question." She raised her hand to summon the owner.

"Ha?" The man bowed slightly in greeting and looked around at the three of them with a nervous smile. He turned to Visha. "You normal?" Julius read the English pronunciation on the man's lips.

Julius's eyebrow sank low, and his shoulders tensed as Visha addressed the man in Hindi. *Normal!* he thought. *Does that mean these people consider us Deaf people abnormal?*

He glared at the man who shot a nervous glance in his direction after Visha asked him a question. Julius read the name 'Poonam' on Visha's lips. He touched Amy's arm. "Do you know the Hindi word for 'Deaf'?" he signed quickly.

"No idea," Amy responded between bites of food. "Ask her when she's done talking with this man."

"It doesn't bother you that all these people are staring at us as if we are animals behind a cage at a zoo? Plus, this man just called her 'normal.' In this country it seems everybody thinks Deaf people are abnormal."

Amy set her food down. "Look! I am here for one purpose. That is to find my mother." She pointed to Visha who continued to talk with the owner. "It looks like she is getting the information we need to do that." Casting a dismissive look at the other people seated around the café, Amy shook her hand in a shooing motion. "I don't care about these people. I just need to find out why I was abandoned and the name I was called."

Visha waved for their attention. "He tell me he might know how find your mother."

Amy perked. Julius glared.

Visha continued. "He say he met woman name P-O-O-N-A-M here at café. Some time ago, she move here from Mumbai. A little time ago, she came here to café with friend who live not far from here." Visha pointed at the owner. "He friends with woman's husband."

Amy stood and placed a hand on the café owner's arm. "You know my mother's husband?" she signed.

The owner stepped back. It seemed he was startled at this sudden touch of a woman who moved her hands in strange ways. He smiled sheepishly and shrugged.

Visha voiced Amy's question, and the owner responded back to Visha. Several conversational turns ensued, appearing as though Visha was clarifying information.

Amy returned to her seat.

Julius reached across the table and tapped Visha's arm. "Can you please interpret what you are talking about?" He pointed to the owner. "Amy asked him a question directly. Why can't you interpret while he answers Amy directly?" In front of his face, Julius flashed the DARK sign in ASL. "What is the ISL sign for **I-N-V-I-S-I-B-L-E**? It's like we Deaf don't exist!"

Amy and Visha signed nothing. Amy twisted her mouth and her beaded bracelet. Julius knew she was angry. Visha's narrowed eyes and face was a mask he couldn't decipher.

The owner glanced nervously between the three of them.

Now more of the other customers stopped and stared.

Visha lifted her hand, palms out at Julius. "Hold!" she signed and held up a finger. "I try to help." The finger pointed to the owner and herself. "He tell me important information to help find Amy's mother." The finger pointed around the room then back to Julius. "This anger not help. Now they all look at us." Visha glanced at the owner. "Now maybe he report us to the cops," she signed quickly, her mouth closed. "So stop! Let me help you." Visha's eyes widened and she nodded once.

Amy jabbed her elbow into Julius's ribs. "You are getting us in trouble!" she signed with tense hands.

"Okay," Julius agreed and glared around the room at the staring customers.

"What did he say?" Amy pointed to the owner.

"He not know your mother's husband. He know husband of your mother's friend." Visha pointed to her watch. "Tonight he call his friend, ask about Poonam. Find out how we meet her. Tomorrow morning he let us know." She nodded at the man to confirm she had interpreted the message.

Apparently having enough of the tension, the owner bowed stiffly and went back to his seat behind the counter.

Amy slapped Julius on the arm and quickly formed his name sign over the eyebrow. "Julius! Stop your anger!" She pointed to the man behind the counter. "If the cops inquire about us here, because of you, for sure he will know they are looking for us!"

"Ironic!" Julius retorted. "Aren't you usually the one who is angry and out of control? In fact, aren't we all in this mess because you couldn't control yourself and had to go and try to kill Sybil? This was supposed to be a summer break trip. Why couldn't you just be patient and wait until you moved into that apartment by the college? Had you done that, we wouldn't be like escaped animals in a zoo being chased around by the keepers!"

Amy huffed and ripped off a piece of chapati. With an angry twist, she dipped it into the dal. She chomped on the food and looked at her plate.

Chai was served.

Amy took a sip then stared into the brown liquid.

Visha pointed to Julius's plate. "Come, eat b0efore food cold," she suggested.

As Visha and Julius dug into their food, Amy held her cup with both hands. Her eyes were unfocused as in a trance.

Julius paused a bite and watched her blank face. It seemed her mind was in a different realm, searching through the cobwebs of memories, emotions, and anger to find the source.

"Amy." Julius waved his hand in front of her face.

Amy's eyes blinked, and her body shuddered as if awakened from an intense dream. She put the cup on the table. "What?"

"What are you thinking?" Julius signed. "Do you have an answer for everything I just signed?"

"I am sorry for this trouble." Amy placed a hand on Julius's arm and squeezed. "I just need to know why I am the kind of person whose mother would abandon me in the middle of a train station. What is it about me that would attract a controlling b**ch like Sybil to adopt me? Am I this helpless victim that seems easy to control?" She raised an 'A' handshape and placed it on her cheek, forming the name sign that Sybil gave her.

Protruding her tongue, Amy forced a gagging reflex and pushed away her plate. "I'm not hungry anymore. I want to puke out this stain that is attached to me. Nope. I will no more use this name sign. I will find out what my mother called me."

Julius scooped the rest of the palak paneer onto a piece of naan and ate it. He stared at his plate. The damage was already done. They needed to move forward. He knew they couldn't go back to the previous week and undo Amy's actions.

The words from John 15:13 in the Bible popped into his head. *There is no greater love than to lay down one's life for one's friends.*

He drained his chai cup and nodded slowly as he placed the cup on the table. "Okay, A-M-Y." Julius fingerspelled the name. "Fine. Wewill continue to look for your mother." He turned to Visha. "Did you understand all that?"

Visha's intense eyes softened. "New name she need. Tomorrow, maybe we find answer."

Chapter 32

JULIUS

The next morning the café owner set a plate in front of him. The smell of the simple scrambled eggs and chapati breakfast comforted Julius. As he sat with Amy and Visha on the front patio of the OYO Divine Hotel, this aroma brought the familiarity of countless scrambled egg breakfasts back home in America.

"A-M-Y." He fingerspelled. "I think we should ask him what he found out about your mother."

"Okay." Amy waved a hand in front of the café owner.

He stepped back like a dog avoiding an unwanted hand reaching out to pet its head.

"S-I-R," Amy fingerspelled. "Your friend. You ask him about my mother?"

The man looked at Visha who voiced in Hindi.

Julius and Amy focused on their food as they waited for the several turns in the interpreted conversation across the table from them.

Visha waved for their attention. "He say last night he call his friend name L-A-X-M-I-K-A-N-T live not far from here. Poonam live near him. Laxmikant say Poonam did live in Dharavi. Move here to Kalyan. Move here about ten years ago."

Amy took a sip of water and wiped her mouth with a napkin. "Did you ask—" she addressed the man, but paused when he looked at Visha. "Hey! Can you please look at me and not her when I sign?"

Visha said nothing as the man continued looking at her.

Julius tapped Amy's arm. "I'm not sure Visha understood the last thing you said. Go-ahead. We need to get this information from him."

Amy rolled her eyes. "Whatever! Did you ask Laxmikant if he told Poonam about her Deaf daughter who is here in Kalyan and wants to visit her?" she signed to the side of the café owner's face.

Julius sighed and glanced at Amy. He wondered why she didn't follow her own advice from the prior evening. It seemed ironic that she was not controlling her own anger. He shook his head before taking a few more bites of his breakfast.

They patiently waited for Visha to interpret. No point in drawing attention to Amy's hypocrisy. It would trigger more of her angry emotions. From his outburst the previous night, he knew they must swallow their frustration and be patient if they were to survive this ordeal.

'Café owner did not tell," Visha began. "Only ask Laxmikant about Poonam. Said visitors want to see her."

"You didn't tell the café owner I am Poonam's daughter?" Amy addressed Visha.

Visha closed her eyes and nodded. "I did." She held up a hand as if to ward off Amy's frustration. "I told him that you are Poonam's daughter. Not sure why he did not tell."

Amy jammed an egg-covered piece of chapati into her mouth.

"Can we find out where this Laxmikant lives?" Julius asked. "Ask him if he can guide us to Poonam's house?"

"I will ask," Visha responded and made the request to the café owner.

The man took out his cell phone and spoke into it.

Visha interpreted, "Julius and A—" she began to form Amy's old name sign but stopped. "A-M-Y," she fingerspelled. "This is difficult. I not know your language ASL well. Only know ISL." She pointed to the café owner who continued talking on his phone. "He not know

Deaf people. You-two are first Deaf people he meet. Please be patient. I try help interpret best I can."

Amy placed her piece of chapati on her plate and grabbed Visha's hand. "I'm sorry," she signed.

The man deposited the phone in his pocket and said something. Visha turned to him. She listened with raised eyebrows and pursed lips, a sign she was trying to make it through the tough interpreting ordeal.

After a few quick turns in the conversation, Visha took out her own phone, typed into it, then turned to the Deaf couple. "Okay, he call Laxmikant and give me address." She pointed to her phone as the café owner left their table. "I record it here. Breakfast finish, we go meet Laxmikant." She tilted her head toward the street. "He live that way. We take rickshaw."

Fifteen minutes later, the three of them crammed in the backseat of the vehicle. The seat of the rickshaw vibrated, tickling Julius's backside. He saw the driver's thumb repeatedly press the horn button as they scooted and maneuvered past the traffic circle where a cop's mouth tightened around a whistle in a vain attempt to demand the attention of the horde of drivers who passed his way.

Julius imagined the cacophony of sound emanating from the countless horns, vibrating engines, and the policeman's whistle.

Visha yelled something to the driver and reached forward to show him her phone which contained Laxmikant's address. The rickshaw veered sharply onto the side street of Gauripada Road.

Amy grabbed Julius's arm to prevent a tumble onto the street. They bumped along the cobblestones which were a few inches below their feet. Brown, flat-topped residential buildings whizzed by.

Soon the rickshaw pulled into a cul-de-sac and approached some gated residences.

"There!" Visha tapped the driver on the shoulder and pointed to a gate at the very end of the street.

The vehicle emitted one last vibration and slowed to a stop. Nearby, a small crowd of women gathered around a cart, fussing with a fruit vendor.

Visha paid the driver before they stepped onto the street.

Julius noticed a figure on the other side of the cul-de-sac and stiffened. He grabbed Amy's leg and pointed to the location.

There, leaning against a parked motorcycle, was a local police officer observing the scene while casually puffing a cigarette.

What's he doing here? Julius thought as he squeezed Amy's leg before she exited the rickshaw. "It might be safer if we stayed here," he signed out of the officer's view.

"Come-on," Visha beckoned but paused when she saw the expressions on their faces. She looked across the street and saw the cop. "Oh!" she mouthed. Her face assumed the hard, tough veil of protection. "Come, be normal."

Amy stepped out first, instinctively pulling Julius by the arm. He sensed the stares of the women near the fruit cart.

As the three of them approached the gated entryway to Laxmikant's household, out of the corner of his eye, Julius saw the cigarette-holding hand pause in front of the cop's face. He fought the urge to run away from the prodding eyes of these people.

Visha rang the bell attached to the gate post.

There was a stir in the people as an elderly woman dropped a mango onto the fruit cart and approached the newcomers.

"Hello," she greeted Julius in English and looked at the two Indian women next to him. Apparently deciding that Amy's face presented a more inviting interaction than Visha's hard demeanor, the woman uttered a Hindi inquiry to Amy.

Visha stepped forward and responded.

Julius recognized the names of Laxmikant and Poonam on Visha's lips as she pointed past the gate to the home beyond the entry courtyard.

"Ha!" the woman responded affirmatively and called to an elderly man who exited the house and approached the gate.

As the man fussed with the gate latch, Julius felt the back of his neck tingle. He sensed the suspicious eyes behind him. The cop was probably wondering about the sudden appearance of this foreigner accompanied by two Indian women, one of whom interacted in a strange, non- responsive way.

After a short introductory conversation in Hindi with the elderly couple, Visha turned to Julius and Amy. "He L-A-X-M-I-K-A-N-T. She his wife D-I-V-Y-A." Visha pointed to the visitors and introduced their names to the elderly couple.

"Velcome!" Laxmikant said, bowing his head slightly while looking around at the still-observing crowd. He pointed to his house and said something. Julius lipread the word 'chai.'

Divya opened the gate and waved for them to follow.

Passing the edge of the gate, Julius glanced and saw the police officer beckon Laxmikant. The old man crossed the street while Julius, Amy, and Visha followed the woman up the slight rise of the courtyard and entered the house.

They found themselves in a greeting room, pleasantly lit by flame-like bulbs within ornate wall sconces. Having removed his shoes just past the entry, Julius now felt the soft threads of a red and blue patterned oriental rug.

Divya said something to Visha and lowered her palms to indicate they should sit on the red, velvet-upholstered couch next to the intricately carved coffee table. She left the room as they sat.

"She will get chai as we wait for Laxmikant," Visha signed.

Across the room, a rather large window afforded a view of the front porch. Just past the fence, Julius saw only the tops of the neighbors' heads as they continued their negotiations with the fruit vendor.

He clearly observed Laxmikant talking with the police officer.

Both nodded and pointed toward the house.

Julius elbowed Amy and pointed out the window.

Chapter 33

AMY

Amy sat, tensed, as she looked out the window. She saw the cop nod goodbye to Laxmikant.

The officer flicked away his cigarette and spoke into his shoulder-mic. Then he mounted his motorcycle, twisted the start key, and puttered out of the cul-de-sac.

The door opened.

Laxmikant entered, his wide smile and raised, bushy-gray eyebrows betraying no hint that something was amiss. "Hello, sorry," he said in English and turned to Visha, addressing her in Hindi.

From his neatly pressed, button-down shirt and trousers, it seemed that perhaps this man was a professional. He probably owned a nearby shop. However, from the high-end decor and furnishings of the home, it appeared that he was more than just a shopkeeper. He probably owned an entire business. But there was nothing in the immediate environment of the sitting room to clarify the industry of the business.

All Amy could think about was that this man knew her mother's husband. So many questions swirled in her mind. She fought an urge to interrupt with questions as Visha explained in Hindi the purpose of their visit. To calm her nerves, Amy grabbed at the bracelet on her wrist and fidgeted with the beads.

Visha waved Laxmikant in their direction. "I explain about you. He is ready for your questions," she signed. "I will interpret the best I can."

Laxmikant looked at Julius and Amy as he waited for their questions.

"Go-ahead, ask about your mother," Julius signed to Amy.

Amy let go of the beads, shifted her weight, and straightened her posture on the couch. "Do you know my mother, or just her husband?"

After Visha's Hindi interpretation, Laxmikant replied to Visha, but she pointed to Amy.

He looked at Amy while she glanced between him and Visha. "I personally not know Poonam well. Just know her husband, Rohit. I own textile business. He work with me as manager."

"I see." Amy made sure to look at Laxmikant as she signed. "Does my mother live close by?" Amy paused and pointed to her ear then shook her thumb in the HEAR-NOTHING sign. "Does she know she has a Deaf daughter who wants to meet her?"

Laxmikant shook his head and replied in Hindi. His face remained pleasant, almost apologetic.

Visha listened then signed. "I not yet speak to Rohit or Poonam about you. Last night and this morning, I receive call from café owner friend at hotel. He say you want to visit Poonam. I just tell him yes she live close by. This morning when he call, I surprise you come visit now."

Amy raised her eyebrows. Her shoulders stiffened as she turned to Julius. "My mother has no idea I'm in her neighborhood," she signed rapidly and pointed to Laxmikant. "I thought he talked to either her or her husband to confirm it is okay for us to visit her."

"Maybe we should wait a bit and let her confirm," Julius

responded. "However, we have no idea what that cop is up to." Julius glanced at Visha to make sure she wasn't voice interpreting their conversation. He tilted his head and subtly pointed his thumb at Laxmikant. "I don't want to raise his suspicions by asking what he told the cop. So, I think we'd better make it quick and meet your mother ASAP."

Visha, Laxmikant, and Divya observed with blank faces.

"I have no idea if my mother even remembers she has a Deaf daughter somewhere in the world. Also, I wonder if I even have a father. How did my mother become pregnant with me?" Amy signed quickly to Julius, "I doubt Laxmikant knows anything about that," then turned back to Laxmikant. "We really need to see my mother today. Could you make sure she is home so that we can visit?"

Laxmikant listened to Visha's interpretation, tilting his head in agreement. He dialed a number into his phone and brought it to his ear.

As questions swirled in her head, Amy imagined the scene on the other end. Was there confusion in the voice on the phone? Was her mother shocked and in denial of having a Deaf daughter whom she abandoned long ago? Would her mother refuse to see her? Amy shifted forward in her seat as she watched Laxmikant talk on the phone.

For some reason, Visha did not interpret Laxmikant's voice. Depending on what he disclosed, perhaps the response on the other end was not positive.

Laxmikant pressed the 'hang up' button. "That was Poonam," he explained. "She is home and said you can visit. She surprised."

So little information. Frustrated, Amy looked at the others, shook her head, and raised her arms with palms up. Such lack of details regarding the two-minute phone conversation.

What was this man was hiding? Didn't he understand that she needed to know more information about Poonam and her own identity? Did he not realize that she had just journeyed across the world to finally meet her long-lost mother?

Amy considered these questions for a moment.

"Did you explain she has a Deaf daughter who wants to see her?" Amy asked, **wiggling her finger with the question mark**.

Laxmikant's face returned to the apologetic expression. "I tell her she have daughter who want to visit. I say nothing about Deaf." "Well, so…um…" Amy searched for the words to sign, but instinctively looked down at her wrist and grabbed the bracelet, rolling one of the beads between her thumb and forefinger.

Julius placed a hand on hers. "I know this is a lot to process. We will help you. You will be okay." He turned to Laxmikant. "What now?"

Laxmikant stood and beckoned for them to follow. "Come, we walk. I take you to your mother."

In Amy's mind, a glimmer of hope sprang up. Any love her mother had for her was still alive.

Chapter 34

AMY

Five minutes later, metal grille and a door-sized security gate confronted Amy. She touched its rusting steel, visible in patches, covered with paint flecks. Concrete steps rose to the left just beyond the cement wall. Very soon, she would meet her mother.

"Well, here goes," Julius said.

They watched Laxmikant pull at the gate, which clicked open with ease, a sign that visitors were expected.

Amy blinked in the darkened stairwell, lit only by a barred window at the top. The sunbaked concrete heated the small interior space like a crucible through which she must pass. Her destination awaited at the top landing of the stairway.

As she ascended the stairway, Amy wondered what lay beyond the door at the top. She hoped it was Poonam, her birth mother, yearning for a connection with her long-lost daughter. Amy took a deep breath and stared at the door. Behind it she wondered if her mother would offer love, indifference, or hostility. Would her mother welcome her presence, or would it disrupt the lives of the people in the household? She knew it was her mother, and the man she married, who lived in this house. Amy wondered if they had children, who would be her half brothers and sisters.

Amy wiped her brow with a shaky hand as they stepped onto the top landing.

Laxmikant rapped on the door. She held her breath.

The door opened.

Amy froze, eyes transfixed on her mother's face as a battle of conflicting emotions pricked at her heart.

In front of her appeared the same face Amy had seen those many years ago, just before she fell asleep on the train station platform. Here was the same thin frame, defined jawline, and shifting eyes accompanied by more pronounced wrinkles, which became crow's feet with advancing age.

Laxmikant uttered a greeting and stepped aside.

"Sita!" the woman exclaimed and covered her mouth in surprise.

Amy's heart skipped a beat.

She saw the wide eyes and surprised expression on her mother's face. But there was no evidence of the relief and longing that should have been there in the discovery of a cherished, long-lost loved one.

Part of Amy wanted to rush forward and embrace her mother. The other part wanted to punch her in the face.

Sita—her given name. The name her five-year-old self had only grasped in portions on her mother's lips on the flooded street by the train station.

Sita—the name she was called by the only person in a position to love her and cherish her.

Sita—the name this woman used in reference to her only child, but didn't show the awareness or even the capacity to care that this child could not access and understand such an important word in her life.

Sita—her name. Her true identity. What did it mean? What did it define?

As these thoughts of confusion percolated in the crucible of her mind, Amy didn't know what to do. The thought of renewing a relationship with this woman was overwhelming. She searched back in a mental quest for a possible connection she ever did have.

All she knew was what she saw—a thin woman who was in fact her birth mother, standing in front of her, frozen in surprise, with her hands covering her mouth.

Despair pricked at Amy's heart. She felt the futility of her quest for clarity. The confusion she felt gave space to the bubbling anger rising in her chest, and she had the sudden urge to lash out, demanding answers to all of her questions.

Visha stepped into Amy's view. "Do you want me to interpret?" she signed.

Poonam blinked, looking at Visha with a confused expression.

"Well…yes," Amy answered, but Visha held up a finger.

"I speak in Marathi, not Hindi now," Visha explained, turning to Poonam and Laxmikant.

Julius stepped forward. It seemed he was trying to read their lips.

Amy saw Visha speak their names and point to them.

Laxmikant moved aside to observe.

Apparently understanding Visha, Poonam tilted her head slowly, looking at Julius, clasping her hands, and nodding in greeting. Then she faced her daughter and did the same.

"How are you?" Visha interpreted Poonam's question.

"Um…I am good." Amy shrugged her shoulders and looked at her hands, which lied about her true feelings. She looked at Julius, biting her lip. "What do I say?" she signed to him.

Amy turned to Poonam. "I came to India to see you." She paused, not sure how to ask the next question. "You remembered my name after all these years?" She looked to Visha to interpret, then back to Poonam.

"Ha," Poonam responded but hesitated and glanced back into the front room of her house. "Come in," Visha interpreted Poonam's welcome.

Laxmikant stepped forward and interrupted. He spoke to

Poonam. "Your husband, he at factory?" Visha interpreted.

"Yes, he left early for work," Poonam responded.

Laxmikant nodded then pulled out his phone, dialed a number, and spoke. After a minute, he hung up and looked at the others. "I spoke to your husband, Rohit. Told him you here. Now I go to factory myself." He clasped his hands together and bowed. "Namaste. Call me if need anything." He exited the home.

They all entered a modestly furnished living room.

"Please sit." Poonam swept her hand in the direction of a thinly upholstered couch and easy chair at the end of a low coffee table.

Julius and Amy sat on the couch while Visha positioned herself on the chair.

Poonam's eyes darted into the adjacent room. Amy remembered these shifting eyes from her time on the streets.

Amy leaned forward in her seat. She was itching to ask her mother many things, but saw a stir of movement as two school age children, much younger than herself, stood in what appeared to be a kitchen-dining area and peeked into the living room.

Poonam said something and waved for them to enter the room.

A girl and a boy entered. They both wore matching blue and white school uniforms. Amy saw that the girl had similar wide, brown eyes and small, round face as herself. The boy was rather thin and appeared tall for his age.

"He my son, Virat. She my daughter, Parul." Poonam introduced them as Visha interpreted. Their mother glanced nervously between Amy and her other children.

Amy observed the children. They were obviously her half sister and half brother. The boy nodded politely, but the girl lowered her eyes and squirmed. Perhaps she was too shy to give a proper greeting.

Poonam moved her hand in a shooing motion toward the door. "Now they go to school," she explained and gave a few commands to her young children in rapid Marathi, which Visha did not interpret.

With furtive glances at the newcomers, the children picked up their school bags near the door and exited the home.

Poonam looked at Visha and asked a question. Visha responded quickly with her voice and turned to Amy and Julius. "She ask me how I related to you. I explain I am friend. I am here to interpret for you." Visha looked at the woman and nodded for her to continue.

Amy sighed in frustration. She wanted to get past all this misunderstanding, confusion, and discomfort. She wanted answers to her questions.

Poonam pointed toward the kitchen and then at her guests. She tilted a thumb toward her mouth and imitated bringing a cup to her lips. Amy lipread the words 'pani' and 'chai.'

"Water or chai?" Visha interpreted.

Julius signed, "I would like to have," but Amy placed a hand on his arms.

"No. We just had chai at Laxmikant's." Amy looked directly a Poonam. "I have many questions to ask you."

As Poonam sat in the chair at the end of the coffee table opposite from Visha, Amy raised her eyebrows and took a deep breath. Finally, she would get answers. She looked at her right hand. "S-I-T-A," she fingerspelled to herself. "So that is the name you called me when I was a little girl?"

Poonam looked at Visha. "Yes, I call her Sita in Dharavi. I see she have different name now. What name they call her now?"

Visha formed Amy's name sign given by Sybil and explained to Poonam in Marathi.

Amy's eyes narrowed. Her shoulders tightened. She was tired of the barriers that even Visha presented.

Julius placed a hand on her thigh and nodded with encouragement.

"Okay." Amy took a deep breath and dropped her shoulders. "First of all," she addressed Visha, "we will no longer use that name sign given by Sybil. Remember, we are fingerspelling A-M-Y from-now-on." Then she turned to face Poonam. "It is better if you look at me and speak to me directly. Visha is our interpreter. You can listen to her, but please look at me."

Poonam nodded. Her eyes narrowed slightly and the crow's feet became more pronounced. She turned and looked at Amy.

"Thank-you," Amy continued. "The name A-M-Y was given to me by the woman who adopted me."

"Oh! She American?" Poonam asked. "She take good care of you? Who is he?" She pointed to Julius. "You have better life now, correct? Before, you lived on streets in Dharavi. Now you have friends and good support in America."

Amy's shoulders rose, and she felt Julius's hand squeeze her leg. She grabbed his arm and lifted it off her leg. "I am fine, Julius," she quickly signed to him. "Look, I am finally getting the answers we came here for."

Julius glanced at the door and pointed. "Good. But don't forget about the cops. I suspect Laxmikant disclosed some information about us to them. We don't know what is going on out there." He raised his  eyebrows and circled a hand with the **MOVE-ALONG** sign. "Let's get the answers you need, then get out of here."

"Fine!" Amy scowled and looked at Visha to make sure she had the wisdom to not interpret their conversation. Shaking her head and gathering herself up, Amy turned to Poonam. "Yes, she is American. Did she take good care of me? What do you mean when you ask that?"

Poonam shrugged, appearing to consider what to say next. "Did you get love from your mother?" Poonam asked.

With a start, Amy kicked at the coffee table with her foot, shifting it sideways a few inches.

Poonam sat straight and grabbed the armrests of her chair, a surprised expression on her face.

Amy raised both hands, palms out in the direction of Poonam.

The hypocrisy of this label of 'love' from the Indian woman who had abandoned her!

Amy looked sharply at Poonam, feeling she must push back at the attribution of 'love' attached to the American woman who abused her. "No. She did not love me. She controlled me. The only reason why she adopted me was to satisfy her need for belonging. She is a very selfish, bad, and controlling woman. Why did you—"

Poonam turned her face and looked in the direction of the door. She raised one hand, palm up, as if to protect herself from Amy. The deeply accented crow's feet extending from her eyes betrayed a long-buried fear.

To Amy, it seemed that Poonam wanted to escape out the door. Perhaps it was a fear of who might enter the home and discover her hidden secret of the daughter she abandoned long ago at a train station near Dharavi.

The woman's hand lowered, and her eyes diverted to the floor as if deep in thought. Then, taking a deep breath, she sat up and looked at Amy.

"Okay," Poonam said, Visha interpreting. "Your questions, I ready."

Chapter 35

A-M-Y

"I remember you and I lived on the streets in Dharavi," Amy began, Poonam watching her. "How long did you end up here in Kalyan?" Amy watched Visha confidently translate with her voice.

Poonam gestured with her hands as she began to answer. She spoke with stiff-jawed, teeth-gritting enunciation. "I in Dharavi for a while, maybe five year after you." She paused and seemed to consider the choice of her words. "Then I meet Rohit. Soon we married. His family help him find job with Laxmikant here in Kalyan. That why we move here, maybe ten year ago."

Amy took her eyes off Visha to observe her birth mother.

Poonam looked up at a nearby wall.

On the wall was a picture of Poonam's little family with her, Rohit and the two children, poised in the stiff, unsmiling manner of posing for portraits common among Indian families. In spite of their rigidity in the formal pose, there was no question that they belonged to each other. In the picture, Poonam's arm was draped around the shoulder of her daughter, Parul. There seemed to be contentment and belonging as the girl posed in a lean close to her mother.

Amy's fingernails dug into the couch as resentment clutched at her heart. She imagined herself being in the picture and realized this little girl replaced her, the abandoned daughter, in the heart of Poonam.

Poonam smiled and pointed to the picture. "Soon after we move here, my children born. You will like them."

Amy observed the tall man standing next to Poonam in the picture. Above the man's strong, broad shoulders, the intense eyes exuded stability, an unspoken statement that this was his family, which it was his duty to protect and take care of.

Amy grabbed her bracelet and held it tight. Then let go of it so she could sign. "Now I would like to ask about my own father. Do I have a father? What is his name?"

Poonam looked at the floor and furrowed her brow. This seemed to be a topic she really did not want to discuss. As Poonam bit her lip, Amy sensed that her mother felt their presence—especially her probing questions—as a disruption and intrusion into her established comfort.

"Before you born, I had companion in Dharavi. His name Sanju. Surname I forget. After you born, he stay with us for very short time until—" Poonam's eyes shifted, her furrowed brow betraying an agony connected to the memory. "Until we find out you not normal."

Amy's mouth gaped open as she took a sharp intake of breath. She squeezed Julius's arm. The knife of her mother's words dug deep into her heart.

There it was, the reason why she was abandoned.

Not normal.

Amy's eyes narrowed, and her teeth clenched as she looked into her mother's eyes. Her hands raised to reply but hesitated. She did not know how to respond. She wanted to yell and punch Poonam in the face, but the shock of full disclosure paralyzed her.

That someone could label her Deafness as the abomination of being 'not normal' seemed an act of extreme hypocrisy.

Slowly, Amy let out her breath and clenched her jaw. It was probably this woman's genes that caused the Deafness in the first place.

"Soon Sanju left me alone with you." Poonam's eyes searched in a plea for understanding.

Amy looked at Julius and shook her head. He also shook his head, and she saw that he felt the same jolt she experienced. Yes, she was getting answers, but the effect was not what she expected. She curled her lips in frustration. Tears formed in her eyes and began dropping down her face.

Amy placed both hands on her knees and took a deep breath. "I need to ask, Why in the name of God did you abandon me?"

Poonam's shoulders twitched as if she was jolted into the same agony which Amy as a little girl saw on the train platform when her mother made the choice to let-go.

Poonam's face twisted into a mass of wrinkles. She shut her eyes and sobbed. Tears streamed over the dark folds of the wrinkles. Her shoulders shook.

Amy didn't want to wait for this woman to compose herself. In spite of the pain, she wanted answers. Her time of waiting was over. A minute passed. Two. Three.

Poonam opened her eyes and dabbed them with her kameez.

"Why did you abandon me?" Amy leaned forward when the woman's eyes finally met hers.

"No money I had." Poonam rubbed her fingers together in the universal sign for money and flicked her hand several times, shaking her head. "I alone, hungry. How I take care of a child? On the streets, parents struggle to take care of child. Later, when child older, they help parents survive." Poonam moved her hand up and down. "Beg, find food, do small work." She paused, shaking her head. "How not-normal, mute child do that?"

"Whoa!" Amy shook her head in disbelief and raised her hands as if to protect herself from the heart-piercing label. She imitated dropping something. "You just abandoned me? Left me at that train station because you couldn't figure it all out? We could have found a way to survive together. You say I am not normal." She set her jaw and nodded resolutely while thumping her chest with an open palm. "Actually, I am better than normal. I am strong, smart, and much more capable than you think I am."

Poonam's body stiffened. Her eyes shot wide. She gave no response. Only a sharp intake of breath signaled that Amy's questions overwhelmed this woman like the putrid stench of long-buried garbage suddenly unearthed for examination.

Finally, Poonam wiped the tears from her face, gathered herself, and faced Amy. "All work out well in the end, no?" She pointed out the front window then to Julius. "You have good life in America. You have man who take care of you. In past, if I take care of you, all these good things not happen, correct?"

"**No!**" Amy stood, jabbing the sign forward. "You left me to be snatched-up by the absolute worst person who could have adopted me! Had you tried to take care of me and given me a chance to help you survive, at least I would have known my true name and been taken care of by a person who cherished me, not a witch who controlled me!"

Now, tears flowed down Amy's face. Her lips quivered and her hands shook. She slowly lowered herself on the couch.

This was not how it was supposed to feel. This finding her true identity and her birth mother.

She should be getting answers and clarity, not this confusing jumble of anger, bitterness, and disappointment.

"Sita!" Amy read her given name on Poonam's lips. Then the word 'deva' was pronounced with a few other syllables and another Marathi term.

Amy looked at Visha for clarification.

"God's will." Visha raised a fist above her head and slowly opened her hand. Both Julius and Amy observed Visha as she tried to add clarity in the tense situation. "I think she mean to let-go. She say it all work out the way God wills it. Need to accept."

"I can't!" Amy wiped the tears from her face and dried her hands on her kameez. "Don't you know what you have done?"

For a long moment, Amy twisted her beaded bracelet while looking at her mother. Finally, she knew what she was looking for—her mother's admission of guilt and shame for the thoughts and actions which caused the abandonment of the daughter she should have cherished.

She could not read her mother's face. There was no evidence that Poonam desired the connection which Amy sought. In the slumped shoulders and defeated look on this woman's face, all Amy could see was self-pity. Panic and confusion gripped Amy's heart as if she were toppling off a cliff and trying vainly to grasp at a tree branch just out of reach.

All of a sudden, the front door opened. In stepped a tall man with intense eyes and broad shoulders.

It was Poonam's husband, Rohit. His eyes narrowed as he looked at his wife and the visitors. Then his eyes shifted to the open door.

Chapter 36

JULIUS

Julius bolted to a standing position.

Officer Steele's muscular frame filled the space just inside the doorway.

Julius stepped close to Amy, holding her hand tight.

Officer Manish stepped in and stationed himself near the door. He placed his hands on the utility belt on his hips.

A short, thick-bodied female officer brushed past. She held a long police wand. She rapped this stick once on the palm of her other hand and looked around with an expressionless mask of toughness. It was a cue for all to freeze.

Julius looked around the house for an escape out a window. All were covered with bars. Resigned but guarded, Julius stood in front of where Amy sat. His shoulders raised in suspicion as he looked at the authorities, Officer Steele, Manish, and Stick Holder, with narrow eyes and waited to see what they would do.

Officer Steele's dark eyes swept the room. The face remained still as the eyes moved.

Visha stirred, slid sideways, and stepped toward the door.

Manish extended an arm, blocking Visha's path out the door.

Visha protested in Hindi.

Manish squared his jaw and jerked his head at Visha's defiance.

Stick Holder elevated her weapon, poised to strike.

A flurry of heated words flew back and forth between Visha and Manish.

Julius lipread the word 'Poonam' as Visha and Manish gestured toward her.

Poonam slid off her chair, collapsing into a cowering ball on the floor. Rohit stepped forward, gesturing wildly, inserting himself into the argument.

Words flew. Stick Holder glared at Visha.

Julius grabbed Amy's shoulder. He expected fear in her eyes but saw something else—intense observation. She sat still. He knew not to say anything. It would distract from her search for clues which would determine her fate.

Jesus. Please be with us now, Julius prayed.

The squabble between Visha, Rohit, and the police officers continued.

Officer Steele's eyes met Julius's. The US marshal shifted his weight, his chest heaving in a sigh. He looked between Amy and the argument fight near the door.

Julius guessed that Steele was annoyed because he did not understand the conversation.

Steele stepped forward, placing one hand on Rohit's shoulder. The other hand he placed on the revolver holstered in his belt.

Rohit turned his head in surprise. He glared at Steele, yelli ng something in Hindi. Rohit squirmed in an attempt to escape, but Steele's clamp remained firm.

Steele addressed Visha in English. She responded back.

Rohit stared at the three officers with his jaw open and slack.

His wife continued to cower on the floor.

Stick Holder stood near the door and glared around the room.

Julius knew that the only people who understood this English were the two male officers and Visha. He tugged at Amy's shoulder.

"They seem distracted," he signed. "I think I can run and escape out that door. Think you can make it?"

Amy looked between the arguing people and the door. "I can try," she signed.

They both stepped around the coffee table.

Stick Holder saw their movement and blocked the door, pointing her wand at them, barking an order in Hindi.

Steele released his grip on Rohit and turned his attention to Amy and Julius.

Rohit shook his head, seeming to mutter some swear words, and walked over to his wife. He grabbed her arm and pulled her up.

Poonam stood unsteadily and watched the officers, a look of complete dread on her face.

"Okay," Visha said in English. She faced Amy and Julius. "They agree not arrest me." She pointed to the cops. "They say they let me go if I interpret for you."

With no escape possible now, Julius knew it was time to face their consequences. This moment had rushed too suddenly upon them. He wasn't prepared.

His heart beat in his chest like it did during his running races. Placing an arm around Amy's shoulders, he pulled her close. He felt the warmth of her body as her shoulder pressed into his ribs. Her arms were stiff as one hand grasped the bracelet on her wrist. Her eyes remained in that intense, observant focus like an animal cornered by its predators.

All Julius could think about was protecting her. He couldn't bear the thought of her being alone, led away in the rough hands of these cops. He knew they both would be arrested. He hoped they would be together.

Visha's face morphed into the neutral, businesslike interpreting expression. "Officer Steele will ask questions. Please be patient. I will interpret in sign language, Hindi, and English."

Stick Holder positioned herself near Amy and Julius.

Officer Steele began his questions. "Both of you are F-U-G-I-T-I-V-E-S from America," Steele said. "You will be handcuffed, and then we will ask some questions."

Stick Holder dropped the stick, whipped a pair of stirrup-shaped handcuffs from her belt, and yanked Amy out of Julius's embrace. She clamped one handcuff on Amy's wrist, picked up her stick, and pulled on the other end of the chain. She raised the stick in a threat.

"Hey!" Julius reached toward Amy, but Steele stepped forward and grabbed his arm. With one fluid motion, Julius's arms were twisted around to his back. Handcuffs clicked shut on both wrists.

Steele spoke. "I need to ask if you know why you are being arrested."

Visha signed the question then interpreted in Hindi for the others.

Amy gritted her teeth and raised her hands to sign. "Yeah, I attacked Syb—"

Stick Holder jerked on the chain as Amy's arms exaggerated the  'attack' sign. The stick raised in a threat.

"Would you quit it!" Amy yanked on the chain. "I need to sign my answers!"

Stick Holder's mouth curled and her eyes shot wide. She poised to strike at this defiance.

"Stop!" Steele let go of Julius and grabbed the woman's stick, twisting it from her grasp. He threw the stick on the floor. "Let her answer!"

Stick Holder's face went blank as Visha interpreted in Hindi.

Steele nodded toward Amy. "Go ahead."

"Like I was trying to say," Amy continued. "I attacked Sybil, the woman who adopted me. But I know she is still alive. So yeah, that is why you are here."

"Okay. Later at the police station, we will let you explain why you did that." Steele waited for Visha to finish the Hindi translation then turned to Julius.

Julius saw restrained patience in the tightening of Steele's square jaw.

"What about you?" Steele asked. "Do you know why I am arresting you also?"

Julius raised his eyebrows and shrugged. He twisted his body to show the handcuffs at his back.

Visha said something in English, and Steele glanced at her. Oh!"

Steele unhooked one side of the handcuffs, let Julius bring his hands out in front, and re-attached them.

"Thanks for this, I guess." Julius awkwardly moved his hands, wondering how best to sign with the severely restrained, handcuffed movements. "Yes, I am supporting her. I think you would call me an A-C-C-O-M-P-L-I-C-E." Julius looked at Visha to make sure she caught the fingerspelling. "If you ask why we came to India, I hope you consider that we are not trying to escape from the law." He pointed to Amy's birth mother, still in the encompass of her husband. "We came to India to find her mother, Poonam—"

Rohit interrupted, gesturing wildly with one hand. He uttered a string of Hindi sentences. "Do not speak my wife's name! She have nothing to do with this. Don't you dare spoil my family reputation with police. My wife innocent." Rohit's eyes bugged wide, and he pointed out the door. "Leave my house now!"

Amy stepped up to Rohit and squared her shoulders. "Sir! You need to know that this woman"—Amy pointed at Poonam and paused, allowing Visha to interpret in Hindi—"this woman abandoned me! Long before she met you, she left me: a little five-year-old Deaf girl!"

Tears welled in Amy's eyes as she shifted her gaze from the man's enraged eyes to the petrified face of her birth mother. "Back in the streets of Dharavi"—Amy pointed out the window—"back on that cold, hard platform at the Mahim train station, she left me."

Amy pointed sharply at Poonam. "She left me completely **alone!**"  She gestured toward Visha. "Instead, this woman who stands in front of you. This woman—not my mother—who found me and took care of me when I needed it the most. And most importantly—" Amy pointed to her ear and shook her thumb. "HEAR-NOTHING. She cared enough to give me a name that I could recognize with my eyes."

Rohit's eyes shifted angrily between Amy and Visha.

Poonam cringed next to him as if she were about to be burned by a flame thrower from her biological daughter.

Amy extended a hand, moving it up and down in front of Poonam. "This woman did not cherish me enough to risk the discomfort and effort of learning sign language." The hand pointed to Visha. "This woman did"—Amy looked directly at Poonam—"and she cherished your Deaf daughter in the way you did not!"

During Visha's lengthy Hindi interpretation, Julius observed the scene in front of him. He saw the power of his little friend, and his love for her deepened far beyond the point he had previously experienced.

Chained in place, yet in a position of control more than previous situations, Amy's firm stance in front of the anger and confusion from the people she confronted, solidified her conviction.

In the eyes of Julius, the actions of this little woman named A-M-Y—or Sita—verified the fact that in his heart, she was far more than a companion.

He was hers, and she was his. Nothing could ever separate them from here or the future. He knew that something needed to be done to solidify that fact.

Visha kept speaking, interpreting, and speaking again until she was through to the end of the conversations. Such a tough, multifaceted interpreting task, especially compounded by the need for Visha to explain her own role in all that transpired those many years ago.

Now it was time for Rohit and Poonam to respond. The man let go of his wife's arm, shook his head, and looked angrily at Visha. His hands gestured wildly. He pointed at Amy, then to his ear, and covered his mouth while emitting a stream of Hindi words that didn't seem friendly.

Visha's eyes widened and her shoulders raised. She glanced at Amy and Julius with a look of complete revulsion. "How you sign A**H-O-L- E?" she signed, then squared her jaw and faced Rohit. Out of Visha's mouth spewed a long string of Hindi words that clearly smothered any of Rohit's offending language. With an angry flourish, she twisted her head, closed her fist, and stepped forward, thrusting the side of the fist in the direction of Rohit. It was an obvious insult.

Rohit took a deep breath, balled his fists, and stepped toward Visha.

"Stop!" Steele released his grip on Julius, grabbed the stick from the floor, and thrust it between Visha and Rohit. He pointed to the wall opposite the door and looked at Rohit. "You! Go stand over there!" Julius read the command on Steele's lips.

Rohit scowled but did not protest. He collected his wife and guided her next to the wall.

The US marshal motioned for Visha to come and interpret for him. Facing Julius and Amy, his neck was less rigid. His face carried a new expression. It seemed he had a better understanding of the situation and knew what to do. "We need to leave," Steele spoke to them both. "We will now go to the police station."

He handed the stick to Stick Holder.

Chapter 37

A-M-Y

Her power restored, Stick Holder jerked on the handcuffs. Amy lurched forward. The handcuff squeezed her wrist.

Like a captive zoo animal led by a chain, Amy tripped and stumbled down the steps in the rear of the procession. Just before turning to exit through the gate in the wall, she looked back where she knew her birth mother would be standing.

From this distance, she saw the hatred in the eyes of Rohit. Next to him, Poonam appeared small and utterly powerless. Fear remained etched on her face, but in her eyes was a longing, which Amy recognized. A severed mother-daughter connection that could not be recovered.

Amy shivered. Had she gotten all the information she was looking for? Maybe this meeting was enough. Could she live with that?

With a subtle shake, then a nod of her head goodbye, Amy turned to exit the gate.

A crowd gathered outside. People gawked at the scene of a mixed-race couple in handcuffs being escorted to a police jeep by law enforcement officers.

Stick Holder pressed down on Amy's head and shoved her into the jeep.

At the Kalyan Police Station, Visha and Officer Steele conversed, sitting in metal chairs in the main section of the station, across from Officer Manish. He occupied the swivel chair behind his desk.

Kitty-corner from this desk, near the entrance to a narrower hallway with smaller cells lining each wall, Amy peered between the bars to observe their interactions. She looked across the hall to the cell which Julius occupied, which was around the corner and out of sight from Manish's desk. "They are asking Visha questions," Amy signed.

"Can you tell what they are talking about?" Julius asked. "Are they interrogating her?"

"No, just asking her questions, and she is calmly answering." Amy shrugged. "She is not signing, so I can't tell what they are discussing."

Julius gripped the bars and tried pushing his face between them in an attempt to see the interaction at Manish's desk. "Can't see them." He popped his face back into the cell. "Visha knows so much about us. Do you think we can trust her to share the right information? I don't want her to put us into more trouble than we already are."

Amy watched the interaction at Manish's desk. Officer Steele perched on the edge of his seat and leaned forward to write notes on a small pad placed on the edge of the desk. His mouth moved in apparent questions. Visha answered to the side of his head, listening as he wrote. Manish rocked his chair slightly; hands folded in his lap as he listened to the English conversation across his desk.

"I have no idea what Visha is telling them," Amy explained. "Her face is turned away from me so I can't try to read her lips. She doesn't look at all agitated. Seems pretty cooperative."

Julius leaned against the bars and looked at her. It seemed he was contemplating what to say next. "Now that you have met your mother, have you found what you are looking for?"

"I'm not sure. I think so." Amy's mind occupied a surreal, turbulent space. Somewhere buried in her consciousness, she knew there were answers. This brought a spark of hope.

She felt the cold iron bars that imprisoned her and stroked her bracelet for comfort. But the strong stench of human refuse from the nearby, curtained-off toilet hole in the floor presented a stark reminder of her predicament.

"Back there"—Amy pointed out the small, barred window, high in the wall of her cell—"at Poonam's house, I guess I was looking for some kind of connection, hoping that she had wanted to find me, too. I kinda saw that in her face at the end when we left." Amy pointed to her bracelet and then to Visha in the other room. "But I always have things to remind me of the damage my mother caused. In a way, this bracelet reminds me of it. So does Sybil. The fact that I don't belong here in this country where I was born reminds me of what my mother threw away. I also wanted to see her shame and guilt from abandoning me."

"**That**"—Julius held the sign—"I see that you called her 'mother.' Did you see that shame and guilt in her?" 

"No, not really." Amy squinted as she tried to remember. "All I saw was a terrified little woman wallowing in self-pity as she cowered next to her a**hole of a husband."

Julius nodded. "I saw that, too. But you know you can't control that. All you are in charge of is yourself, Amy." He pressed his palms together and looked up. "I was praying that whole time we were at your mother's house."

"I know, but it seems that the choices and actions of other people, like our teacher, Jolina, back in Spokane, Sybil, and my birth mother, have defined who I am. Fighting against them and their oppression is all I know. That is my default. I want to be free and move on, but have no idea how to do that."

Julius pointed across the hall to Amy's wrist. "I know you have things like your bracelet and that crucifix necklace that you got—"

"Oh crap!" Amy exclaimed. "That necklace is in my purse. In all this confusion, I left my purse at Poonam's house!" She looked at Manish's desk but didn't see her purse. "I wonder if they've kept it somewhere?"

The people at Manish's desk nodded in agreement and stood.  Amy's mind crashed in a wave of panic. Eyes wide, she looked at Julius and **wiggled her fingers**. "They're coming toward us!"

Stick Holder appeared out of nowhere. A large set of keys hung from her belt. She grabbed one key, unlocked the cell, entered, and clamped one end of the handcuffs on Amy's wrist. With a sharp tug, Stick Holder jerked Amy out of the cell and into the hall.

Visha stepped forward to interpret.

"We will now go to another room and ask you questions," Officer Steele explained.

"One second," Amy interjected. "Do you have my purse? I think I left it at Poonam's house."

Steele looked at Manish who nodded.

"I will call her now and tell her to bring it here." Manish took out his phone, dialed a number, and spoke into it.

As they walked down the hall past the individual prisoner cells, Amy glanced back at Julius. His forehead rested on a bar of the cell's door, and his hands moved in small movements. She knew he was praying for her.

An office door opened. They entered a windowless, white-walled room.

Stick Holder attached one end of the handcuffs to a ring jutting from the center of a metal table and left the room. "Sit," Steele commanded.

Amy sat on a metal chair, her handcuffed wrists on the table.

Manish sat near Steele on the other side of the table.

Visha stood between the two officers across from Amy.

Amy looked to Visha for support. But the woman's detached, professional expression and neutral stance brought no verification that she was there as a protector.

Amy grabbed the chains of the handcuffs and fidgeted with them.

She really was alone. And she was thankful that Julius was now praying for her. *God, I know I haven't always liked you, but would you please help me?* she prayed.

Manish leaned forward then pointed a finger at Amy. "Why did you try to kill your mother?" he demanded.

"Hold on!" Steele addressed Manish. "I know I am in your country, under your laws and ways of doing things." He pointed to Amy. "But she is my subject. I need the power and freedom to talk with her in the way I need."

Steele's raised eyebrows and intense stare met Manish's slight frown. The Indian officer shrugged, leaned back in his chair, and waved for Steele to take over.

"Yes, we do want to know why you assaulted your mother." Visha interpreted Steele's tone as calm and measured.

Amy let go of the chains. "First of all, she is not my mother. I call her Sybil." She produced the "S" name sign on the chin. "You probably know she adopted me when I was five years old — no — rather, she snatched me from this country and dragged me to America. She is not my mother. She is the woman who took me away so she could control me to meet her own selfish needs of love and belonging."

Steele took his notepad from a shirt pocket, opened it, and scribbled some notes.

Amy appreciated it when he looked at her before speaking. "Are you sorry that you tried to kill Sybil?" Steele asked.

Amy looked at the chain attached to her wrist. "I am sorry I took the actions I did to physically harm her." She held up her wrist and pointed to the handcuff. "It certainly has not got me to the place where I need to be. But I am not sorry for my message to Sybil." The chains clanked as she hit the table with her fist. "From-here-on-forward, I will

NOT be controlled by her! Nor will I be controlled by anyone else!"

From Visha's facial expressions, it seemed she was accurately conveying the intensity of Amy's signs.

Steele scribbled on his notepad as he listened. He paused, tapped the pad with a finger, and looked up. "One thing I need to know is if you really came to India to find your birth mother. Or was it a way to escape from the law in America?"

Amy scooted back in her chair. "No! Like I explained back at Poonam's house, I needed to find her. Why? To understand the reason she abandoned me." She looked at her hand. "S-I-T-A," she fingerspelled. "Now I finally know my name, the one I was called when I first came into the world."

Amy regarded Officer Steele, and did not know the thoughts of this brown-attired US marshal. His questions and actions seemed fair. The fact that he gave her a chance to explain was an encouraging sign that, given the circumstances, perhaps he desired the best for her. But in her mind, that didn't matter.

All she knew was now she had a name that was given to her by a person who brought her into the world. It was not a name forced upon her by a self-serving person like Sybil, whose main purpose was to control all those in her sphere of influence.

But was this name, 'Sita,' really hers? Should she take ownership of it in spite of the fact that it was given by a person who should have taken care of and cherished her, but instead, made the choice to abandon her?

What should be her name—Amy or Sita? She did not know. Looking at Visha, Amy sighed deeply, pointed to her ear, and shook her thumb. "Hear-Nothing is what I shall be called for now," she signed.

Visha's eyes narrowed slightly in recognition within her poised, professional face.

"One last question," Steele said. "What do you think should happen with you now?"

Hear-Nothing raised her hands, palms up, and thrusted them forward. "I'm in your hands. I know there are consequences I must face. I will face them."

Manish opened the door and called out into the hall. Stick Holder entered the room and unhooked the handcuff from the ring in the table.

"We will take you back to your cell," Steele explained.

They filed out the door and walked the short distance down the hall.

Amy entered her cell.

Julius lowered his right eyebrow with worry. "Are you okay?" he asked.

The line of sight between the two Deaf people was cut as Stick Holder exited into the larger room.

Manish opened Julius's cell, clasping a handcuff around one of his wrists.

Steele beckoned for Julius to follow. "Your turn," Visha interpreted.

Standing alone in her cell, Hear-Nothing felt a slight stirring of air as the entry door opened at the end of the large room. A small, thin figure of a woman entered the room, holding a bundle. The backlight from the door and surrounding windows made her features unrecognizable. She approached the first desk and asked a question. The officer pointed to Manish's desk.

The woman dropped the bundle on Manish's desk, turned back toward the door, and hesitated. Her head turned to look down the hall of individual cells. With a slight lowering of the head and drop of the shoulders, the woman walked toward the hall, her figure becoming clear to Hear-Nothing's vision.

On the other side of the bars, Hear-Nothing looked into the eyes of Poonam who was completely alone.

Devoid of the distractions and intrusions of others, Hear-Nothing observed her birth mother. The small frame was there, but the thin, fragile-looking hands betrayed Hear-Nothing's long-ago memory of the strong grasp on her arm as she was dragged across the flooded street to the train station. A thin, pink dupatta covered Poonam's head, shadowing her face from the dim yellow overhead lights.

The dark eyes widened as a hand pointed to Manish's desk. "___ parsa," Poonam said.

Parsa must mean 'purse,' Hear-Nothing thought and nodded. "Thank-you," she signed and pressed her palms together with a slight bow. It was the only way she could think to gesture the concept.

Poonam pressed a palm on her chest. "___ narawa," she said. Hear- Nothing shook her head. "I don't understand," she signed.

Poonam glanced around as if looking for something to help her communicate. Then she pointed to the small gold ring on her left hand. "S—sa," she said, pointing out the front door and lowering her head in an apparent apology.

Is she apologizing for her husband? Hear-Nothing thought and narrowed her eyes. *Why is she apologizing for him? She should apologize for herself!* She frowned, shook her head, and pointed to the front door.

"Sita," Poonam interrupted and pointed to herself. "S—sa." Her head bowed.

Hear-Nothing grabbed one of the iron bars.

Forgive.

Out of nowhere, the thought entered her mind.

Forgive.

Like the recurrent flash of a phone notification, the word popped into her mind.

Forgive.

Hear-Nothing fought the thought, then tightened her hand on the bar.

Forgive.

Tears welled in her eyes. She released the bar as her mind succumbed.

"I forgive you," she signed. She pressed her hands together and bowed her head while briefly closing her eyes. Next, she raised her palms and extended her hands toward Poonam. "You are forgiven."

The worry lines on Poonam's face diminished and her shoulders relaxed. It seemed she understood. A tear trickled down her face as she looked at her daughter.

Hear-Nothing knew there was not much to say.

In the new, strange connection with this woman, somehow her heart felt light. It was as if a weight lifted, a barrier removed from her path forward.

It was not the connection between a daughter and her mother. The dearth of a relationship history and the layers of cultural and communication barriers prevented that connection. Rather, Hear-Nothing's heart was freed as she busted through the wall of anger, resentment, and shame to release her birth mother from the chains of guilt.

Poonam stepped close, nodding her head with a questioning expression.

Confused, Hear-Nothing stood still.

"Sita," Poonam said with an affectionate smile and reached into the cell to place her hands upon the head of her daughter, and with a slow, soothing motion, the hands moved down the side of Hear-Nothing's head and rested on her shoulders, squeezing softly.

For a long moment, the mother and daughter looked at each other. It was not a look of love. It was a realization and acceptance of the way things were.

The daughter knew that her mother was not equipped to forge the intimate connection that should occur between a mother and daughter. It seemed that the mother knew her daughter would soon be whisked far away, with little chance to visit and connect.

They both nodded in mutual understanding, and Hear-Nothing understood it was for the best.

"Namaste," Poonam said, wiping the tears from her face. She walked down the hall, becoming a silhouette in the backlight of the large room as she left the jail building.

The blessing, for the first time in seventeen years, her own mother had touched her. And Hear-Nothing knew it would be the last. Sadness weighed her heart.

She felt the natural wish for the time and space to develop a relationship and thus a connection with her mother.

But it was not to be.

The lingering touch of her birth mother comforted her in the confirmation that her main task was to truly forgive. Only then could her heart find the freedom it so desperately sought.

Chapter 38

JULIUS

The door down the hall opened. Officer Manish led Julius by the handcuffs, followed by Officer Steele and Visha. Manish held open the cell door across the hall.

Julius ducked his head under the low head jamb and entered the cell.

"Everything okay?" Hear-Nothing asked.

"Yes, they just asked me questions about what happened with Sybil and how we ended up here in India," Julius explained. "I told them—"

Visha waved her hand, stepping between the two cells and pointed to Officer Steele.

"Here's what's happening next," Steele began. "Tomorrow you both will be ___ America." He paused as Visha questioned a word he used.

"He say you be E-X-T-R-A-D-I-T-E-D tomorrow," Visha clarified. "Means he bring you back to America." She looked at Steele. "Go-ahead."

"Tomorrow morning you will be transported to Mumbai." Steele arched a hand in the air. "I will fly with you back to Spokane in America. You two will stay here tonight." Steele waved toward the large room, then both officers walked to Manish's desk.

Visha stayed in the spot between the cells and watched the officers settle into their chairs.

Hear-Nothing and Julius observed closely. It seemed Visha paused to transition out of her interpreting mode. The street-wise, shifty-eyed expressions returned.

Visha turned her back to the officers and stepped aside so that the Deaf people on both sides of the hall could see her. "Whew!" Visha sighed deeply. "I tired!"

Julius saw that Visha did indeed look exhausted. Her eyes drooped with a weary expression.

She raised an arm and sniffed at the armpit. "I stink. Need bath." She looked back and forth between Julius and Hear-Nothing. "You-two okay if I go now?" She pointed to the officers in the other room. "They put me in a Kalyan hotel for tonight. Will be back tomorrow morning to interpret."

Julius looked at Hear-Nothing who nodded. "Fine. Nowhere for you to sleep here," he signed.

"Visha, come-here." Hear-Nothing beckoned.

Visha stepped close to the cell. "What you need?"

Hear-Nothing reached her hand between the bars and touched lightly on the side of Visha's face. "Thank-you so much for your help."

Visha took a quick breath. "Oh!" Her shoulders shuddered with a small sob. A tear trickled down her face. She wiped the tear away. "I need go now. Will see you tomorrow," she signed, then walked quickly through the large room and exited out the entry door.

"Julius," Hear-Nothing signed. "My mother came to see me while you were being interrogated."

Julius lowered an eyebrow. "Alone?"

"Yes. Her husband was not with her."

Julius looked at his girlfriend and sighed, nodding slowly. "This time I see you signed 'mother' like you really mean it."

Chapter 39

JULIUS

"I miss toilet paper!" Hear-Nothing sat on the jail-supplied blanket folded on the floor in a front corner of the cell across the hall from Julius.

It was late that night, long after the simple dal and rice meal supplied on metal plates had been passed through the small shelf in the middle of the door. Several men lay in their own cells along Julius's side of the hall. The dim, yellow overhead lights illuminated their faces enough to show that they slept. A single police officer slumbered in the large main room of the police station.

The jail was still, and Julius welcomed the quietude as he sat on his own jail-supplied blanket. He was grateful for sign language. Its lack of sound permitted safe conversation with his companion in her separate cell across the hall.

Julius looked at the curtain in the back, opposite corner of his cell. "Yeah, my toilet is just a hole in the floor. Do you also just have a spigot and bucket of water to clean yourself?"

Hear-Nothing raised her left hand, turning it over and examining it. "Yeah, I used this hand. Instinct, I guess. I remember my mother teaching me to use my left hand to wipe in the outhouses on the Dharavi streets." She raised her right hand. "Here in India, they use the right hand for clean actions like eating and shaking hands."

"Oops!" Julius looked at his right hand. "I recently used this one."

Hear-Nothing wrinkled her nose and stuck out her tongue. "Gross! I'm never letting you touch me with THAT hand!"

Julius's heart softened, grateful that Hear-Nothing's quirky humor arose even in the midst of these dire circumstances. He reached through the bars with his left hand. "Can I touch you with this one?"

"Sure!" Hear-Nothing reached between her own bars and stretched her arm into the hall. "Can't reach you. Gonna take a rain check on that for when we get out of here."

For a long moment, Julius looked at Hear-Nothing. "I really want to give you a hug now."

"I'm imagining you doing just that!" she signed and wrapped her arms around herself. "But why are you saying all this when I have caused so much trouble? Are you angry with me for destroying your life?" She swept her hand around the jail. "I mean, if it wasn't for me, you wouldn't be stuck in a jail in India."

He pulled his blanket closer to the front of the cell. He noticed a thread on the hem of his blanket was loose. "Ever since your troubles started, something Jesus said keeps reminding me of what is happening with us. I think it is John 15, verses 12 and 13 in the Bible." Julius squinted, searching his memory for the verses. He began picking at the loose thread. "Jesus says we should love each other in the same way He has loved us. He says that there is no greater love than to lay one's life down for one's friends."

Hear-Nothing nodded, as if agreeing with him.

Julius swept his arms in the direction of Hear-Nothing. He imagined she was right in front of him. He also wrapped his arms around himself in a pretend hug. His body swayed slowly as he sat on the blanket, thinking. "What now?" he asked.

"Well, it is strange. When my mother was trying to apologize for her husband's behavior, all of a sudden, I got a message to forgive. Out of nowhere, it just popped into my mind."

Julius nodded, glad to hear this news. "What did you do?"

"No matter what I thought or did, that word 'forgive' remained. So, I did. I forgave her."

"How did you do that? I mean, you don't exactly know each other's language."

"I signed it, then acted like this." Hear-Nothing pressed her hands together and bowed her head.

"I see. I do remember praying for you before you went into the interrogation room. Prayed that Jesus be with you and help you through this." Julius pointed to the ceiling. "It looks like He was with you, telling you what to do with your mother."

He knew now he wanted much more than this commitment to be together as companions through their troubles.

But he didn't have a ring to propose. An idea formed in his mind.

"Amy," he signed.

Her hands flew. "Hear-Nothing."

Nodding, he signed, "Okay. Hear-Nothing. I am proud of you because you forgave your mother. That was a difficult thing to do, but I know you did the right thing." He pulled at the strand, and it unraveled until he ended up with a two-foot length in his hand. "You are so much more than Hear-Nothing."

"What are you doing?" Hear-Nothing gestured wide. "You are so distracted!"

"Be patient. You will see." He joined the ends of the strand and twisted so it became a thicker cord.

Her hands flew again. "Hurry up. It's late, and I am tired. I am ready for sleep after a very long day."

Julius smiled at his girlfriend's impatience. She was right. It had been a very long day. "S-I-T-A." He fingerspelled her new name and paused for emphasis. "I say this because I love you."

She looked at him, her face recognized as confusion. "Sita?" she signed. "You love me? Why do you call me 'Sita' and say that?"

"You showed bravery and confidence in the past few days, and you forgave your mother for abandoning you long-ago."

A slow, warm smile crossed her face. "Julius, I love you, too."

Julius knew his companion confessed this from the bottom of her heart.

Then she nodded. "I don't know. Maybe I can be called 'Sita' from-now-on." Hear-Nothing yawned. "I'm tired. I need to get some sleep. We leave early in the morning for the airport."

"Wait." His chest clenched, and he waved, the thread dangling from his fingers as he worked it around his pinky finger and tied the ends. "I have something for you."

"What is it?"

"S-I-T-A." Julius removed the chorded ring from his finger and held it up. "Will you marry me?"

Her hands froze. Her eyes shot open wide. In the dim, yellow light, her facial expression was not clear. "Marry?" Her hands joined then questioned.

Seeing this, a twinge of panic pricked his chest. "Actually, for a while now I have wanted to do this…" He pointed to the ring as his mind searched for the appropriate words. "I planned to ask you to marry me during our planned summer—"

"**Yes!**" Sita interrupted with an emphatic movement of her hand. A smile formed on her lips, her eyes remained wide in surprise.

Julius saw a tear start to trickle down her face. "Yes," she said again.

He reached between the bars and held the ring in her direction. "Do you really mean that?"

Hear-Nothing looked at the ring and then into Julius's eyes. "Did you really mean to ask me to marry you?"

They laughed.

"I did," Julius signed. "Will you marry me? Do I need to ask again?"

She nodded her head. "Yes, Julius. I will marry you."

In their universe, their connection was the only thing that existed. For a moment, the cold steel bars and hard concrete floor of the jail evaporated away as Julius and Hear-Nothing allowed their eyes to remain connected to each other in a deep understanding.

Julius knew it in his heart, and he saw in his new fiancée their love that had evolved over the years of an entwined identity, forged through a common bond between soul-mates who were always meant to be.

Chapter 40

HEAR-NOTHING

A movement in the other room broke their connection. The police officer stood and stretched while his mouth gaped open in a yawn.

Hear-Nothing shooed her hands at Julius. "Police officer waking up!"

Julius closed his hand around the ring and brought it back into his cell.

The bored, sleepy eyes of the officer glanced around the jail. Apparently satisfied that no one was trying to escape, he settled back in his chair and resumed his slumber.

Hear-Nothing reached her right hand through the bars of the cell. "I wish you could put that ring on my finger now." She stretched her arm as far as it would go. "But I don't think you will reach it across this hall."

Julius looked at the ring and shrugged slightly. He raised his right hand to place the ring on his pinky finger.

"Wait!" She wiggled her fingers and brought her hand back into the cell. "I think it's supposed to be the left hand." She formed the **FIANCÉ** sign on her left hand. "We are engaged. Not married yet."

Smiling sweetly, Sita looked across the hall at Julius. "So, my fiancé, go-ahead and put it on your left hand. Later, when we get married, you can put it on mine." This seemed surreal to be labeling her longtime boyfriend as fiancé.

Julius placed the ring on his left pinky and caressed it.

Hear-Nothing saw his right eyebrow lower a bit as he looked at his hands. "What are you thinking about?" she asked.

Julius looked at her with a serious expression. "I am sorry to change the subject, but want to return to the 'forgiveness' we were talking about before. It looks like you forgive your mother. Do you also forgive yourself?" he asked.

"Well, based on what you just did with asking me to marry you, it seems you forgive me for everything I've done to mess up your life. You probably will be kicked out of Gonzaga University and because you now have a criminal record, probably won't be able to get a job. Do you really forgive me?"

Julius shrugged. "I will deal with it, but yes, I forgive you."

"Then I forgive myself."

"That is good." Julius leaned forward and grabbed one of the bars. "Now for the hard part. Do you forgive Sybil?"

At the mention of this name, her shoulders tensed and her fist balled around the blanket hem. The mention of that name spoiled her mood. "I'm not sure about that. Yes, my own birth mother abandoned me. But it is because of Sybil and her tight control of me that I've been so angry and messed-up."

"I agree." Julius nodded. "I can't stand her either. But what do you need so you can forgive her, too? What can we do so you are not so bound and chained by the effects of her control that has messed-up your life?"

She squared her shoulders. "Have nothing to do with her for the rest of my life."

Julius stared at her, then his pinky finger sprang at his temple. "I got an **idea** what we can do to free Sybil from her control on your heart. It's about your name."

"How is my name going to kick Sybil out of my life for good?"

Julius pointed to his ear and shook a thumb. "Hear-Nothing is what Visha named you." He placed an 'A' name sign on his cheek. "Amy is what Sybil called you. S-I-T-A is what your birth mother named you." He moved a hand in a downward arch out from the  other. "**From-now- on** what name will you use?"

Hear-Nothing paused. What Julius said whirled around in her mind. She looked at her hand as she fingerpelled "S-I-T-A." she nodded with conviction. "Yes. The name my mother gave me shall be my name from-now-on"

"S-I-T-A…" Julius paused and stroked his chin. He formed his own name sign, a 'J' on the eyebrow. "Remember you gave me this name sign when you were a little girl? Well, we will no longer use the 'A' name sign on the cheek which Sybil invented. How about this?" He extended a pinky finger and moved it backward in an 'S' motion on the top of his wrist.

Sita copied the motion. "Why this?"

"Well"—Julius pointed across the hall to Sita's wrist—"you know that bracelet Visha made and you are always fidgeting with?"

"Yes." Sita looked at the wrist and stroked the bracelet beads between a thumb and forefinger. Even though she now knew Visha as a woman, the long-ago memory of the girl with the tough face but caring eyes whom she knew as 'Bisha' remained etched in her consciousness. Sita remembered the action of Bisha giving her the bracelet was the first time in her life that someone showed she was valued and cherished.

Julius repeated the motion on his wrist. "It is related to a memory you cherish related to that bracelet. Plus, it has an 'S' movement representing your new name S-I-T-A. Will you accept it?" 

Sita formed the name sign and patted her wrist affectionately. "Yes! I accept it! Especially because it is given by you."

Sita realized that Julius, the person she cherished most in her life— indeed, the very same person to whom she granted his own name sign long ago when she was a little school girl—joined the connection between these divergent parts of her life with the cherished identity of a name sign that uniquely defined her identity.

"Sita." Julius used her new name sign. "Now you can be free because you have a new identity that is uniquely yours." He patted his chest and pointed upward. "You are loved by me. Most importantly, you are loved by God. That is enough. No one else can control you or drag you down. I think that is why you got the message to forgive."

A stillness enveloped the jail. No words were spoken by the snoring police officer and slumbering prisoners.

Julius stroked the ring he made. Sita repeated her newly given name sign. No signs were needed between the two Deaf people in the cells on opposite sides of the hall. Somehow it didn't matter that they could not touch. Their companionship bonded in a spiritual peace enhanced and solidified by each other's presence.

"Julius," Sita signed, her eyes wide with worry.

Julius shifted on the blanket and narrowed his eyes. He seemed worried about this sudden shift in her mood. "What's wrong?"

"When we get to America, if we are imprisoned separately, there's no way we can be together. What will we do?"

Julius shook his head slowly. "I don't know, but I do know that if we walk this path together, nothing can separate the two-of-us. It will probably be very difficult, and yes, we may be physically separated for a while. But please"—he pointed upward—"pray to Jesus and keep your faith in Him. That way we will ultimately end up together."

Sita clasped her hands together and closed then opened her eyes. "I pray that tomorrow, at least we get to sit together on the plane ride back to America."

Chapter 41

JULIUS

In the back seat of the police jeep, on the way to the airport, Julius smelled the strong, spicy sent of Steele's cologne and looked across the thick body of Officer Steele to the other side of the vehicle. Sita's left hand rested on her lap.

Julius touched the threaded ring on his finger. He really wanted to place this ring on his fiancée's finger. The thought occurred that he could simply remove it and hand it to her.

His chest constricted. But the handcuffs chaining both of them to bars of the back doors made this handover impossible. Perhaps later at the airport, he and Sita would have a chance to complete the actions of the marriage proposal.

The brown police jeep passed a sign, announcing the entrance to the Mumbai airport, and veered right, entering the lane designated for 'official' vehicles.

"Okay, here's what will happen." Visha sat sideways in the front passenger seat and interpreted as Steele gave instructions from the back seat and Officer Manish drove.

Sitting between Julius and Sita, Officer Steele pulled a key from the retractable chain on his utility belt. "I will now take off your handcuffs, but I expect your full ___."

"How you sign **C-O-O-P-E-R-A-T-E** in ASL?" Visha asked as Steele reached across Julius to unhook his handcuff from his wrist.

Julius joined his thumb and forefinger of both hands to demonstrate the sign.

Steele unhooked Sita's handcuffs. The bulk of Steele's brown bullet- proof vest prevented Julius from seeing Sita's facial expression.

Steele pointed to the approaching concourse entrance. "When we get out, you must stay close to me. It will be crowded." He patted the handcuffs which were now attached to his utility belt. "If you separate from me, I will need to put these back on." Steele jerked his thumb to the jeep's hatch area behind them where their suitcases were. "We will go directly to the ticket counter and check in your suitcases."

Sita lifted her purse from her lap. "Can I bring my purse with me on the plane?"

Steele nodded and pointed to the backpacks which both Sita and Julius had placed on the floor between their feet. "Yes, you can also bring your backpacks as carry-ons. After your suitcases are checked in, we will go straight to security. I have your documents with me and will present them to the border control officer."

The jeep drove past the crazy congestion of rickshaws, taxicabs, passenger vehicles, and the packed crowd of people jostling to enter the main doors of the airport. The vehicle jerked to a stop next to a street sign labeled 'Police' in both Hindi and English.

Manish got out to open the back hatch and take out their suitcases.

"Let's go," Steele commanded.

Manish whistled, and two baggage wallas ran to grab their suitcases.

Steele grabbed his black locked briefcase which Julius assumed to contain their documents and perhaps an extra hand gun.

The group entered a side door with the baggage wallas following. Once in the airport's public area, they avoided the long lines of passengers as they walked straight to the international flight ticketing area. People in the line stared at them.

Julius realized it must be strange for them to see a mixed-race couple's bags placed on the scale next to a ticket attendant as a tall African American officer spoke, while an Indian woman and a Mumbai police officer watched.

Julius poked Sita. "I feel like you and I are zoo animals before they are placed inside their cages. All these people are gawking at us as if we are on display."

Sita looked at the line of people gawking at them. "I know. I don't like it either. I try to ignore them. But at least we aren't stuck waiting for hours in that long line." She pointed.

Julius grasped Sita's hands and looked around. It was the first time he had touched her since they were at Poonam's house. "I was really hoping to—" Julius paused and looked at Steele who was observing them closely from the ticket counter area.

"Hoping to do what?" Sita asked.

"Later." Julius let go of Sita's hands and pointed to his finger. "I want to give you this ring now, but there are too many people watching. It is not the right time."

"I want that, too. Hopefully on the flight, sometime, we will have a chance to do that." Sita frowned and looked toward the counter.

Manish stood to the side. Visha watched as Steele resumed talking to the female ticketing attendant.

"How come Visha is not interpreting for us?" Sita asked.

"That's a good question," Julius responded. He looked at Visha.

Her face was set in that businesslike expression. She seemed to be concentrating to catch the fluent English conversation between Steele and the ticketing attendant.

Julius waved to get her attention. She blinked. "Yes?"

"Would you mind interpreting for us?"

"Oh!" Visha's hand flew to her chest. "**Sorry!** Officer Steele explain to make sure your luggage go to correct flight. He say you already have ticket. US Government pay for it."

Julius thought of the irony around their original one-way ticket. They were so intensely focused on their quest to evade the authorities and find Sita's mother that they didn't put much thought into what would happen afterward. A return ticket was not purchased when they changed the original flight. Now it was the very same authorities they were previously trying to avoid who would provide their ticket to return.

"That's right." Julius sighed.

The attendant handed Steele their boarding passes.

Steele motioned for them to follow.

Adjacent to the public ticketing area was another large room with an even longer, densely packed line of people. They were waiting to have their documents checked by security before being admitted to the international flight concourse. Officer Manish led them past this line, and they approached a row of counters with stern-looking border control officers sitting behind thick plexiglass windows.

Officer Steele held up a hand. "Do either of you need to use the bathroom before we go in?"

Sita signed, "I do."

Steele pointed to a female police officer standing sentry to the side. "Can you tell her we need a female escort to the bathroom?" he asked Manish.

"Come." Manish waved for Sita to follow.

At least she's not holding a stick like that annoying woman at the jail, Julius thought as he watched the female officer escort Sita into a nearby bathroom.

Chapter 42

SITA

After exiting the bathroom, with a stern nod in the direction of the people waiting at the front of the line, the female police officer sent Sita on her way.

Approaching the line, Sita felt like a special first-class passenger with the privilege to bypass the long line and approach security at her convenience. It seemed ironic that the Indian border control officers needed to check the documents of her own escort, who was also an officer of the law.

Manish stood several yards away as Visha waited next to Steele and Julius.

Sita hoped Visha would accompany them to the departure gate. She was not yet ready to say goodbye to her friend.

"Okay, we will now go through security," Steele instructed. "I will present your documents and your arrest warrant so they understand why I am escorting you." He held out his hand toward Visha as she interpreted. "I understand these security officers are fluent in English, so we will no longer need your services. Thank you for your cooperation."

Visha shook Steele's hand after interpreting what he said.

"Wait!" Sita interrupted. "This is goodbye?" she signed to Visha.

"I think yes," Visha responded in sign language without voicing. "I not have documents or permission to go through security." She pointed to Manish. "He waiting to take me home. I must cooperate with him."

Sita held up her hand and looked at Steele. She pointed her finger between Visha and herself. "Goodbye?" she asked with her voice.

Steele nodded, and Sita grabbed Julius's arm to pull him toward Visha.

"We want to thank-you for being our friend." Sita touched the bracelet on her wrist. "I will always wear this bracelet to remind me of your love and how you cherished me when no one else did. I want to show you something."

Sita extended her pinky finger and produced her new name sign on her wrist. "Last night Julius gave me this new name sign. It honors you and is connected to this bracelet you gave me and what it represents."

Sita pointed to her ear, shaking her thumb and head at the same time. "Hear-Nothing. No." She placed an 'A' next to her cheek and shook her head. "Amy. No." She drew the 'S' on her wrist and nodded her head. "S-I-T-A. Yes," she fingerspelled and nodded. "From-now-on, my name will be Sita."

The softening of Visha's eyes and the single tear that trickled down her face indicated she understood.

Sita felt herself embraced by a long, warm hug as Visha's tear dropped on the top of her head.

Visha did not let go. She held Sita's shoulder and signed with one hand. "You, me, we keep in contact, okay?"

Now Sita's tears flowed. "Definitely!" She gave Visha another hug. "I will probably not have contact with my mother in the future," she signed, wiping the tears from her own eyes. "I need family from my country of birth. Can you be my sister? You-me, we are Indian sisters, okay?" Sita joined her hands together in a plea.

Visha's expressive eyes looked deeply into Sita's. "You always my sister in past. Always will be." She placed both hands on Sita's head in a blessing. "Sita, yes, you my sister."

EPILOGUE

Like a bulldozer clearing a path through the crowded streets they arrived from, Officer Steele's large frame led Julius and Sita down the right-center aisle of the SEA-Air jumbo jet. In the midst of mostly Indian passengers, along with a number of Westerners, there was no mistaking the authority of Steele as he moved down the aisle.

Julius held Sita's hand as they passed the previously seated passengers. They stopped at the window section of row twenty-seven.

Steele pointed to their backpacks and then to the overhead bin. "Put here," Julius read his lips.

Julius stuffed his backpack into the bin. Sita stretched on her tiptoes. Her backpack couldn't quite reach the bin. He moved toward her to help, but Steele stepped between them, grabbed her backpack, and stuffed it into the bin with one strong arm.

Steele pointed to the window seat and then to Sita. "You sit there."

Sita moved sideways to the seat next to the small oval window. Julius began to enter the aisle, but Steele's arm interrupted him. The officer sat in the middle seat with Julius next to the aisle.

Frustrated, Julius shook his head and sat hard in his seat. He realized he would be stuck for hours next to this man whom he and Sita had recently spent many days trying to avoid. He wondered when he would ever have a chance to be with Sita, give her the ring, and connect in the romantic way he wanted and needed. His elbow brushed the cold, hard metal of Steele's revolver latched into the holster of his utility belt, and he jerked his elbow away.

Julius wondered what he would face on the other side of the Atlantic Ocean in America. It seemed so far away and yet so close. In less than a day, he would probably be behind bars in a Spokane jail. Or worse, in prison.

All of a sudden, a very pleasant smell entered his nostrils.

The perfume of an attractive, Caucasian female stewardess walked from behind and stopped a few aisles in front of him. Her smile enhanced the oxygen mask and emergency exit demonstrations of her arms following the PA instructions from the steward at the front of the plane.

With a quick glance, Julius saw Steele's expressionless face and eyes regard this woman, then he leaned forward to see past the officer and check on Sita who was looking out the window.

●　　●　　●　　●　　●

Outside the window, airport workers bustled about their tasks. Sita sensed something behind her and looked at Julius peering around Officer Steele. Her fiancé's eyebrows raised, and she recognized a pleading look on his face. Her heart elevated as she felt the longing for his presence.

"We need to sit together," she signed, then tapped Steele's shoulder, pointing to Julius when the officer looked at her. "Can he and I sit together?"

Steele's eyebrows furrowed and he shook his head with lack of comprehension.

Sita pointed to Steele's phone which he kept in a front pocket of his vest. He took it out, typed in it, then handed her the phone. She typed and handed it back.

Steele straightened, his eyes looking forward, taking a moment to think. Perhaps it broke protocol for prisoners to sit together on a plane. He stood to switch places.

Sita grabbed Julius's hand and, for the first time, felt the twisted threads of the ring on his finger. Her heart now raced.

Julius placed his hand on hers and caressed, lovingly regarding at her eyes.

In this little section of the plane, they were in their own little universe.

"Let's do this again," Julius began. "Sita, will you marry me?"

Sita's eyes widened with a smile as she nodded emphatically. "Yes, Julius, I will marry you."

He removed the ring from his pinky finger and placed it on the ring finger of her left hand. It fit perfectly.

They embraced with a lingering kiss.

With a contented sigh, Sita held Julius's hand, their fingers intertwined. She felt the rough wool as the ring rubbed on her finger. A movement, and she glanced at Steele whose eyes turned quickly to his phone.

"You know, Julius," Sita freed her hand and signed. "I remember building a wall when Sybil flew me to America."

Julius's right eyebrow lowered. "A wall? What do you mean?"

"Well, on that plane Sybil was sitting next to me just like you are now. But I hated her. Not even a day after meeting her, I detested her." Sita used the PUKE sign. "I took all the pillows and blankets I could and built a wall on the armrest between us. Boy, she hated that!"

"I bet!" Julius chuckled. "I don't think she's going to be much of a factor anymore. Now we have each-other, and I don't think we need to build any more walls in the future."

The seats vibrated as the plane began backing out of the gate.

Sita looked at Officer Steele checking something on his phone.

She wrinkled her nose. "Ironic, isn't it? Now Steele is the wall between us and everyone else out there."

"Yes," Julius responded. "Unlike before with Sybil, you are not alone. I don't know what will happen when we land in America. But I do know that whatever happens, we will face it together."

Sita squeezed Julius's leg. "But what if I am locked away for a long time in a jail, separate from you?"

"Yes, that is possible. Even I may be locked away for a while because I supported you." Julius clasped his hand around hers. "As God is my witness, I vow that I will never leave you alone as long as I live." Sita placed her hand against Julius's cheek and caressed. "I vow the same."

"I have one more thing for you." Julius dug into his pants pocket, pulling out a closed fist. When he opened his hand, Sita noticed two bracelet beads.

"What for?" she asked.

Julius reached for her wrist that wore the bracelet with fad ed, colorful beads. He showed her each bead as he explained, "For your bracelet, two new beads. A bright blue bead for your new identity, meaning secure, and a yellow bead to represent the belonging in finding Poonam, your birth mother."

Sita gazed at Julius and then down at the beads that wobbled in his palm. She looked at her bracelet, which meant so many things of her past, her present, and now her future. "Where did you find these beads?"

Julius smiled sheepishly. "At one of the shops back in Mumbai. You did not know I was out shopping, did you?"

She laughed. "No, I did not know you were shopping. Many times today, you surprise me!"

Grinning, he asked, "Want me to put the beads on your bracelet right now?"

She let him carefully remove the old bracelet and slip the new beads on and retie it onto her wrist. Caressing the bracelet, she said, "Julius, thank-you for surprising me and showing me love in this way. You care for me. I love you so much." She placed her hand in his.

The seat suddenly pressed on her back as the plane took off.

Sita's eyes turned to her hand which now held Julius's. Fingering the thread, she realized that the wool thread of her engagement ring matched the bracelet thread on her wrist.

She no longer needed, nor was she bound to, the people or the things in her life beyond who she saw right here.

Mostly Sita felt free, the freedom of hope here within and there beside her.

Yes, it was enduring love.

Acknowledgments

Resilient Surrender; A Deaf-Experience Suspense Novel is a journey that was sparked almost forty years ago during the year I lived in Pakistan and continued years later when I married into the Indian culture. The journey got rolling with the publication of *Resilient Silence*, book one in the Resilient Silence Series and this second novel is a culmination of the inspiring teamwork of some very creative, talented and dedicated people. As seen in *Resilient Surrender*, the adventures of Sita and Julius are not just a story; it is a mix of people, themes and events which are derived from my own life and experiences. These involve many interpersonal connections and the crucibles as well as rich rewards that come from committing ourselves to the forces that guide us and the people who are with us on this journey through life.

Both *Resilient Silence* and *Resilient Surrender* would not be near their finished quality without the publishing team who have worked with Quintessential Deaf Press (QDP). I honor Tisha Martin Mills for your belief in the impact of the messages within my novels and your dedication, skill, and the work you put into being a top-notch editor, guide, and project manager in the journey toward publication. Since our work with the first book in the series, you have been a key part in the refinement of these stories into the quality that God intended for them to be. Thank you, Kim Autrey, for your attention to detail and providing your skill and knowledge in the proofreading as well as excellent interior design, formatting, and finishing steps of publication to launch these stories into the world. Thank you, Francine Platt, in partnership with Augusto Silva, for your excellent work in developing a high-quality cover for *Resilient Surrender* based on a difficult-to-create concept. The end product communicates the essence of a central character around whom this story revolves. In the development of a logo which communicates the Deaf-focused aspect of the QDP imprint logo, I thank Justin Van Valey for your wonderful skill and graphic design efforts.

I would like to thank the members of the Deaf community, of which I am a part, for welcoming me wherever I live and for providing rich material which has become part of my stories. I thank the Deaf people and our allies who are followers of Jesus and have supported me and my family along this path toward publication of novels which include elements of faith and an examination of how different people respond to spiritual forces. Thank you to the people of Deaf House Fellowship and Rock Creek Church for your prayers and encouragement.

I honor the members of the Deaf Author Group, who have been instrumental in taking the time to read chapters and excerpts of these novels in a collaborative approach to develop dialogue representations of the various communication styles found within and in association with the Deaf-World. Thank you to my fellow Deaf authors Linda Drattell, Karly Waldrip, Rachel Zemach, Steve Baldwin, Tonia Fehrenbach, Kat Hartwell, Christina Pean, and others for your support and encouragement. As a special ally in supporting us Deaf authors, I thank Jennifer Alford for the enthusiasm and skill which you demonstrate in the web design and marketing guidance you provide to us all.

I honor Rebekah Covington for your creativity and wonderful collaboration in the development of stunning illustrations which bring to life the characters and themes in these novels. The visual elements of sign language and facial/body expression as well as the unique bonds that Deaf people share are skillfully incorporated in your illustrations.

For her support of me in life, I must honor my wife. Thank you, Pratibha, for your never-ending support and belief in my work as an author and the graciousness in which you share your Deaf Indian heritage which is a central theme in this second novel of the series. Finally, I give all the glory and honor to Jesus Christ for His grace and the guidance He provides in my life, giving me the freedom to operate in ways that allow the love and peace needed to thrive.

Author's Note

Resilient Surrender: A Deaf-Experience Suspense Novel is about American Deaf people who interact both within a Deaf-world and with society at large. It is a story told from the perspectives of the Deaf characters themselves. The English language is used as a medium to show dialogue the Deaf characters experience. Much of this dialogue is presented as English language representation of the fluent American Sign Language used between the Deaf characters. However, these characters also interact with others who converse using a variety of signed and spoken language forms.

Here is an explanation of how each form is represented in the story:

Fluent American Sign Language (ASL) between Deaf characters

Because the Deaf characters have an in-depth, complex and complete understanding of their ASL dialogue, this is presented in regular, grammatically complete English language quotes with 'he/she signed' taglines accompanied by short descriptions of the particular signs, facial expressions, hand and body movements used to produce the concepts in ASL.

Example: "What's up?" she signed and held the handshape, waiting for his response.

Individual ASL signs explained in taglines

Taglines are the phrases such as 'she said' used to clarify who is producing the dialogue. Because the majority of the complex dialogue in this story is produced by fluent, ASL signing Deaf characters, short descriptions of the methods and sign choices used are often substituted to avoid the over use of the 'he/she signed' taglines. It also allows the reader to see and experience individual character traits as demonstrated by how the Deaf characters choose to react, converse, 'verbally' retaliate, and make their points. Often this requires the use of ALL-CAPS to identify the individual sign choices of the characters. At certain points in the novel, QR codes are linked to video demonstrations of the targeted signs.

Example: Amy glanced down at the stylistic 'New York' letters printed on her shirt. "Okay. I agree but," she formed the HONORIFIC-YOU sign. "You are very white." She exaggerated the WHITE-PERSON sign in front of her face. "Does this mean you will color your face brown so you blend in better?"

Individual fingerspelled words

Within regular quotes, the fingerspelled words themselves appear with ALL-CAP letters separated by individual dashes. The most common function of these fingerspelled words in the dialogue is for the characters to clarify sign and concept meanings to others who do not have a complete understanding of the ASL and/or other language produced.

Example: "M-O-T-H-E-R," Visha fingerspelled.

Signing Exact English (SEE) as Deaf Characters experience it

SEE is an invented code of communication using signs and following spoken English sentence structure. The Deaf characters experience this as a string of visual signs presented in a linear order as opposed to the rich visual grammar and structure of ASL. In this story, SEE dialogue is presented as English words separated by ellipses.

Example: Sybil raised her hand, interrupting Amy's advance. "I…hear…the…garbage…truck."

The understanding of spoken English accessed via lipreading

From the perspective of the profoundly Deaf characters, only about 40 percent to 60 percent of spoken English is understood via lipreading. These dialogue sentences are presented using the English words the Deaf characters understand with underscore representing the inaccessible or non-intelligible parts of the sentences.

Example: "I___partner___past," she said.

Non-fluent ASL produced by hearing people

At certain points in the novel, the Deaf characters interact with others who possess a beginning level of ASL, but are not yet fluent. The signed dialogue produced by these non-ASL-fluent characters is represented with ALL-CAPS words placed in the word order in which they are signed. Although this dialogue is often not grammatically complete ASL, it is presented as the Deaf characters see it.

Example: He looked at the bedroom door then at Julius. "NIGHT TWO-YOU SLEEP WHERE?"

The understanding of foreign, Indian Sign Language (ISL) sentences and signs

One of the unique aspects of this story is the fact that the American Deaf characters interact with other characters who are fluent signers in a sign language foreign to American Deaf people. The foreign sign language represented here is Indian Sign Language (ISL). Capital letters separated by hyphens represent fingerspelled words in both ISL and ASL alphabets. Regular quoted sentences in English with the words arranged in syntax showing that which the American Deaf characters understand and underscores embedded to represent the incomprehensible words is the style used for this dialogue.

Example: Visha pointed in the direction of the slum. "We tell___Q your___," she produced what appeared to be the ISL letter for 'Q' and pointed to her nose.

Dialogue presented within cell phone text messages

At times, the Deaf and non-fluent ASL signing characters will revert to communicating via text messages passed between them on their cell phones. The characters choose this method when they must use more complicated language regarding topics requiring much clarification and explanation that the spoken and signed language barrier prevents. Such dialogue is presented in regular quotes with English sentences exactly as typed in the text messages.

Example: She typed and handed the phone to Amy. "Let's communicate this way for now," the message read in English. "It seems you two are discussing something serious. Would you mind letting me know that that is?"

Character thoughts

Character thoughts are in italics, often with 'he/she thought' taglines.

Example: Amy's eyes followed this river and peered into the darkness. *Will I find my mother there?* she wondered. *Are there people out there who may remember my name?*

Author Bio

Peter M. Quint is the author of two novels in the Resilient Silence Series. His books create an accessible pathway for people to examine the struggles, joys and triumphs experienced in the lives of Deaf people. These books also encourage introspection with exposure to characters who face life challenges as they demonstrate various levels of faith and anchors to something bigger than themselves.

A teacher of the Deaf and American Sign Language for over 30 years, Peter has infused his novels with characters who exhibit the traits and values experienced in this rich field of experience. He is also a leader in the Christian Deaf community as the founder of Deaf Heartlight, a Christ-based recovery program for Deaf people, and a founding member of Deaf House Fellowship in the Pacific Northwest region of America.

Peter actively supports Deaf artisans in his work by including illustrations created by a Deaf artist. Throughout his life, he has been involved with Deaf sports, holding the American record for the Deaf in the track and field steeplechase event. He has been a high-level competitor in distance events, including a placing in the top 20 of the Bloomsday race in Spokane, Washington state, an event featured in his first novel.

Visit Peter M. Quint at www.peterquint.com.

Purchase Books, Obtain Companion Course/Workbooks & Leave a Review

Congratulations on finishing *Resilient Surrender!* I hope you enjoyed Sita's and Julius's journeys together through India.

Please scan the following QR codes to complete your journey.

A concluding message from the author

Visit Liinks (scan the QR code below, or go to http://www.liinks.co/ peter.m.quint) for more information and to purchase novels in the series and to purchase companion courses/workbooks that accompany the series.

Reader, are you on Goodreads? Add your book to your Reading List.

Leave a reader review on Amazon, Barnes and Noble as well as wherever books are sold, read, and enjoyed.